WAR CRY ON THE PURGATORY

It was coming now. Just as he feared. Just as he once saw.

With an aching heart he pushed free of the crowd of women and immediately broke into a run.

He ran fast, feet barely skimming the broken ground, lungs burning, shattered heart pounding.

He could hear the roar of fury as the war cries of his people sounded behind him.

Before him lay windows and lights and people taking their ease in the early evening.

Behind him the men had blood on their hands and blood in their hearts and a raging appetite for more blood in their voices.

Rivers West
Ask your bookseller for the books you have missed.

RIVERS
WEST

THE
PURGATORY RIVER

Frank Roderus

BANTAM BOOKS

NEW YORK · TORONTO · LONDON · SYDNEY · AUCKLAND

THE PURGATORY RIVER
A Bantam Book / July 1997

ISBN 0-553-56795-0

Published simultaneously in the United States and Canada

Bantam Books are published by Bantam Books, a division of Bantam
Doubleday Dell Publishing Group, Inc. Its trademark, consisting of the
words "Bantam Books" and the portrayal of a rooster, is Registered in
U.S. Patent and Trademark Office and in other countries. Marca Reg-
istrada. Bantam Books, 1540 Broadway, New York, New York 10036.

PRINTED IN THE UNITED STATES OF AMERICA

OPM 10 9 8 7 6 5 4 3 2 1

For Magdalena
Always

Prologue

THEY'D TOLD HIM the water would be cold. They said a man's feet fair froze off from standing hip deep all the day long, wading from one set to another so as to keep his manscent from being detected by animals ashore or animals a-swimming.

Well, they'd lied. Or anyway been mistaken as all billy hell.

Could be it was the time of year, he supposed. Late in the summer when the snowmelt was long since drained off and there wasn't much to feed the stream except some springs and the like. Whatever the reason there was hardly any water at all in this nameless little river off somewhere south of the big Arkansas.

The truth was that Devon Jenks had no idea of where he was. That wasn't so bad. But he didn't think Captain—the man did like that title—Big Jim Mahoney knew where they were either.

All they were for sure of was that they'd left the States a month or so back. Ran out of navigable water and left the boats a week and a half ago. Now, Jenks suspected, they were leaving their senses.

They were a party of eleven. Trappers formed into a company to take fur in the far western country. Except the closer to the great mountains—and Lordy, those mountains

ahead were something for the eye to behold—the closer
they got the less Devon thought any member of the company knew what it was they were supposed to be doing here.
Or how to go about it.

Setting traps in sand with scarcely enough water running over it to make the riverbed moist. Now wasn't that
foolish.

And what the hell were they trying to catch anyway?
Devon didn't know beans about beaver. He admitted that. It
was said there used to be beaver back home in Pennsylvania
but they'd all been trapped out a long time ago. Devon
never his whole life long saw a live beaver nor a beaver-
built dam still in useful repair.

So he couldn't exactly claim to be an expert on the
subject of beaver, like some people he could name.

Just because he wasn't no beaver expert, though, didn't
mean he was a complete idjit in the woods. And Devon was
certain-sure positive that the tracks Big Jim Mahoney got so
excited about were plain old raccoon tracks. There were still
plenty of 'coons in Pennsylvania, b'damn, and Devon was
more than a little familiar with those.

Besides, weren't beaver supposed to eat saplings and
succulent bark and like that? There weren't any saplings or
small trees along this stretch of near dry river for beaver to
feed on. And it was Devon's experience that wild things
aren't generally found in places where there's nothing for
them to eat. So why in hell would Big Jim—Captain Big
Jim, that is—think they were going to catch beaver along
this stretch of river? Just because they'd reached the first
greenery they'd seen in days? Maybe. But the grove of trees
here was tall and mature and there wasn't all that much in
the way of undergrowth beneath those spreading limbs. The
place was pretty. But there wasn't nothing here for beavers
to eat. Nor was there anything like a beaver dam. Nor bark
cuttings gnawed down low to the ground like they said
beaver left when they fed. Nor any other beaver sign that
Devon could make out.

Big Jim said to set traps regardless. This here was
prime beaver country to his mind. He could feel it in his

bones. Yeah, sure he could. Especially in the big, solid bone
that sat atop his neck. Devon could accept that.

With a grunt and a grimace he spread the steel jaws
of his trap, set the pan trip, and gently placed the trap in
enough water to barely cover it. He didn't bother trying to
hide the trap. If he did he might actually catch something, a
muskrat or opossum or some such dumb critter, and what
was the point in that?

He made his set, hefted his sack, and found he still had
two traps yet to place and wandered ankle deep through the
water in search of a couple more places to lay his traps.
Places where he could be sure of two things, first that he
couldn't catch anything and second that he could remember
where to find the traps come tomorrow. Dang traps were
expensive things, and most of Devon's worldly wherewithal
was tied up in them and in the rest of the gear he needed to
make this journey into the far western mountains. Devon
figured to make his fortune on this trip. Make his fortune
and go home to marry—he knew who the lucky girl would
be although it was knowledge that he hadn't yet passed
along to her—and roam no more.

But first he had that fortune to make.

Devon stifled a yawn and reached to slice another
chunk of deer meat off the haunch that was scorching over
the fire. Big deer in this country, he had to give them that.
The meat wasn't so sweet as the corn- and barley-fed farm-
land deer back home, though. The deer out here tasted
mildly of sage. Which was not altogether bad. Just different.
He cut away a goodly hunk, offered his knife to Harold
Brantly beside him, and went to set his teeth in the hot, dripping venison.

He was interrupted, along with all the other boys in the
party, by the appearance of a soldier coming at them unexpected out of the gloom of the dusk.

It looked pretty much like a dressed-up wooden toy soldier, complete with knee-high shiny boots and buff-colored
breeches, scarlet sash and blue coat with shiny brass buttons, gold epaulets big as serving trays, a domed helmet

with a monster big plume of purest white . . . and a sword. There had to be a sword and of course there was one. Long and slightly curved and hanging thick with golden tassels and knobs.

"God, ain't he pretty?" Devon observed from behind his hunk of venison, punctuating the comment by taking a huge bite of meat.

"If I looked like that I bet I could have half the women in Bedford County," another said.

"Jerry, you already had half the women in Bedford County."

"I meant the other half." Jerry Mixon grinned.

Meanwhile Captain Mahoney was rising and puffing his chest and blustering something to the toy soldier who'd showed up amongst them.

While Mahoney was talking the soldier boy was carefully removing his gauntlets, tugging on one finger at a time and slowly working the fancy glove off his right hand. He seemed to be paying no attention at all to Mahoney, who now was standing smack in front of him and still running his mouth.

The officer finally got the glove off, gave Big Jim a calculated look . . . and whacked Jim Mahoney across the face with the back of his glove.

Big Jim let out a roar and balled his fists. Then dropped them quick again when two, maybe three dozen soldiers tromped loud into view. The soldiers—they weren't dressed halfway so fancy as their officer but didn't have to be in light of what else they were carrying—had muskets with them. Muskets with long, sharp, wicked-looking sword bayonets attached to their front ends.

And those muskets, each and every damned one of them, were pointing at Big Jim Mahoney. And at Jerry Mixon. And at Harold Brantly. And at Devon Jenks and all the other boys.

"Hey now," Devon protested. "Hey now."

The officer, who must've been a general to have so much gold and brass on him, said something in Spanish. But hell, none of them spoke any of that weird tongue. Not Mahoney nor anybody else.

The officer tried again, this time in French. Devon recognized that it was French but that was all he could make out.

Finally the toy soldier asked a thick-tongued, one-word question. "Papers?"

Big Jim smiled and bobbed his head. They had papers. Damn straight they did. Bought them off a whiskey pedlar back in the States. The man had papers but had gone and started drinking up his inventory so was willing to part with the trading permits in exchange for a small addition to his stock. Big Jim smiled and held up one finger indicating the officer should wait. He went to his pack, rifled through it for a moment until he found what he needed, and carried the document back to hand to the officer. Big Jim smiled.

The general scowled. And slapped Big Jim with the glove again.

It was lucky for the toy soldier that he had those bayonets to protect him. But then he'd made the gesture already knowing he was safe from retaliation. There wasn't a damn thing Mahoney and his trappers could do against this many armed soldiers.

"What the hell's the matter with you?" Big Jim demanded.

"No good," the general said.

"What d'you mean no good? O' course it's good. Permit to trade. Permit to trap. O' course it's good."

The general pointed to something on the document and read it aloud. Not that any of the Americans knew what the hell he was saying but he read it out loud anyway. The officer turned his head and spat. "Permit to . . ."—he searched for the English word he wanted—"permit to marry. You bride?" He laughed and pointed. "You?" He pointed this time at Devon.

Devon felt his cheeks going hot. Why the hell did he always get singled out in a situation like this? Well, all right. He knew why he did. But he wished that once, just once . . . He sighed. It was one of the prices a man had to pay when he was blessed with a head of bright red hair.

Having red hair is sort of like wearing a lantern atop one's head. Nobody misses spotting it. Not ever.

"You marry?" the officer asked.

"Say yes, dammit. Tell him we're on our way t' meet your damn bride," Harold hissed under his breath.

Unfortunately Big Jim Mahoney—Captain Mahoney, if you please—was not so quick-witted as his minions. Big Jim stuck his chest out all the farther. And spat square in the general's face.

It was, Mahoney himself conceded afterward, the wrong thing to do at that particular place and time.

Jeez, but it hurt to walk. Devon wouldn't actually swear to it, but he thought he could feel the pain when he turned his eyes from one side to the other.

What they all needed was to lie down, hole up, sleep and rest and lie about until they healed some and could move on in comfort.

Unfortunately that wasn't possible. Not without food, and the damn Spanish hadn't left them with much of anything. Their traps were gone. Their guns. Their ammunition. Their food supplies.

Just damn near everything was gone.

And the general, his English getting better and better the more he used it, the general said if he caught them in the King's territory again they would all be hauled down to Santa Fe and thrown into prison for five or ten years.

Devon wasn't sure, but a few years in prison might not be such a bad swap considering how close to his back his front was getting.

Two days they'd been without food and there wasn't much prospect for getting any now until they got back at least to the Arkansas. That meant getting downriver along this stupid, no-named creek far enough to recover the boats, then floating them and getting back to the Arkansas. And after that, well, it would just depend on whether they encountered any other parties moving on the lower Arkansas at this time of year. Either find another party of white traders or make their way all the way back to civilization.

Of course once they reached the Arkansas they could probably catch some fish. Poor food but marginally better than boiled moccasin.

Devon sighed. Back in Pittsburgh where they put the company together Big Jim promised excitement and adventure here in the western lands. Devon hoped this wasn't what Mahoney'd had in mind, else he just might feel compelled to add to the beating the Spaniards already gave the good captain.

"Jenks!"

Devon's head came up, and his wandering attention returned to the struggling company of trappers strung out ahead of him.

"You're falling behind again, Jenks."

Devon stifled an impulse to reply the way he really wanted to—if only because he didn't have strength enough or, really, any true inclination to back up a hot response— and mutely nodded.

"You're lagging, Jenks. Now hurry."

"I'll be right along. I got to take a dump." It was a lie, but he just didn't feel like arguing at the moment.

"How?" Jerry Mixon asked. "We ain't none of us eat anything since Tuesday a week ago." It hadn't been that long, of course. And anyway none of them had any idea was this Tuesday or Christmas Eve. There wasn't any reason to keep track of time now. Jerry was just being funny anyhow.

"I'll catch right up," Devon assured Captain Mahoney. "You boys go on."

The others marched slowly onward, feet dragging. Devon decided there was no sense wasting a perfectly good opportunity. He veered away from the riverbank they were following and selected a rock to sit on so he could rest for a minute. Just a minute. That was all he needed.

It felt good to sit still for a few minutes. He could . . . He blinked. He might well have been losing his reason due to hunger, but he could almost swear that he could smell food. Onions, to be precise about it. He would swear that he could smell raw onion.

Frowning, and paying attention now, he began to search the ground around the rock where he was seated.

There, he thought. Was that sprig of green an onion top? A wild onion? Was there such a thing as a wild onion? He didn't know.

Devon slipped off his rock and onto hands and knees. He poked the hard, sun-baked earth with a finger. Then dug so hard around the wisp of green stalk that his fingers hurt.

But it was. It really was an onion. Had to be a wild one. No one would have reason to plant anything out here in the middle of empty hell.

Devon rubbed some of the dirt off the thin, elongated bulb and, hesitantly, bit into it. It was an onion. For damn sure it was. The taste of it was bright and biting on his tongue. He grinned and looked up to tell the others about his good fortune, but they were all out of sight now. They'd rounded a shallow bend and marched on toward the Arkansas.

No matter. Devon would catch up with them. And he'd have food with him when he did. Because there were onions here. Lots of them. All right, maybe not lots exactly. But quite a few. Now that he knew what to look for Devon could see onion stalks sticking up out of the ground every little whipstitch or so.

He needed a stick so he could dig them easier. But there were plenty enough onions that he could gather a bunch of them for himself and plenty enough to share and . . .

He frowned as the sound of yelling came to him from somewhere in the direction the fellows had gone.

Yelling, screaming . . . had they reached the boats? Surely not this soon. What then? Found a party of hunters? A dead deer or buffalo not rotted yet? What?

Devon stuffed the remainder of that first onion into his mouth and started off at a lope to catch up with the rest of the boys.

He . . . he stopped. Froze was more like it. His heart missed a beat and jumped into the back of his throat.

Sweet Jesus!

It was . . . awful. Unbelievable.

Indians. Wild Indians. They hadn't seen a single Indian the whole way out. Now here was a bunch of them.

And no guns. No knives. Nothing they could use to defend themselves with.

The Indians were everywhere. Swarming. More of them than there'd been Spaniards.

And the Indians weren't interested in giving the Americans a whipping and sending them home.

The Indians were . . . God, it was too horrible to watch. War clubs, great lumps of stone tied onto limber sticks, crushed skulls with all the ferocity of foxes attacking a box of chicks. Laying about in all directions and killing for the sheer, mad joy of it.

Devon saw Harold die with a spear in his back. Watched while three of the Indian sons of bitches toyed with Jerry Mixon, two of them poking at him from in front while the third crept around behind and bashed his cranium in with one of those terrible war clubs. Saw Big Jim Mahoney standing like a cornered bear, his belly sprouting feathered arrows until he became too weak to stand upright any longer. Big Jim's legs gave out and he sank slowly to his knees while his tormentors laughed and chattered in some ugly language of their own and finally, mercifully, finally came in and finished the foul deed.

It was . . . awful. And for the first few seconds of watching Devon observed the scene as if he were no part of it, as if the Indians who were so gleefully murdering his companions were somehow disconnected from him.

Then, belatedly, it occurred to Devon that he was in every bit as much danger as the others.

Except, Jesus, the others were dead now. Dead or dying. All of them save himself alone.

And it remained to be seen whether he would escape.

Devon dropped to his hands and knees, dropping out of sight, and scurried hard and fast for the nest of rocks where he'd rested minutes earlier.

He could hide cowering among those stones, and if the Indians did not come too near, if they did not see him there . . .

Devon covered his head with his arms and tried to

muffle his sobs lest noise give him away to the savages who were murdering his friends.

Oh, Jesus God, he thought. If he could just get away now, if he could just make it safely back to the States, to Pennsylvania, to home . . . he would never ever venture west again. Not one step west of his own county line. Forget fortune and excitement and adventure. He was done with all that. He wouldn't even *talk* about anything like that again. If only he could live to get home.

Somehow.

He would . . . he didn't know. Eat wild onions or anything else he could find or catch. Walk only at night so the savages would not see him. Get to the boats. If he could only get one boat afloat and let it carry him down to the Arkansas, down to civilization and safety.

He didn't know.

And he was afraid. Oh, God, he was afraid.

He could still hear the savage, evil shrieking and chanting. Devon covered his ears in a vain attempt to block out the demonic sounds. He lay trembling within his nest of rocks and did not move throughout the entire night, through the heat of another day and the bitter chill of yet another night, did not move out of the place of safety until maddening thirst drove him out to the nearly dry river.

And then, thirst finally slaked, he ran. Ran blindly eastward until his chest burned with pain and his stomach ached and the wind of his passage wiped the moisture from his eyes. He ran until he could run no more, and after that he walked. East. Only east. Unwilling even to look backward toward the terrors in the West.

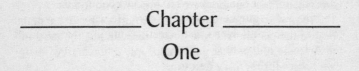

Chapter One

I

Talks To Ghosts felt the pull of the hillside in the muscles of his thighs and the feel of it was good. He was strong. Young. It was good to walk here, the tall grass swishing over the skin of his lower legs and the effort of climbing bringing out the sweat on his body even though the sun was not two hands high from the horizon before him.

But then he had been walking for many hours now. He rose in the chill of the night to stand and fill his lungs with the last of the mountain air, then slipped away from the Plum Camp where each year for far longer than Talks To Ghosts had memory the people stopped to gather wild plums and gooseberry and piñon nuts. But that was on the journey back into the mountains each fall. At this time of year, coming down from their mountain homeland onto the wide-open grassland for the summer hunting, the people stopped at Plum Camp to rest and relax within the protection of the last of the foothills before coming out into the open where enemies might find them.

Today the people would break camp and come down to Horse Camp. It had been how many years ago now that

Horse Camp got its name. Many years ago that was, but the people still spoke of it, the time the Arapaho from the north raided them only to have the valiant warriors of the people follow them back to their own camp and cleverly steal all the Arapaho horses, then get quickly away into the mountains where the Arapaho were too cowardly to follow.

That was a fine year, a fine thing to have happen, because the people had few horses then. It was the herd of the Arapaho raiders that gave the people a fine herd of their own horses for the very first time.

Now every one of the people was used to riding horses always. Every one, even the women. Every one except Talks To Ghosts. Talks To Ghosts liked the ease of riding a horse as well as the next man, but there were times when it was better to feel the power of one's own long muscles and to feel the tickle of sweat.

And there were times when Talks To Ghosts simply liked to be alone.

This was one of those times, this morning when the people would come to Horse Camp. For Horse Camp was Talks To Ghosts' most favorite of all the many places where the people went.

There were places of greater beauty and there were places with more food to eat and more water to drink and to bathe in. But there was no place, not in any of the thousand places the people wandered, where Talks To Ghosts' heart sang so sweetly as at Horse Camp.

And now the last rise was before him. He stopped below the crest, teasing himself and adding to the anticipation of his pleasure with this momentary delay, pulling the clean air deep into his lungs and pretending to rest while in fact he forced himself to wait. A moment and a moment more. Then, smiling silently to himself, he stepped up so that he could peer over the final ridgeline and look down to Horse Camp, there on a bend in the small river, there in the shadows of the tall cottonwoods, there below the ford where the river could be crossed by those wanting to go south into the land of the black robes.

It was as fine as Talks To Ghosts remembered. Fine lush grass for the horses in the rich bottomlands along the banks of the river. Shade for a man to sleep in through the heat of the day. The white-mantled Two Peaks to the west. Jagged, rocky crags to the south protecting the people from the black robes and from the pale-skinned ones of the broad hats who lived with the black robes. Vast grasslands to the north and the east, grasslands where the buffalo grazed in summer, brought there at this same time each year by the spirits for the use of the people. Brought to the land east of Horse Camp every year so the people would have meat, meat to feast on during the summer hunting and more meat to dry, to preserve and keep for use through the long mountain winters.

Talks To Ghosts stood atop the last ridgeline looking down onto the beauty of Horse Camp.

He found an outcrop of bare rock and sat on it, closing his eyes and lifting his head to the sky, opening his heart to the spirits above and those all around. Talks To Ghosts found great joy and peace among the spirits. They held no terror for him. In his heart he talked to them without words, extending his feelings outward and upward, neither expecting nor needing any response.

He sat like that for perhaps as long as it would take the sun to rise another four fingers, then opened his eyes.

The smile that had been on his face froze and was abandoned.

Down below, amid the branches of the cottonwoods at Horse Camp, Talks To Ghosts could see the thin, white rise of a stream of smoke. Someone else was at Horse Camp. Someone had to be. And yet he could see no people and no movement.

He knew very well the people were not here ahead of him. Every one of the camp was asleep when he left them this morning, and the long line of horses and dogs and people could never have gotten here ahead of him.

Scouts coming fast by horseback? He did not think so. Surely none could have passed without his knowledge.

Arapaho then. Possible, of course, but unlikely. The Arapaho had not been so far south in many years. Voyageurs? Also possible, but unlikely. They seldom came into this country and never strayed far from the Arkansas when they did. More traders here than trappers, there was no reason for them to come up the small river that the old black robes called the River of Lost Souls and that the voyageurs called the Purgatoire and the bearded men of the long rifles said was the Purgatory. Surely there was no reason for any of them to foul Horse Camp with their presence.

Surely, though, Talks To Ghosts should determine who was there. It might be necessary to warn the people about this.

He sat where he was for a time and concluded that as he was already in the open he might already have been seen. And if he was not seen then it was safe to remain within view because in that event the party below would consist of blind men anyway.

Grunting unhappily that the pleasure of solitude seemed to have been interrupted, Talks To Ghosts stood and made his way slowly down the hillside toward Horse Camp.

It occurred to him, many hours too late, that perhaps he should have brought a weapon with him. Something more effective than the small knife suspended from a thong at his waist that was his only means of defense. The knife, that is, and the swiftness of his feet.

He came slowly down the hill and past the ford.

It was odd but he could no longer see the smoke. Had the fire been dying? That could be. The ones he sought could have left with the coming of day, leaving their fire untended to die on its own.

That seemed entirely possible, Talks To Ghosts somewhat hopefully decided. There was that possibility and a hundred more just as likely.

His sense of caution becoming more acute the closer he came to Horse Camp, Talks To Ghosts slowed and dropped to one knee. He lifted his head to a puff of breeze, and his nostrils flared as he tried to catch some hint of scent that would tell him if anyone remained at the camp. But there was nothing. Not even the sharp odor of hot coals and fresh ash from a recently living fire.

Talks To Ghosts hid in the grass and slithered on his belly like a great, lumpy snake.

He reached Horse Camp without sound, without being seen. And, puzzled, came reluctantly to his feet. He was certain he was not seen. Because there was no one here to see.

No man.

No fire.

No embers where a fire recently had been.

Nothing.

Talks To Ghosts shivered even though the sun was high in the sky and the day was anything but chill.

No fire. No source of smoke. None.

He trotted back and forth along the riverbank for more than an hour, seeking, smelling, trying to find some place where a fire had been. The only fire pits he saw were the same ones the people used year after year. And if any of them had been used anytime since the people left Horse Camp late last summer, it was not possible for Talks To Ghosts to tell it now.

He thought back, trying to bring to mind the exact sights he had seen from the top of the final ridge. It was smoke. He was sure of that. He had seen it clearly.

Smoke. But no fire. Nothing here to cause a smoke. And yet he saw, he truly saw, that smoke.

Talks To Ghosts stood on the bank of the river, sheltered by the cottonwoods above, and spread his legs wide apart, flung his hands out to either side. He tilted his head far back and with his eyes closed began a slow, measured chant as he appealed to the spirits above to explain to him this smoke where there was no fire.

There was no answer.

II

"What, no food? Again? You spend the whole morning hunting and come back with empty hands? Bah! You are the worst hunter I have ever known, Talks To Ghosts. Even children with tiny bows and blunt sticks for arrows can find more meat than Talks To Ghosts. All morning. And nothing, nothing at all to show for it. I beat my breast in despair. Do you see?" By way of example Sleeping Fawn hit herself on the hard bones of her chest several times in quick succession, glaring at her husband while she did so to make sure he got the point of her demonstration.

Talks To Ghosts shrugged and looked into the pot to see what she was preparing for lunch now that the lodge was in place and their things mostly in order. As far as he could determine, Sleeping Fawn intended to serve a soup of hot water for the meal. Very thin, water soup. As thin and unsatisfying as the somewhat similar footprint soup that was fashionable during particularly hard winter months when the snow was deep and the game scarce.

"Where are you going, Talks To Ghosts? I am not through talking to you."

Talks To Ghosts pretended not to hear. He left the lodge and the woman who had been his dead brother's wife—although why his brother would have chosen to marry a woman with all the gently sweet disposition of an ailing lynx he would never comprehend—and wandered down to the river.

There in the shade of the cottonwoods he found Black Otter, who was without doubt the best and closest friend anyone, least of all Talks To Ghosts, could ever have.

"Good morning, Talks To Ghosts. Where have you been all day, eh? I saw Sleeping Fawn on the path today but caught no sight of you. Have you been hunting? Did you kill game? Is there meat in your lodge?"

"Do you want me to answer all those at once or may I sort them out and take a day or two to make my responses?"

Black Otter laughed and motioned for his friend to

have a seat on the grassy embankment at his side. "Answer whatever you will. Or not as you prefer."

"I saw a smoke today where there was no fire," Talks To Ghosts said, as much to himself as to Black Otter.

"Truly?"

"Yes, truly. I do not understand it."

Black Otter grunted and, in thought, reached into the pouch at his waist to pull out a pipe and twist of black, molasses-soaked trade tobacco. He used his knife to shave bits of the dark, sweet leaf into his pipe and brought out a burning glass to light the pipe, shifting over a few inches to find a shaft of sunlight for the glass and then rocking back into the comfort of the shade once the pipe was burning.

Black Otter puffed on the tobacco for a few moments, then absently passed the pipe to his friend. Talks To Ghosts shared the smoke, the taste of it sharp and pleasantly biting on his tongue, and returned the pipe to Black Otter.

"This smoke I understand," Black Otter said finally. "But how can there be a smoke where there is no fire?"

"No fire then and not for a long time before," Talks To Ghosts said, reaching over to take the pipe from his friend's fingers and help himself for half a dozen long inhalations before again returning it.

"You are quite sure of this," Black Otter said, pretending it to be a statement rather than a question.

"I am sure."

Black Otter grunted. He smoked the remainder of his pipe in silence, then carefully cleaned the pipe and returned it to his pouch. Standing, he said, "My wife butchered one of the brown bitch's pups today. It was too big, you know. The meat will spoil before we can eat it all."

"You think so?"

"That is what my wife claims. Perhaps you would take some of it. So it will not spoil and be wasted."

"I would do that, yes."

"Come along then and see where she put my lodge."

Talks To Ghosts came to his feet and followed Black

Otter through the swarming activity of the people on their return to Horse Camp.

Life, he thought, was sometimes very good indeed.

III

White, puffy clouds streamed overhead, gliding swift and graceful from west to east, coming from the hills and jagged peaks and moving in silent majesty out across the vast grasslands where the life-giving buffalo were to be found.

Talks To Ghosts crouched in the foliage of the brush beside the river, well downstream from Horse Camp, his bow in his hands, an arrow nocked and ready to pull.

But in truth his attention was on neither the bow nor the patch of open ground he was watching—supposed to be watching—while small, eager boys moved toward the waiting hunters, driving game before them as the boys laughingly and happily made noise and with their small bows whacked busily at the bushes they passed through.

Talks To Ghosts stared intently at the beauty of the clouds that moved far above his head. He knew what clouds were made of. How many times had he passed through them in the mountains, clouds that truly were little different from chill, moist fog when they drifted down upon the mountain slopes that Talks To Ghosts and all the people of his tribe knew so very well and so very fondly.

He understood what the clouds were. But he did not pretend to understand the clouds themselves. What formed them? And why did they lie in the air like that? Was it only wind that moved them? Or was there some other unknown, perhaps unknowable, force that directed them? Where did they go when they were lost to sight so far into the land of the newborn sun? And how could a cloud contain something as heavy as rainwater and yet continue to float upon the air? That question was a great puzzlement to Talks To

Ghosts and one he had pondered at length without approaching any hint of satisfaction.

Think of it, he prompted himself once again. Take a water bag and fill it with rain. A good-size water bag can weigh so much it takes a strong woman to carry it. Or a stout pony. Yet that much water and how much more will fall from a single cloud in a single rainstorm. How much would all that water weigh? As much as every man, pony, child, and woman of all the tribes of the people. Or even more. And yet all of that, so much it was beyond the mind of mere man to comprehend, all of that rode inside the belly of the clouds until the spirits told the rain to descend.

Talks To Ghosts peered at the clouds and thought about them at length and then, reluctant but resigned that this was a mystery he would never unravel, he muttered a small complaint to the spirits around him and shifted his attention upstream, to the thin columns of smoke that rose from the grove where Horse Camp and the people now were.

The smoke he saw there was much like a cloud when seen from this distance. In appearance, at least, if not in substance. For after all, while both seem white and soft and rise on the air, a cloud is moist and can be felt upon one's cheek. Its moisture will collect on a man's eyelashes and its wetness can be tasted on his tongue. And yet a cloud has no odor while dry and insubstantial smoke has scents peculiar to whatever is burned to produce it. And smoke does not remain together on the wind but is whipped apart and made to disappear if it is carried by a wind.

Talks To Ghosts sighed. These smokes, at least, he could understand. And these smokes he knew were caused by fires. Real ones.

He could walk back to Horse Camp. Smell the smokes, see the fire pits, feel the heat of the coals. These smokes were real. Not like the one he saw so few days ago.

That smoke was . . . but no, what if the smoke he saw then was no smoke at all?

Talks To Ghosts had never seen a cloud so small and

so low standing on its end like a column of rising smoke. But because he never before saw such a thing, did it necessarily therefore follow that there could not *be* such a cloud?

Of course not, he told himself. He never saw a spirit either, but that did not mean there was no such thing. Everyone knew that.

So perhaps the great mystery of the smoke without fire was not a mystery after all but merely something new to Talks To Ghosts. Perhaps it was only a new sort of cloud. Or a wisp of the ordinary sort of cloud that somehow lost its way and was turned on end by a swirl of breeze. That was entirely possible, Talks To Ghosts conceded. Unlikely perhaps, but possible.

He grunted softly to himself, glad to think that there might be some explanation for the strange thing that he had seen.

He looked back up at the clouds. Now if only he could . . .

"Talks To Ghosts."

He blinked, looked about to see who was speaking to him. Then he smiled. "Yes, Burnt Finger?"

"Why didn't you shoot, Talks To Ghosts?"

"Shoot what, Burnt Finger?"

"Those rabbits. Three rabbits I saw pass in front of you not ten paces distant. And those were only the ones that I saw. Everyone else has meat, Talks To Ghosts. The beaters are bringing many rabbits to us. Have you not shot a single arrow yet?"

"I'm sorry, Burnt Finger. I didn't see them." Which was entirely true. He hadn't noticed a thing so far this drive.

But then it is also true that very few rabbits travel in clouds. A rabbit shape now and then perhaps but rather few actual rabbits.

Talks To Ghosts frowned and told himself, quite harshly, to pay attention from now on.

Unfortunately it was already too late for that, for the giggling, jumping, brush-whacking boys were already coming into view from the direction of Horse Camp, and all the game they were frightening ahead of them had already passed this place and by now would be scurrying through

the undergrowth well downstream from Talks To Ghosts'
place of ambush.

This was a shame, Talks To Ghosts conceded.

On the other hand, his thoughts today had brought
to him a possible explanation of the unexplainable. That
seemed quite enough of an accomplishment for one day.
And there was always tomorrow in which he might hunt. He
gave Burnt Finger a grin and a shrug and picked up his
spare arrows. He wondered what Sleeping Fawn was
making for their lunch. Time to go see.

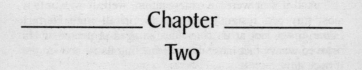

Chapter Two

I

Love is good. Love in the absence of a duenna would be even better.

Hernan Eduardo Salazar-Montoya glanced past the perfect features of his beloved to find—as he all too well expected—the somewhat less lovely but unfailingly watchful eyes of her tia Immaculata. The old woman's fingers moved in a swift and rhythmic dance and the needles of her knitting clacked and clattered in time to some unheard refrain, but the eyes, dark and expressionless and without hint of mercy or moderation of kindness, remained fixed on Hernan Eduardo and, more to the point, on the porcelain beauty of Maria Magdalena Mendoza.

Well, no wonder. Hernan Eduardo himself could not bring himself to look elsewhere when Maria Magdalena was near. Why should the old aunt of his beloved prove any different? For after all, was Maria Magdalena not the center of the known universe? In truth, yes. Of course. No other could begin to compare.

They sat side by side on the cold stone bench. Not too closely side by side, of course. Close enough that the hand laid ever so casually at rest between them encountered the stiff, embroidered cloth of her overskirt. Close enough that he could imagine the warmth that radiated from her glorious flesh. Far enough apart that the dragon duenna would not open her maw and belch fire.

And if that were an exaggeration, well, it was only a most tiny and insignificant one, for in all truth Hernan Eduardo was not at all sure that the aged protector of his beloved was in fact incapable of expelling flame and smoke if once aroused.

A sensible man, any sensible man at all, should surely choose a beloved whose aunts were all blind tipplers and of a benevolent nature besides.

But then what man, sensible or otherwise, had the power to exercise control over his own choice of loved one. A man felt the stirrings of his heart. Or he did not. It was not a matter he could determine of his own volition. It was a path some mighty—and ofttimes fickle—power led him onto whether he would will it or otherwise.

Hernan Eduardo listened attentively as Maria Magdalena spoke in her clear sweet voice about the troupe of musicians lately arrived from far-off Hidalgo del Parral. It was rumored that the duennas there were kindly and of a tolerant disposition, unlike here. In the staid and dreary northland modern influences *never* seemed to penetrate, neither in fashion, in thought, nor in indulgence. Santa Fe. Bah! It was hidebound, impossible.

He listened to Maria Magdalena with openly rapt attention, but his gaze wandered skyward, past the sheltering branches of the tree where they sat and into the night sky.

He blinked, glanced once more toward Tia Immaculata, then with a feigned gasp reached out to grasp Maria Magdalena by the softness of her dainty hand.

He felt the warmth of the contact, flesh upon flesh and skin upon skin and, before the dragon had time to pounce, he exclaimed, quite loudly, "Look there, Ma-Lena. A falling star. Do you see it?"

And of course no swain could be faulted for such a

moment of small excitement when seeing something so wondrous and luck-giving as a falling star, no?

"Where?"

"There. No, closer to the horizon. Did you see it? Really? Or was it too quickly gone?"

"I think . . . I may have caught a glimpse of it, yes."

He smiled. And was pleased. Because in the excitement their hands remained joined.

And of course there had been no star for either one of them to have seen.

Over on the adjacent bench Tia Immaculata gave up searching for the now disappeared star, or what she thought to have been a fleetingly visible star, and cleared her throat with an appropriately disapproving grimace.

Hernan Eduardo obediently remembered himself in the wake of his momentous discovery and allowed Maria Magdalena's sweet and tiny hand to fall from his grasp.

But, oh, he retained the memory of it. That, he was quite perfectly sure, he would never relinquish, never ever in all his days.

He could still feel the warmth of her flesh, the softness of her skin, the smooth and wonderful feel of touching his own truly beloved.

He committed each tiny morsel of sensation into his memory, to hold and to savor and to draw upon in the long and lonely hours of nights yet to come.

"Did you see it?" he asked. "Did you really see it?"

"I think so, yes. Yes, I really did." And she smiled and the evening air was scented with the perfume of fresh blossoms. Or was that the scent of simple happiness that so thrilled and pleased him?

Ah, he thought, it cannot be much better than this.

Well, upon reflection perhaps he would have to admit that indeed it *could* become better than this. But it would be better not to dwell upon that possibility lest he embarrass himself.

He shifted position minutely on the hard surface of the sandstone bench, searching for a moment of physical discomfort to cut through the unwonted lust that flickered and stirred within his loins and threatened to burst into active flame unless he brought it quickly and most firmly under control. For after all, duenna or no, there are some things that a man of decency and honor does not permit, not of himself any more than of others. And disrespect to one's own beloved is perhaps foremost among those things that are truly and totally beyond the permissible.

Idly, as if rambling about things of no particular interest or consequence, their previous conversation resumed. But in and through and beneath the things that were said wove all the things that were unsaid.

And Hernan Eduardo was almost deliriously happy in the cool of this most beautiful of all evenings.

II

No need to worry about tripping over an uneven cobble in the dark. Not on this night when his feet floated so lightly above the paving. Not on this night when it was certain that Maria Magdalena did truly love him. And on this most glorious night, yes, this was most assuredly of a certitude, for Hernan Eduardo had been able to see her affection so clearly, so plainly, so beautifully.

It was there in the softness of her gaze. She displayed it in the warmth of her smile. She showed it to him in the flutter of her lashes, the sultriness of her whispers, the daring closeness of her hand to his—not touching, no, but oh so very close to it—when the dragon's attention was diverted for one precious moment or two. She showed it to him in so very many ways.

And Hernan Eduardo responded with a heart that soared, responded with a mad rush of blood through his veins, responded with a joyous fullness the like of which he never before had known.

Was there ever before a night such as this? Never. No man had ever known its match. Of this he was certain.

He drifted through the shadows and along the narrow

alleys as light as a wraith and as carefree as a songbird. And indeed there were songs within his breast as he made his way through the maze of paths and small streets to the high wall and ornate iron gatework that hid the Salazar home from rude view.

He turned in there, happy and gay, and allowed the gate to close behind him with a huge clatter of announcement. The son, the heir, the most fortunate of fortunates was returned. And while he would make no declaration of the things that had taken place on this night, surely all in the family would know that tonight, now, their Hernan Eduardo was changed and would never again visit feckless childhood. This they would sense in him. This he was sure of.

The gate clanged shut as if it were a bell sounding forth. But no one came into the courtyard. Not a servant, not his father, no one.

So odd, this was. So very unusual. Lamps blazed and candles guttered, but the courtyard and the garden were empty.

Hernan Eduardo paused, uncertain, and came unbidden to a halt as the silence enveloped him. There was . . . something . . . an ominous sense of uncertainty . . . that held him in a chill grip. For a moment, a moment only.

And then from somewhere inside the grand house that his grandfather's grandfather had built there was a muffled shriek. And for the second time on this very same night Hernan Eduardo's life was altered.

III

His father sat in icy silence, a statue at the dining table while around him there was . . . nothing. No Josephina peeping out from the kitchen doorway to see the approval of her works. No shy Angelica bustling in and out with steaming dishes. In fact, there was neither food nor scent of food despite the lateness of the hour when normally the family should be gathered for a shared evening meal.

Tonight there was none of that. Tonight there was but a cold and stony emptiness that invaded the huge room and hung like a shroud about his father's immobile shoulders.

No sign of Hernan Eduardo's mother nor of his baby sister. No sign of . . .

"Father?" Hernan Eduardo stepped out of the shadows and into the light. "Is something wrong?"

His father continued to stare blindly forward, not acknowledging the son and heir in the slightest.

"Father?" Hernan Eduardo repeated, this time perhaps with a faint tremor in his voice, for such a thing as this had never happened before, never in all his twenty-four years. Father was stern, yes, and proud, as was right and proper. But always, always fair and kind and loving within the privacy of the family. But now . . .

"Father?"

"Your father cannot hear you, Son."

He turned. His mother stood in the doorway that led down from the upper floor where the breezes drifted softly through to cool their bedrooms even on the warmest of nights.

His mother stood there, her face as strange a mask as his father's. She spoke to her son, but her glare—glare? Yes, so indeed it was—focused upon her husband, who sat as if waiting without true expectation for the dinner to be served. She glared at her husband, who continued to ignore both wife and son but who did not deign to look in the direction of the kitchen where the errant staff should have been but were not.

"Mother, what is . . . ?"

"Your father cannot answer, my son, because he has become deaf. He is blinded. He has departed from reason."

"But . . ."

"Tragedy, Hernan Eduardo. A great tragedy afflicts this house."

"I do not understand." That was more than merely true. It was a masterpiece of understatement. Hernan Eduardo looked unhappily from one parent to the other and back again, but that did not provide him with answers.

"We are disgraced, Son."

"Disgraced, Mother?"

"Everyone will know. Everyone. The town, this entire region, will look at us with contempt. We will become the butt of rumor and scorn and, worst of all, we will be the objects of small and ugly jokings."

"What happened, Mother? Can't you please tell me? Please?"

"It is your sister who—"

"No!" His father's voice was the great and rasping roar of a jaguar, a lion, a fierce and fearsome gargantuan although he was but scant inches more than five feet in height. Hernan Eduardo always saw his father as a large man. And never more so than at this moment when the old man's fist towered high in the air, hung there for one awful moment, and then descended full force onto the polished surface of the table. Crystal rocked and cutlery jangled and for a second Hernan Eduardo was sure the great pine table would be split apart by the force of his father's blow.

"No!" the old man stormed. "My son has no sister."

Hernan Eduardo gaped, speechless, as with a terrifying power his father repeated that lie. In loud, carefully spaced words the old man roared out, "I ... have ... no ... daughter."

IV

Elena was not in her room, and for a moment Hernan Eduardo's heart failed to beat. It stopped dead in his chest. Until he noticed with a surge of relief that the doors onto the balcony were open. She was out there, a shawl covering her head from the cool of the air, leaning on the stone railing and staring blindly, forlornly into the night.

Hernan Eduardo approached and lightly touched her elbow. His beloved baby sister, seventeen years of age at her last birthday and more beautiful than a sunrise, saw who it was and spun, throwing herself onto him with a sob. She pressed her face into his shoulder, and he could feel her breath wet and hot against his flesh, even through the fabric of his tunic.

"How?" he whispered.

Elena pulled back, aghast, and gave him a startled, doe-eyed stare.

Hernan Eduardo blushed and shook his head. "No, I . . . I didn't mean *that* how. I mean . . . I know how such things happen. What I meant to say . . ." He stopped, quite thoroughly miserable, for in truth he did not know really quite what it was that he did mean to say.

Elena managed a small, brave smile and kissed the side of his mouth as lightly as if he were brushed by the wings of a butterfly. "Love," she said simply. "Just . . . love." The smile reappeared but somewhat twisted this time into a wry and dear little face. "Or so I thought at the time."

"And now?"

She shrugged. "My valiant prince was unprepared for, shall we say, the responsibilities of parenthood. Besides, he finds it necessary that he make a visit to a relative. A rather distant relative."

"Ah," Hernan Eduardo said softly. "Perhaps I should discuss this with him."

"With what, Brother? A sword? A knife? A gun perhaps? No, let it go. I was the one who was the fool. He took no more than I permitted. The fault is mine. So must the punishment be."

"When?"

Again Elena shrugged. "Your father did not tell me. I would assume . . . tomorrow at the dawning? He is a decent man, this father of yours. He would not turn a stranger into the street at night. It is a thing better done in the light of the day, no?"

Hernan Eduardo felt the pain stab deep into his chest. Elena, sweet and innocent Elena. Out. Thrown upon the mercy of . . . Who? The mercy of what? Lord God Almighty, sweet Mary and Joseph and all the saints above . . . thrown upon the mercy of what or of whom? Where would Elena go? How would she live, she who never in her life had been required to lift a hand except perhaps to an embroidery hoop. What was to become of her now?

"You look sad, dear brother."

"And would you not if our positions were reversed?"

Elena's face twisted into a caricature of a smile and she lightly jibed, "Hernan Eduardo, for shame. You? With child?"

But the lightheartedness was feigned, and poorly so, for bitter tears streamed from Elena's dark and beautiful eyes, tears that flowed hot and salty around the mouth that formed that mockery of a smile. Salty, Hernan Eduardo knew for a certainty, because he hugged Elena close to his breast and kissed the softness of her cheek and so he could taste the salt of her tears upon his tongue.

Dios, oh, Dios, he murmured silently to himself while brother and sister stood locked in anguished embrace. What, oh, what shall become of her now? What, oh, what can the future hold?

Hernan Eduardo had no answers to his own questions. Which, he reflected sourly, was probably just as well. He held Elena tight to his bosom and rocked gently to and fro just as long ago he had held and rocked her when she was but an infant and he the protecting big brother. The big brother who now had failed her so very, very badly. Aye, if only he could confront . . . but no, done was done. To find the man and to punish him would be to become no better than their father's fearsome retribution, would that not be so? The thing that was needed now was to think about Elena and what was to become of her.

And for that he had no inkling of an answer. None whatsoever, and thus he grieved and soon began to weep, his own tears mingling with those of his dear sister as the two of them stood on the threshold of the unknowable and the unanswerable.

"Dios, oh, Dios," he whispered softly under his breath, and with the faint sound Elena began to cry all the harder, her whole delicate frame shuddering and shaking with the force of her despair.

V

There was but one solution. And that was no solution at all. A lifetime of disgrace and contempt seemed harsh payment for a moment . . . a moment? Better not to ask, better not to know if it were but one moment or a hundred. Of some things a brother should not inquire. For some things a gentleman does not seek. Who, how . . . those things were no longer of importance. Now the only question remaining was what to do toward the future and never mind the past.

But, oh, his heart ached so fiercely. Hernan Eduardo bled for this child who was of his own blood, this girl whose flesh was part and parcel of his own.

The two sat together throughout the night. And both knew of a certainty that come the dawn the order would be brought—not delivered personally, no, for that would necessarily involve requiring his father to speak directly to a person whose existence the man would not, could not, ever again acknowledge—but come the dawning the order would be brought by some heartbroken servant, and Elena would be cast beyond the door, abandoned forevermore by the family that once cherished her.

"Where will you go?" Hernan Eduardo asked. Foolishly.

Elena shrugged. There was no answer. None she could speak of. There were no choices. She knew that as completely as did Hernan Eduardo. There was but one possibility. That or death. And Hernan Eduardo knew that to Elena the one would be the same as the other.

At least he thought he knew this to be so.

He was mistaken. For after a lengthy silence Elena sat upright, squaring her shoulders and her jaw. "I will live," she said slowly but firmly. "I will survive. For my small one. For the child of love that I carry in my belly."

"But . . ."

"You do not know, dear brother. You cannot. No man could ever know. But this . . . I have known for several months, you see. And I suspected before that. Five months almost I have been with child. Five months. And while I should feel disgraced, a whore, a slattern, and the worst sort of scum, I . . . I feel for the baby a thing that I never could have felt for its father. A joy, a closeness, a completion such as I never knew was possible. You do not understand, my poor confused brother." She gave him a small smile and reached up to lightly caress his cheek. "Never mind trying to comprehend, Hern'ardo dear. I will not do what our parents expect. I will go . . . somewhere. It does not matter where. I will change my name. I will do whatever I must to remain alive, to have this child . . . to love and care for it for the rest of my days. I will do what I must, Hern'ardo my sweet."

"You would even . . ." He could not finish it, could not speak of such an enormity as this.

"Yes. I would do anything. Do you understand me? I would do *any* thing that is necessary for the good of my child. I would and indeed I shall. Anything that I must."

There was a firmness of resolve in little Elena now that Hernan Eduardo had not seen, indeed that he had never before suspected. It was a strength—and a flaw—that he had not known she possessed.

He held her hand in his, and together they wept. For all that had been, for all that was, for all that would be.

VI

"No," Hernan Eduardo said, his voice firm and strong now that his thoughts had come at last to a conclusion. The two of them, he and his beloved Elena, stood together sleepless and dry-eyed on the balcony. Far to the east, beyond the arid plains, the sun was creeping toward the horizon to begin this most bitter of all days.

But no, some things are not permissible. Some things simply cannot be allowed to be. And for his own Elena to become a vessel of public convenience, no. Of a certainty no. This would not be.

"No, Hern'ardo dear? Would you stop the sun from rising?"

He smiled and shook his head. "Not even if I had the power, for that would trap us both here and now, would it not? And this I would not wish for you. No, Elena, we must put yesterday behind and seek tomorrow. Is that not what we have always been taught? Seek for the good. Pray for divine grace. But do not neglect to work for what is desired."

"You have been a good brother," Elena said. "I loved you. In my heart I always will. Now, Hernan Eduardo, help me pack a few things. I must be ready, and I—"

"You are not listening to me," he chided softly.

"There is no time now to—"

"How many times must I tell you, eh? Listen while I speak."

"I do not understand."

"Of course you do not understand. How could you when you speak instead of listen." He smiled and bussed her lightly on the cheek. "A woman alone, with or without a child, is a woman without honor. But a wife, with or without child, a wife is a glory to her husband and to her god."

"Yes, Hern'ardo, but . . ."

He laughed, all his uncertainties falling away now to be replaced by a surging joy. He laughed and he grabbed Elena's two hands in his own and squeezed hard, then dropped her hands and gathered her to him in a hug. "It will be fine, little sister who is no longer to be my sister. It will all work out well. For you and for the child of your heart."

"But I do not—"

"Do you love me, Elena?"

"You know that I do."

"Do you trust me?"

"Of course, but—"

"No but, little one. I know what we must do, you and I." He paused, then laughed again. "No, not us two. Us three. You, me, the baby within you. The three of us. It will be fine. Depend upon it. I promise you, Elena. The three of us shall be fine. Now go. Pack. Money if you have any. And whatever you own of value, anything that can be sold for cash. For what I have in mind, baby sister, we will need all we can gather. So go now, quickly while you can, eh?"

"But . . ."

His mood was infectious. He could tell from her expression that for the first time in hours, for the first time since he had come home to find the world torn apart, Elena was beginning to hope. And not grimly but almost with an eagerness. She was beginning to accept Hernan Eduardo's lead.

And his attitude most certainly now was that this greatest of all disasters could also be viewed as a challenge. A challenge of most magnificent proportion, true, but a challenge nonetheless.

"Go," he told her. "Pack. And do not, I tell you do *not* allow anyone to put you out of this room until I return. You hear me?"

"I hear you, Hern'ardo."

He grabbed her. Hugged her briskly, joyously, then turned and plunged off toward his own cluttered quarters, for he too had preparations to make.

And quick packing to accomplish.

Chapter
Three

I

It was a sound that woke him. A—he had to reach for it—a gasp, that's what it was. He was mildly proud of himself for having worked that out. Until he heard another one. This time right into his ear.

He came halfway to a sitting position at that explosive little outburst, and even while he was moving, the awful realization swept through his mind to stop his heartbeat—well, sort of—and to chill his marrow.

And that was the truth. Chilling, that's what it was. No, stupid was what it *really* was.

He had gone and fallen asleep. How in the world could he have been so dumb as to go and drop off to sleep, for crying out loud. Sleep!

Letty's folks never came upstairs until nine-thirty, sometimes ten o'clock. They'd had all the time in the world. Used it mighty darn well too if he did say so.

But then to fall asleep? Sheesh! They were in for it now, darn it.

Not that he couldn't handle it now that necessity arose. Of course he could. He had that one time before, hadn't he?

Not here, of course. Not with Letty and her parents. But back home that time. It hadn't been so hard. Confess. Cry a little. Pray a whole lot. Ask for mercy. In the end they'd all cried together, the girl and her mam and her pap and before they were done the little sisters and baby brother too, all of them including Aaron bawling and praying and carrying on. They'd done all that and he'd promised to marry the girl, and a couple days later he was on the road making dust.

Which was how he came to be here with a wild-eyed woman staring down at him from the doorway to Letty's bedroom.

Dammit.

Aaron rubbed at his eyes—he still couldn't hardly believe he'd been so dumb as to go to sleep like that—and cleared his throat ready to start on the first step, which would be to apologize and confess and to say how much he admired and respected and truly, deeply loved this little old girl.

Then the world kind of came to a screeching halt.

Screeching in that it was Letty doing the screeching. Also screaming, snuffling, whimpering, and assorted other stuff in the same vein.

"Mama Mama get him off me don't let him make me do those disgusting things to him no more *help* me Mama don't let him hurt me no more." It all came out in one tumbled, crazy rush. Letty didn't so much as stop to take a breath. She just sucked in a lungful and then let the lies fly, damn her.

Lies? Lordy, he reckoned they were lies. Damn girl hadn't been no virgin when he got there. Why, she was the one wanted it the most. Pretty much. For sure she was every bit as eager and ready as he was. Every time. Why, it wasn't like this here was anything new neither. He'd been working for her pap for, what? three months? closer to four? Either way, he'd been a contented employee since the second week or thereabouts, even if the old bastard did overwork a fella.

Huh. It was his fault Aaron fell asleep. He'd been so tired from all that labor that of course he'd dropped off. It was all the fault of that damned old man.

And now Letty was screaming that he'd forced her. Why, he ought to . . . tell? Tell who? Her folks? Now that he had half a second to ponder the truth it occurred to him that it wasn't real likely that anybody in this house was gonna pay mind to anything Aaron Jenks had to say. Not so long as the damn girl kept bellowing and carrying on like she was.

"Make him quit Mama make him leave me be Mama he hurt me Mama he hurt me awful bad." She paused. Gulped in a deep breath ready for another go. Pointed toward the mound of quilting that covered the big, soft feather bed. "Down here Mama it hurts awful bad from what he made me do help me Mama please help me don't let him do me no more or . . ."

Not that Mama was listening. By now she was doing some shouting her own self. She'd turned and was leaning out into the hallway and shouting. "Get your gun, Curtis, that snotty hired boy is raping our baby, Curtis, get your gun and come quick."

Gun! Lordy, that was serious. Gun. Jesus Crippled Christ on a crutch. Gun!

Aaron sprang out of bed, realized he was naked as a hardboiled egg, and made a pass as if to duck back under the covers, then remembered that even the nicest-made color quilt won't do much to stop a bullet and decided that being seen naked by Letty's mam wasn't half as bad as some other things might could be. He came off the bed like a jack-in-the-box gone loose and made a sweeping grab for his clothes piled on the knitting stool by the window.

He bent down, thinking to find his shoes, which seemed to've been kicked under the dust ruffle someplace, but he could hear footsteps, mighty heavy ones, at the bottom of the stairs.

Barefoot wasn't so bad. Considering.

Aaron skinned out of the window and onto the roof of the back porch—the way he always came and went from that lying dang Letty's bedroom—and threw his clothes over the edge, following them half a heartbeat later. If there

were any splinters on the porch post he never felt them.
Time enough to think about that later.

Aaron grabbed up his clothes and went larruping
across the farmyard in the direction of the barn where he
slept and where his little bundle of stuff was. He ran at a sort
of humped-over lope, hopping on one foot at a time and
trying to get into his britches while he went.

Behind him he heard a roar. A deep and masculine one.
And the hollow, fearsome sound of a gunshot. It was only
the shotgun though, thank goodness, and not the squirrel
rifle. Birdshot peppered the ground all around and stung him
on the shoulders a mite, but it wasn't so bad as it could have
been, like if the shooting was done from a close-up distance.
Up close even birdshot would mess up a fellow's entire day.

Aaron disappeared inside the barn before the old man
had time enough to loose his second barrel—and damn the
man who invented two-shoot guns anyway—and ran right
on through.

He knew what they'd be expecting him to do, and
that sure as snuff wasn't what he was fixing to let happen.
No sir.

Instead he jumped over the railing into the hog stall,
dropped to hands and knees, and scooted underneath the
open bottom of the half-door out into the feed lot. Generally
he would have been cussing about getting covered with the
filth of the hogpen, but at the moment he wasn't much worried about that. Later maybe.

Once back outside in the chill night air he splashed
ankle deep through the cold hog crap to the gate and
unlatched the thing, pushing it open.

Then where a less thoughtful soul would have hurled
on into the dark, Aaron turned back and commenced hazing
the startled sows and their broods of part-grown pigs out
into the lane that led through the neighbor's woodlot.

It was clear to him now what needed to be done, and he
was busy going about it.

Behind him he could hear the puffing, huffing, lum-
bering approach of Letty's father. The one with the gun and
the big mad. Ha!

Aaron chased the last squealing litter of pigs out of the lot and into the night, then threw himself down darn near nose deep in the muddy slop behind the water trough.

Lordy, he'd never felt anything, and he meant *any-* thing, so cold and slimy as that soupy mud was. But the deeper into it he could bury himself right now the better he would like it, yes indeedy-dee.

He permitted himself a tiny smile as Letty's pap splashed by in pursuit of the noise all those loose pigs were making.

II

Cold? Lordy, he reckoned. But necessary. Just about anything was better than smelling of the muck in that pigpen.

He wallowed neck deep in the water .of the horse trough for a minute or so, so as to work the muck off himself, then crawled out and headed at a slow trot for the back door of the house. He knew exactly what he wanted there.

Inside the kitchen door he took down Letty's pap's woolen capote. It was a beauty of a thing, made from a soft, thick, six-point blanket and big enough to serve as a bed at night as well as keeping a fellow warm on the coldest of cold days. Which there were sure to be more of on the way, never mind that the calendar claimed it was supposed to be springtime already.

Aaron had admired that capote right along, ever since he'd got to the farm, and now he couldn't see any reason why he shouldn't help himself to it. As recompense for the lies that were being told about him, so to speak.

He took it down and then for good measure stepped into the boots that were set on the floor under the hook where the capote hung. The boots weren't such a good fit, but not such a bad one either. The error, fortunately, was on the big side of things so he could wrap his feet in some cloths—he spotted some dish towels in the wash basket and took them too, concluding that they would do just fine for foot wrapping—and be comfortable enough in the old man's boots. Or, rather, in Aaron's new boots.

Upstairs there was still commotion going on. He could hear Letty whimpering and wailing and weeping on her mam's shoulder. Which was fine by Aaron. The more noise the two women made up there the less likely they were to hear him down here.

He figured Letty's pap would be some time figuring out that he wasn't going to get another shot at the hired man this night, so Aaron should be able to do this thing right now that the necessity was upon him.

He made himself comfortable in the boots and capote and then set about gathering a sack of eatables to carry on the road with him.

No money, though. He knew where the family kept their pin money, but he left it be. That would have been stealing, and Aaron wasn't one to think of himself as a thief. Taking the things he needed to get away from Letty's false-hoods, that was only a fair and proper restitution, the way he saw it. Taking cash money would have been base thievery, and that he wouldn't do.

He did help himself to some cold beef, a hunk of cold lamb, some leftover biscuits, and a fair-sized burlap poke of new potatoes. Aaron loved potatoes. He liked them raw as well as he did cooked, and there wasn't any way he'd ever heard of to cook a potato that he wouldn't like it. He took about all of the potatoes that he figured he could comfortably carry and a couple extra in his pockets.

And that, as the saying went, kind of seemed to be that.

It had been a good enough place to work. For so long as it lasted. Time now, though, to move along. Either that or hop around whilst Letty's father tried to pot him like a half-wild gobbler at a turkey shoot. That was an image that could be amusing from every viewpoint save that of the turkey, Aaron could clearly see now. And it was one he calculated he would rather avoid.

So he helped himself to the few things he needed, along with a stout basket and straps to carry it all in, then quietly let himself out the front door—it had been a spell now, and one never knew when the old bastard might be coming home to the back door again—and on out to the road.

The only question now was which direction to set his feet once he got the dust on them.

Aaron was grinning a mite as he walked through the deep shadows beneath the front-yard elm. He felt . . . light. Free. Loose and kind of happy.

He stuffed his hands into the big patch pockets on the skirts of the dandy capote and, under his breath, commenced to whistle a sprightly tune.

III

Right, that was the direction. Right, that is to say, toward the west. Toward Pittsburgh and the Ohio. The reason for that was simple. Time and time before Aaron had talked to Letty's father about someday moving on to Philadelphia, so it was east where the old man would expect him to be. Plenty good enough reason to go west, that.

And a modicum of deception would not be a bad thing at all, not if there was any chance a hue and cry could be raised—for after all, who knew what embellishments Letty might think to add to her tale now that she'd started her mouth to running—because it was hard for folks to overlook the passage of a lean, lanky, beanpole of a stranger with bright red hair.

Kind of stood out in a crowd, Aaron conceded that he did. Which hardly seemed reason to punish him for things he hadn't even done. Lord knew he'd done enough things to deserve punishing. Wouldn't it be a real kick in the teeth now to be nabbed for something he didn't do?

But then nobody ever actually said that life was going to be fair, had they?

Aaron chuckled some about that. And put his chin down so as to concentrate on the path before him and holding to a solid, steady pace along it.

What he would like would be to have a goodly distance between himself and this farmstead before the break of the morrow.

That not only was what he would like, it was what he fully intended, and he set himself to the task with all the wiry strength that was in him.

IV

"Well, well, well, if it isn't our old friend Aaron."

"You shouldn't ought to be sarcastic, Barney. It doesn't become you." Aaron set down the mug of cider that he'd been enjoying . . . right up until Barney and his little brother James walked in.

Aaron guessed that Letty's father, and maybe the old man's brother too, had gone east toward Philadelphia where they expected Aaron to run. But just to be cautious they'd sent the boys, Letty's two hulking cousins, sons of her quarrelsome uncle, west along the road to Pittsburgh.

Tough luck, darn it.

And no help for it now but to answer up. If he dang well had to.

Aaron grinned and motioned vaguely toward the pewter tankard. "Join me, fellows? My treat."

"You'd treat us with money you stole from Uncle Jergen?"

"That, James, I did not do. I took no cash."

"And isn't that his cape you're wearing?"

Aaron's grin became a mite wider. "Not no more it isn't. Besides, he owed me something for wages due. And it wouldn't have been right for me to take cash money. I thought this would settle the account nicely."

The older of the brothers, each of whom had shoulders resembling those of a near-grown ox, was not in a humor to be distracted. "The most valuable thing you stole is the one we dasn't mention where others can listen in, damn you."

"Nonsense," Aaron said. "As you well know, Barney,

since you were there afore me." He gave Letty's cousin a knowing wink and then laughed.

Interestingly enough it was James and not Barney who became the angrier over the accusation.

But then it was James who was hopelessly in love with darlin' Letty. And big brother Barney who'd deflowered the girl, or anyway bedded her. Aaron was never quite sure what to believe and what not when it came to Letty's tales of amorous endeavor. At times she'd seemed a tad carried away with the romance of a notion, so much so that he suspected she sometimes gilded the lily. So maybe it was to Barney she'd granted the honor of abandoning chastity . . . or maybe not. It wasn't likely Aaron would ever know for certain sure. But it was certain sure he would not bother himself with caring overmuch.

"You take that back, damn you," James warned with his mouth pinched tight shut and his eyes squeezed half closed in menace as well.

"Or you'll what, Master James?" Aaron mocked him.

For after all there wasn't much doubt in his mind that the boys already intended to thrash him before they carried him back to face the old man's ire. Any threats beyond that could not help but ring hollow.

"Well?" he asked, sliding his cider back out of the way and taking a moment to cinch his belt tighter at the waist of the handsome capote.

Barney hesitated but James did not. The impetuous younger brother launched himself at Aaron in a low and sudden head butt.

Incredible! Aaron could scarcely believe his luck. He stood his ground until young James was fully committed, then quickly sidestepped. James swept past the inviting target of Aaron's midsection.

And right on into the rather solid obstruction of the heavy walnut bar.

Aaron winced at the sound as James's noggin crashed into unyielding wood with roughly the same hollow sound of a melon being dropped onto a puncheon floor. From a considerable height.

It positively hurt just to hear it.

James dropped facedown in the sawdust of the public room flooring, blood flowing generously from a newly opened split atop his scalp.

Now if only Barney would accommodate by being so brash. . . .

No such luck, sadly. The older, and wiser, of the brothers gave his baby bro'er a pitying glance—Aaron suspected the pity had to do not with James's pain but with his stupidity—then turned his head aside to delicately spit once or twice in anticipation of the combat about to commence.

"Rules, Barney?" Aaron inquired pleasantly.

"None, damn you," Barney snarled.

"If you care to reconsider . . ."

Barney spit into his left palm and then into the right— unsanitary in Aaron's view but commendably traditional— and hitched his trousers up, then lifted his fists into *en garde* posture and slowly stalked forward.

Aaron sighed. He'd seen Barney fight before.

Barney, on the other hand, had not seen him in a tussle.

And as it happened, the primary difference between them was that Barney loved little more than the feel of the gristle in another's nose crunching and bursting under the onslaught of his own hard knuckles, while Aaron, on the other hand, regarded himself as something of a coward and was most unwilling to take the pains of a happy-go-lucky pummeling. So much so, in fact, that he was quite willing to cheat in order to avoid physical punishment.

As for instance . . .

Barney lowered his chin behind his high-raised guard and shuffled closer, ever closer.

Aaron waited.

And when Barney was in proper position, Aaron feinted a wild left-handed haymaker while the big boot that once belonged to predictable Barney's uncle lashed out to socket itself unerringly in poor Barney's crotch.

Well, Aaron had asked about rules. The choice of dispensing with them was Barney's, was it not? It was, Aaron somewhat smugly congratulated himself.

Barney joined his brother in the sawdust with scarcely a whimper, the one knocked cold by his own assault and the other doubled into a tight ball and writhing to and fro on the floor like a hog rooting for acorns buried in the litter.

Aaron eyed the cider sitting undisturbed on the bar top . . . but decided that would be a show-off stunt.

Besides, what if Barney got up?

Better not to chance it.

And so, taking discretion firmly in hand, Aaron made good time leaving Barney and James behind.

V

The capote would fetch a good price. Enough, perhaps, to keep him for a month or longer. Certainly enough to carry him over until he could find employment, which in a city the size of Pittsburgh, said to have a population of several thousand, surely could not be long.

And anyway it was only sensible to get rid of the garment.

Aaron was easy enough to notice on his own but all the more so when he was wearing the gaudy capote. So of course he ought to dispose of it at once, before the all-too-visible thing helped lead Barney and James to him for a second attempt at mayhem.

Aaron had no illusions about the outcome should the brothers catch up with him a second time. At that tavern back on the highway they had been unprepared. He could not expect to be so lucky again. So naturally the only sensible course was to bow to the inevitable.

But . . . he *liked* the capote. And, anyway, what had Pittsburgh ever done for him that he should favor the community by adopting it?

Aaron followed his nose—literally, for the stench of the waterfront was unmistakable—to one of the two great rivers that passed by the city—one was the Allegheny and the other the Mononga-something, but Aaron had no idea which of them was which, only that together they formed the Ohio, of which he had heard much—and onto the first quay he sighted.

"You there."

"Aye?" The man was engaged in gathering a bunch of wet rope into a tight coil.

"You look loaded and ready to leave. Where are you bound?"

The riverman gave Aaron a haughty look. "Upstream, where else?"

"Look, I can see as well as anybody that you've no oars or paddles. Of course you're going downstream. I mean to ask where your cargo is destined."

"Cairo."

It was Aaron's turn to deliver a look of disgust. "You can tug on my leg all you want, friend, but you won't make me believe that flat-bottomed contraption will take you all the way to far Egypt."

"Not Cairo, dammit, Cairo."

"Say what?"

The riverman chuckled. "They're spelt the same but pronounced different. The one I'm drifting to is in Illinois."

"Ah, yes, of course. Illinois." Which so far as Aaron had been concerned in the past might as well have been in Egypt too. "Would you be needing a hand on your journey to, um, Cairo?"

"I would not, thankee."

Aaron shrugged. "It was a thought. Thanks all the same." He started to turn away.

"Don't need a hand," the riverman stopped him, "but I could take a passenger."

"I don't have much in the way of money," Aaron reported.

"We might work something out."

"Such as?"

"That coat. It looks warm."

"That it is," Aaron agreed.

"You got your own grub?"

"Some," Aaron said.

"If'n you feed yourself along the way, friend, I expect I'd give you passage in exchange for the coat."

Aaron rubbed his chin. Then smiled. Surely a brawny sort like this river fellow would have the vice of gambling. Or something. Surely they could work out alternate arrangements along the way. Aaron had little doubt that he would be able to manage his passage plus leave the boat still wearing his handsome capote.

And anyway, with Barney and James somewhere close behind, he was willing to accept the risk of losing the capote in exchange for avoiding the risk of a second encounter with the hard-handed lads from Bedford County.

"Done," Aaron said, dropping from the quay onto the low-lying deck of the heavily loaded flatboat.

"Where's your gear, mister?"

"I'm wearing it."

"Do you mean to tell me that coat is all you own?"

Aaron shrugged. But in truth was greatly pleased. The question showed that the fellow was a man of conscience. Why, given a few days to talk about all this and the riverman would take the initiative to look for ways he could leave Aaron the one possession he had and keep from taking the capote in payment.

And as for Barney and James, they would never catch up to him now.

Unless maybe they went to Egypt. Aaron threw his head back and laughed aloud with the sheer joy of being alive and free. And unpummeled, of course.

"You feeling all right, friend?" the riverman asked.

"More than all right. Here, let me give you a hand."

"You're a paying passenger. You don't have to work your way."

"That's all right. I don't mind helping out."

"In that case, friend, you can help me best by . . ."

Chapter Four

I

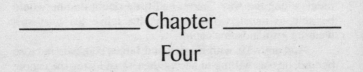

Talks To Ghosts ambled across the top of the ridge, looked closely and carefully at the ground where he stood, and then settled into a comfortable position with his legs crossed and his hands lying slack in his lap, which was a great aid to concentration.

Behind him he could hear Big Stones's rustling, crackling approach through the dried grasses of the winter past. Talks To Ghosts kept his face straight and his expression bland. But he wanted to laugh. This hillside was thick with the rounded, gray-green buttons of small cactus, and he knew poor Big Stones must be filling his belly with their spines. Very uncomfortable, Talks To Ghosts knew. But then so did Big Stones. He could have stood up and walked like Talks To Ghosts had. Buffalo have truly horrible eyesight. It would have made no difference. Not to the buffalo, anyway. Apparently hiding and sneaking and crawling about most uncomfortably satisfied some desire in Big Stones that Talks To Ghosts did not really understand. Another mystery to be pondered when time permitted, neh?

Talks To Ghosts glanced back in time to see Big

Stones wince. It was more difficult than ever to keep from laughing. Big Stones's belly by now must be furry with the tiny spines.

And at that Big Stones was better off than if he'd sat upon the tiny round shapes. Because after all, a man can remove cactus spines from his own belly. But who has a friend so close that he will remove the spines when one sits upon a cactus?

Talks To Ghosts turned quickly back around to hide the expression he could not quite contain. Then he gave himself a firm and forceful reminder to pay attention now, close attention and serious. For after all, this was very serious business indeed.

The leader of the hunt reached his side, elbows and knees thoroughly scraped and stomach nicely tenderized by the intrusion of many wee small stickers. "Do you see them, Talks To Ghosts?"

"I see them," Talks To Ghosts assured the older man. He refrained from mentioning the obvious. It would have been very difficult indeed to not see the small, shaggy herd in the distance. They were dark, slowly moving shapes distinct against the pale background of sun-bleached earth and scarce grass. "I saw them yesterday, remember? They have come to where we expected."

The "we" part of that was said out of respect for Big Stones. In truth there was no one else among the people, not even Long Hair the healer, who understood buffalo and the other living creatures the way Talks To Ghosts did. It was only Talks To Ghosts who could look at a grazing band of buffalo and predict where they would be in twenty-four hours. Or forty-eight. Or more.

Talks To Ghosts himself did not understand how he knew all the things he knew. He only knew what was so, and he had come to trust this knowledge.

And a good thing too, for he was a truly terrible hunter and it was only his ability to direct his betters in the hunt that kept his lodge from being empty of meat even more than was the case.

"Put the young men there, Big Stones, and there,"

Talks To Ghosts said, pointing. "The herd will come past that wallow. Do you see it? They will come by to the north side, very close. Then they will turn there . . . do you see where I mean? . . . to begin toward the river. Tell the young men to wait until the last calves have passed the wallow. Then when the men show themselves the buffalo will run that way. Have the rifles and the best of the bowmen waiting there." Again he pointed. "If they shoot when the buffalo are not yet too close . . . half a bowshot but not much nearer than that . . . they will turn back and the young men too will be able to shoot. But let them get too close and they will burst past the hunters and cross the river at that spot where the bottom is hard, there."

Big Stones pulled at his chin and looked from side to side as if he expected to find someone else nearby to offer counsel. "This is what you think, Talks To Ghosts?"

Talks To Ghosts pretended not to hear.

"Perhaps I should put two of our hunters beside the river. Just in case the herd gets by."

"That would be very wise," Talks To Ghosts conceded. "I did not think of it. I should have."

Big Stones looked pleased with himself. And with Talks To Ghosts for paying him the compliment. "I will do what you say, Talks To Ghosts."

"Do you want me to go down with the hunters, Big Stones?"

The older man hesitated, seemingly careful of the words he would choose for his answer. "I think, Talks To Ghosts, you are most valuable here. I will send a boy to join you. If you see that the herd is changing its march, tell the boy what your new thoughts are and he can run to me with the message."

Talks To Ghosts nodded solemnly. And inwardly was laughing. Very nicely done, he thought. Although that was not a compliment he could so easily convey to Big Stones, who after all was only trying to be thoughtful and considerate of his younger clansman.

The simple truth was that if Talks To Ghosts was lacking as a hunter, he was a menace as a marksman.

The last time they let him carry a loaded musket on a buffalo hunt he ended up shooting Spotted Pony in the backside. A shallow wound, fortunately, but no doubt a painful one. The accident occurred at regrettably close range as well so that Spotted Pony was permanently marked with a dark powder burn in a shape that resembled a prairie chicken in its mating dance. Or so Talks To Ghosts always thought. There were others who found other shapes or symbols in the mark, none of which Spotted Pony himself seemed to find amusing.

But then Spotted Pony had never been able to observe the injury from the same viewpoint as the others, so perhaps he could be forgiven.

"If we are successful, Talks To Ghosts, you will be given a full share of the meat," Big Stones promised.

"Thank you. I will tell my woman to join the others." He had already done so, of course, which Big Stones already knew. The conversation was a matter of politeness more than necessity.

"I will leave you now to tell the hunters where they must be," Big Stones apologized, then began backing away on hands and knees before turning around and once again slithering off through the cactus-studded rocks on the hillside.

Talks To Ghosts watched the older man leave. Then he turned back to face the buffalo but quickly found his attention captured by the dance of a pair of eagles flying far to the south. He was lost in the beauty of their movements when Tall Man's second son came belly-down on the ground—carefully instructed by Big Stones about how to move within sight of a miles-off buffalo herd, no doubt—to sit silent and cross-legged at Talks To Ghosts' side.

II

The herd of buffalo—a small group, with no more than six or seven hundred head among them—grazed peacefully along on the expected course, moving inexorably toward the ambush that was planned for them.

Below the hillside where Talks To Ghosts and his young helper Otter Tail waited, the hunters crouched carefully out of sight with their guns and their bows held at the ready. And away upriver the women of the tribe would be gathered in anticipation of taking the fine, rich, lifegiving meat.

The buffalo moved slowly. But they moved precisely as Talks To Ghosts had said they would.

"May I ask you a question, wise one?" the child inquired.

Talks To Ghosts glanced into the boy's eyes before answering, but if the child was being sarcastic he was doing it so well that Talks To Ghosts could not see it in his expression. "Yes, of course."

"How do you make the magic that tells you where the buffalo will go?"

Talks To Ghosts smiled. "It is not magic, small one. Merely observation. For years I have watched the buffalo and many other animals too. I only know to expect what they normally will do. Here, see, they move along the low path where it is easiest for them to walk and where the grass is good, down low where the rains pool and the water collects to nourish the grasses. You see how thick and lush the grass is . . . no, not there where the herd is now but closer, there, where they soon will be. Do you see how thick and dark it is?"

Talks To Ghosts pointed, and the boy looked and nodded, although whether because he truly saw or simply out of politeness Talks To Ghosts could not be sure.

"They eat now. Then as the heat of the day grows they will come to the water and pass through it, taking a drink as they go, and lie down on a north slope . . . you see beyond the river where those hills are? There I would think if they are allowed to go without disturbance . . . there they would lie down to rest and to chew. Then later, when the sun begins to sink and the heat is not so great, then they would stand again and come down to the grass once more to eat and to roll in the dust to clean themselves and rub some of the ticks from their coats."

The boy raised an eyebrow. He did not openly disagree, but it was clear that he was skeptical.

"Someday when you see a buffalo roll in a wallow, Otter Tail, wait in hiding and when it has gone, take yourself to the place where it has just been. Look closely in the dust or the mud it leaves behind. If you see ticks and other insects wriggling there, think of me and of the thing I told you this day." Talks To Ghosts smiled again and reached out to tousle the boy's thick, close-cropped hair. "If you do not, then come and tell me I was wrong."

Otter Tail grinned. "I think I will not have to tell you that, wise one."

Wise One indeed, Talks To Ghosts thought with a mild pang. It was a pity that a name for the ancient should be applied to a man so young. For surely this was not the compliment the boy thought it was.

"Watch now," he said. "They reach the place where they will either turn to the water and to the place where our hunters wait or they will prove me foolish and graze on in the direction they have been traveling. What do you think?"

The boy shivered, probably in anticipation of a supper of fresh liver sprinkled with gall, and pointed solemnly toward the waiting men with their trade fusils and their most powerful bows.

"Yes," Talks To Ghosts agreed, "let us hope so."

III

It was a thing of great beauty. Two of the mighty beasts fell to the first fire and three more were staggered. The herd turned back in confusion only to meet another volley from that direction. Panicked, they whirled again in a pale maelstrom of dust and once more faced the muskets and the arrows.

This time their run was a mindless, headlong charge

that carried them into the chill water, raising silver sheet after sheet of spray as a thousand hoofs and more churned the clean, sweet water into foam.

And then, finally, from the far bank there was one final volley of arrows as the youngest hunters and would-be hunters loosed their missiles.

Talks To Ghosts clapped his hands in delight and young Otter Tail laughed aloud.

Dark bodies lay scattered over a trail half a mile long, and more shaggy forms bobbed in the flowing water.

The young men at the riverbank dropped their bows— none of the ones so young were entrusted with the valuable and devastatingly effective fusils that the voyageurs traded away—and plunged waist deep into the water to grab the dead and dying buffalo and drag the carcasses to shore lest they float away and be lost.

And from upstream the women and girls appeared now carrying baskets and fleshing knives and behind them the small boys, armed with toy bows and cattail arrows that they would use to proudly kill and rekill the fallen buffalo in anticipation of other days yet to come.

The whole band was there, every man and woman and child, and it was good, for now they had meat enough for a feast of many days and enough meat more to dry some, to make jerky and pemmican, fresh hides to cure and new sinew to use as thread to turn those hides into clothing and robes and parfleche containers, bone to use for awls and scrapers, bladders to inflate and use as balls, intestines to stuff and roast as boudins, brains and urine for tanning, tongues and humps for those most delicious of delicacies, tails for flyswatters, and thick, heavy bones for the taking of marrow cooked in blood.

Ah, it was all a joy to perceive, and now for many weeks the people would be happy and heavy of belly and Horse Camp would ring with laughter and goodwill.

On this night and for many more to come the women would throw open their robes and welcome their men into them, and the children already born to the people would have shiny rings of fresh grease around their little mouths.

And what sight could be better to a man than that of his child well fed and his woman content?

Or so Talks To Ghosts sincerely believed.

If such a thing was not fated for him ever to know by his own experience, well, that did nothing to deny the truth or the beauty of it. After all, Talks To Ghosts could appreciate the loveliness of a bird in flight even if he could not himself rise into the air.

"Come with me," he said to Otter Tail, standing and stretching after the long period of stillness. "I think they need us down there to supervise the butchering."

Tall Man's second son gave him a dirty look. But then even a child no older than Otter Tail would know better than to interfere with the serious business of butchering. Try to tell one of the women how to do that job and even the most respected of warriors would risk being pelted with offal and run off. How much more the punishment for a child or an inoffensive dreamer?

Talks To Ghosts chuckled, his mood fine and his mouth already watering at the thought of what this night's supper would bring, and led the boy down off the hillside toward the distant beehive of glad activity.

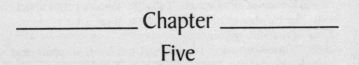

Chapter
Five

I

"**A**re you . . . ?"

"Shhh! He might overhear." The young man turned, smiled, held out both hands to welcome the man who was joining them.

The older man was not so inclined to waste time on frivolous pleasantries. He tapped an open palm and said, "You have the money, señor?"

"I do, my friend, most assuredly I do. But first there is a small matter we must discuss."

"And what matter would this be, señor?"

"The sheep, my friend."

"Yes, what of them?"

"They are only three hundred eighty-five in number. The price we agreed upon was for four hundred."

"No!" The older man managed—no doubt with some small amount of difficulty—to sound quite incredulous, quite shocked and disbelieving.

"It is a sadness but true, my friend," the handsome younger fellow said, regret and compassion syrupy in his voice. "I counted them myself three times over. Each time the number was the same."

"My employees are loyal and decent men, señor," the seller apologized, "but they are not educated. Surely this was but an oversight."

"Most assuredly I agree, Don Obregon. Merely a small error."

"And one I shall hasten to correct," the man named Obregon quickly said.

"No need," the younger returned. "You know, as I do, that our party leaves with the dawn. There is no time to send for more sheep."

"But what shall we . . . ?"

"You will discover when you count the coins in this purse, señor, that adjustment has been made already."

The seller looked stricken. Genuinely this time. "But . . ."

"An honest man such as yourself, señor, will surely amend the bill of sale and allow the matter to drop." The young man smiled. "No need, of course, to discipline the poor peons who made the error, for no harm has been done to either party, eh?"

The seller swallowed back his disappointment, shrugged, and nodded his assent to this most sensible adjustment. He accepted the purse Hernan Eduardo handed him, took a few minutes to fuss over the preparing of fresh ink and a newly trimmed pen nib, then completed and signed a bill of sale. For 350 ewes and thirty-five young rams.

Hernan Eduardo found it illuminating that Don Obregon somehow happened to already know the distribution by gender of a flock whose total numbers were supposed to be a surprise to him.

But then Hernan Eduardo had not really expected otherwise, only found it amazing that the old scoundrel would so forget himself as to give himself away like that.

"My thanks to you for your valuable services, Don Obregon," Hernan Eduardo said.

"And mine to you as well, Señor Escavara."

"Please," Hernan Eduardo demurred with a gracious smile. "Call me Emilio."

II

"Are you sure this is what you want to do, my sweet Hern'ard . . . excuse me, I mean to say of course my dear Emilio." Consuela, who once was known as Elena, sighed and touched the arm of the young man who now called himself Emilio Escavara. And she, she was now known as the señora Escavara, the shy and slender and even younger wife of this Emilio. Except she would be slender and lovely for very little longer. This she—and Hernan Eduardo/Emilio as well—knew. Her pregnancy was not yet noticeable, but soon, in a matter of a few months or even weeks, it would be obvious to all.

Poor Hern'ardo. The sacrifice he was making. It shamed her. But if the truth be known it also thrilled her. She would live a lie, yes, but she would live her lie with dignity. And her baby, her precious and beloved small one, would have a life of dignity also. The child would never be thought a bastard. The child's mother would never become a figure of shame and public disgrace.

But oh, poor Hern'ardo.

Poor, dear Emilio. Never again must she permit herself to call him Hern'ardo, never. And even within her own heart now, for the sake of the unborn one, never again must she think of herself as Elena. From this day onward they would be among people, strangers now but for the remainder of their days to be their neighbors and hopefully their friends. From this day on she must think in the most private of her thoughts that she was Consuela Escavara from far distant Zacatecas, a place so far that surely no one they would ever encounter in the wild northland would ever have been there. Or know anything about the people who came from there. Surely, God willing, no one need ever question the young "couple" who so bravely set out for the frontier.

"Are you sure of this, Emilio?" she repeated. "It is not too late for you to change your mind."

"Not too late?" Emilio laughed, and Consuela delighted in the dear and natural and so long known way in which his eyes sparkled and at the corners wrinkled when he did so, for this was a thing to lighten the burdens on her heart when she could hear him laugh so lightly. "We are the proud owners of a flock of finest sheep, no? And what would our proud father say if we were to return with a gaggle of smelly sheep, eh? Can you imagine the squealing? The indignation? Ah, the thought of it . . ." He grinned and shook his head, and Consuela could not help but join him in the amusement of that thought.

She paused, pondered, and then realized that Emilio's reference to the man who had been their father was very likely a deliberate one. Emilio was making light of the past, trying to take away the sting from it.

And who knew? Perhaps that would work. In time.

"You are really—" she began once more.

"Hush, wife," Emilio said in a mock-stern tone, his eyes alight with teasing as he used that term when neither of them ever had, nor ever would, stand before a priest to receive the blessed sacrament of marriage.

"Wife," Emilio repeated.

"Yes, husband?" his sister answered, her own expression lightened by the same secretive amusement that so pleased Emilio.

He dug into his purse and handed her a satisfyingly heavy weight of coins. "Take this and buy more food for our journey. And thank the good don when you do so, for it is his attempt to cheat us that leaves us with a few pesos to spare."

"We have corn and spices enough, Emilio. What I would like to buy is seed for a garden. Squash seeds and speckled beans and perhaps some chilies if you would permit."

Emilio shrugged. "Whatever you think best, good wife."

"Seed then, Emilio, because we will be far from civilization for all our days. We need to make our way from now on without a town to buy in." Or, she did not have to add, a family to fall back upon. Yet if this was a sadness it was also a challenge and one that brought a rush of eagerness to her breast. It was, she admitted to herself but to no other living creature, a guilty, fluttering pleasure for her to think about making her—no, their—own brave way into the future.

"Do you want me to come with you?" Emilio offered, his tone hinting that the offer was made dutifully but that his true desire was that he be free to do something else.

"No need," Consuela said. "Go see to the burros and the packs or whatever man thing it is that you must do. I will meet you at the inn in time for supper." Which, she sternly reminded herself, would be served at dusk when the poor ate, quickly so as not to waste candle wax and not at the late-night hour of the indulgent dining she had all her life until now taken so for granted.

"Later then." Emilio leaned forward to give his "wife" a chaste peck on the cheek, then turned and headed with a light and cheerful step toward the pens where the pack train of northbound pioneers was gathered.

Consuela too turned, her hand unconsciously fingering the bulge of heavy silver coins in the pocket of her apron. She had said she would buy seed and so she would. What she had not told her brother—her "husband"—was that she would also use a part of the money to pay for a novena. For it could be years before she would again have an opportunity to kneel before a priest. And her sins were many.

III

It was a hopeful group, if not a prosperous one, that gathered in the plaza before dawn that morning. Emilio and Consuela—for so they considered themselves truly to be now—joined them. Consuela looked red-eyed and tired. Emilio understood that full well. His own eyes burned and stung from lack of sleep the night before. His rest was disrupted by excitement about what was to come today . . . and also by a spate of final regrets over what once had been.

But no more. Never again. He swore this to himself even as the soldiers of their escort marched so handsomely to the fore of the confusion.

An escort. Incredible but true. There once was a time when it would have been unthinkable for anyone to set out across the great barrier of mountains to the north. That was when Spain still ruled in the south, and the king was jealously fearful that some miserable peon might earn three pesos without remembering to give the royal one His due. But this policy was no longer. Now the free and independent and generous government of the great nation of Mexico was actually encouraging new settlement on that far frontier.

Most of the pioneers Emilio spoke with accepted the change of heart and policy as simple magnanimity. Emilio, if only thanks to overhearing his father's—that is to say, his former father's—blustering, railing arguments against the change, understood the true purpose of this fostering of development.

The government in Mexico City was becoming increasingly worried that the damned Americanos with their greedy, land-hungry habits would soon begin to covet Mexican territories along the northern border.

It was said they already talked openly about taking Tejas away from Mexico. And surely the empty lands lying below the Arkansas River would soon follow.

Empty, Emilio knew, was the key to that statement.

For hundreds of years Spanish, and later Mexican, settlement ended south of the mountain wall, stopping along the Las Vegas–Mora–Taos–Pueblo axis. Scarcely a crop had been sown or a sprig of grass grazed in all the northern territories.

Oh, there had been a few hardy souls who made their way in the San Luis Valley north of Taos. But not a one, not a single solitary one, in all the basin of the River of Lost Souls, although it was there that the Americanos were most likely to intrude.

Had they not already put trading posts along the Arkansas and on tributaries lying north of that great river? Of course they had. How many times had Emilio heard his former father complain about this intrusion into what was clearly acknowledged to be fully within Mexico's sphere of influence.

Was it not also true that the Yankees were traveling even as far as Santa Fe to spread their trade? Yes, this was so. It was in clear violation of the laws of Mexico, of course. But the Americanos cared nothing about the laws of Mexico. And neither did the officials who were charged with the responsibility of enforcing those laws, not when the damnable Yankees were so free with gold and silver coin, not when they distributed the *mordida* in exchange for the blindness of eye and the approval of spurious forms and permits.

It was all of a sadness, Emilio knew.

It was also, if the full truth be known, something of a joke.

For how ironic it was to Emilio that he and Consuela now would benefit from this new policy, accepting the protection of soldiers when they traveled, more importantly becoming themselves beneficiaries of grants of landholdings. Ironic all the more so because their very forefathers had been among those charged with protecting the king's vast and never used yet carefully guarded territories. Ah yes, the irony of it seemed delicious in the extreme.

And the young Hernan Eduardo no doubt would have joined his never-changing former father in opposing this and all other new policies, even those intended to thwart the despised Yankees. But Emilio Escavara—it was a proud name and one he could justly claim, as it had been that of his maternal grandfather's grandfather, the first of the family line to reach the shores of the New World—was young and modern and very much inclined to accept both the perquisites and the hardships of a pioneer existence. For himself and for his young and pregnant "wife" Consuela.

It all was a joke indeed. And if the laughter had an aftertaste of bitterness, well, that was of small consequence. The point, after all, had to do not with the past but with the future. Aye, the future.

Emilio gave Consuela a wink and a gentle squeeze of

the arm, then responded to a hail from Luis Del Garza who had been elected captain of their little expedition.

"Are the Escavaras ready to depart, friend Emilio?"

"At your command, Mayordomo."

"Then take your place in line, Emilio, you and your animals. We go as soon as all are in place."

With a grin and a genuine rush of excitement, Emilio took up the shepherd's staff Consuela had given to him for a birthday present. He rapped the butt of the crooked staff sharply on the ground to draw the attention of the sheep and began slowly, haltingly—and quite inexpertly—guiding them across the plaza to their place in the long column of new pioneers.

It was all, he reflected, a quite magnificent undertaking.

Chapter

Six

I

Aaron returned to the flatboat puffing and sweating from the effort of unloading cargo. He dropped lightly onto the deck—funny how comfortably familiar that was now after a few weeks afloat when back in Pittsburgh the same act had felt awkward and just a wee bit dangerous—and stooped without thought to recoil a line that had been kicked or trampled into a tangle by one of the cargo handlers.

"It's all right, son, you can leave that."

Aaron shrugged. "Better if things are tidy, Mr. Burnham." He grinned and finished what he was doing, then carefully draped the new-made coil onto a peg so it would not be mussed again by accident.

"I tell you true, son, for a passenger you're the liveliest deckhand I think I've ever had. My offer stands, you know. I'd be glad to keep you aboard."

Now that his cargo was safely delivered to Cairo, Burnham intended to take on another load of whatever proved available and continue downriver to New Orleans.

For the past week he had been trying to talk Aaron into making the rest of the passage with him.

"Tell you what, son. Stick with me on to N'Orleans and I'll pay you a wage. Cash money. I can't afford t' make it much, but . . ."

"You're a kind man and a good one, Mr. Burnham, but my mind is made up. I want to see Saint Louie, not some southern swamp. I'll be heading up the river, not down."

He didn't say, but thought, that St. Louis was a place he wanted to know more anyhow. Rumor was that Aaron's own pap came west one time. Not that Pap ever spoke of it. Never a single word. Still, there were others in the family who claimed it, and that Pap seen something there that turned his hair white. All that made Aaron curious and all the more interested in seeing his old Pap's elephant.

He took a final look around and crossed the deck to give Burnham a big smile and a warm handshake. "I thank you for all you've done for me."

Which was fairly considerable. Aaron's few supplies were exhausted early in the journey down from Pittsburgh, and Aaron had been eating at the older man's sufferance ever since. As it was, he owned nothing now that he needed to gather up before his departure.

Not even, darn it, the warm and handsome cape. Burnham, it turned out, was not a man with any exploitable vices. Not that Aaron had been able to find anyway. And besides, he had come to genuinely like the Pittsburgher. He would stand by his word—not all that reluctantly—and leave the scarlet capote hanging inside the sleeping cuddy as payment for his passage. That seemed the least he could do in return for such freely given kindness.

Burnham amazed and mildly embarrassed Aaron by accepting the handshake but following it with an embrace quite as if they were parting family and not strangers save for a few weeks' travel. "You take care of yourself, son."

"Aye, and you the same."

"If you ever need anything . . ."

They would never see each other again, Aaron was sure. Not in a hundred years. But then Burnham knew that quite as well as Aaron did. Aaron nodded, a small hard knot forming inside his throat, and clapped the older man on the arm. "We'll meet again," he lied.

"Yes."

Aaron turned away. He hadn't reached the gunwale when Burnham stopped him. "Aaron, son."

"Yes, sir?"

"You're forgetting sommat."

"Sir?"

"The coat, son. There's still cold nights ahead, y'know. You'll be needing something warm to wrap y'self in."

"But that's yours, Mr. Burnham. A deal is a deal and I couldn't—"

"No, Aaron, I was only teasing you 'bout that. Right from the start, it's true." Which it was not and the both of them knew it. Burnham smiled. "Besides, whatever would I do with a heavy old thing like that in N'Orleans where it's hot an' humid even through the winter never mind in the balmy springtime season? Do me no good at all down there and be a burden I couldn't possibly rid m'self of, don't you know. So do me a favor an' take it off my hands." The smile became a grin. "Tis my cloak to give as I believe you will agree an' so I give it to you."

"I said it before and I'll say it again. You're a kind man and a good one, Mr. Burnham."

"Ach, go on now. Take the cloak an' go, quick before I press-gang you for a voyage down the river."

Aaron nodded, not sure he could trust himself to speak at the moment. He reached into the cuddy to drag the capote out and leaped ashore without looking back, afraid that if this good-bye were prolonged any further it would turn out to be no good-bye at all.

II

Now just who was it that said St. Louis wasn't but a hop, skip, and jump upriver from where the Ohio joined up with the Mississippi? Or was that just an impression he'd picked up somewhere along the line?

One thing Aaron was certain sure of. If somebody actually told him that he was one lying SOB. And if the knowledge was the result of an impression, well, he'd been wrong before this a time or two. But never so downright footsore-causing wrong.

It took eleven days of walking to get from one to the other.

Not that quite all that amount of time was spent in actual walking. At this time of year there wasn't anything in the fields and the gardens along the way for a fellow to filch in the night to munch on by day, so he had to stop and look for handouts and offer to work in exchange for a mouthful or so.

By the end of the first week he was pretty sure he could have built a corduroy path from Cairo to St. Louis with all the wood he was having to split to earn his meals.

The whole thing would have been much easier if it had been the fall of the year when there would have been potatoes still in the gardens.

But in the spring, darn it, all the potatoes were stored away in root cellars. And to open somebody's root cellar without permission was actual stealing. Taking something from a garden, that was just getting something to eat. But taking from a root cellar was thievery, and Aaron didn't want to do that.

Still and all, he got by. That was the important thing. Cut and split some wood here or some shingles there, tend to somebody's livestock or else help finish pruning a too-long-untended apple orchard, one way and another he managed to get along with his belly full and his feet not too badly worn out.

And at night, of course, he had the thick woolen capote to wrap around himself and sleep in. More than one chill night along the way he had cause to be grateful to Mr. Burnham for allowing him to keep the cloak.

In the end of it he came safe enough to the settlement on the Illinois side of the river and spent a morning splitting already cut stove lengths—the wood was nicely dried and so the work really wasn't all that difficult—in exchange for passage on a ferryboat across to the city.

Aaron was full of excitement by the time he got there. Most of that day he'd been looking across to the chimneys and the smoke plumes that marked the sprawling community, which looked to be even bigger than Pittsburgh, maybe bigger than anyplace else in the whole of the country, certainly bigger than anything Aaron Jenks ever once laid eyes on all at one and the same time.

It was something, it was.

And it was all his for the taking. At least that is the way he looked at it at the time.

He was grinning big when he stepped off that ferryboat as a newcomer to opportunity.

III

Aaron felt like bawling. Felt like sitting down in a dark, dank corner somewhere and just plain busting out bawling like some dang little kid or something.

He'd never been so tired, so hungry, or so damn . . . discouraged. That was the simplest and best way to describe it. He just plain felt discouraged.

St. Louis was so . . . cold. Big, sprawling, serious and . . . cold. Uncaring, that's what the people were like here, at least the way he was finding them to be.

Hungry? Nobody in St. Louis seemed to care that he was. The few he'd gone and actually mentioned it to turned hard-faced and mean-spirited when he said it. The streets were full of bums and layabouts and coffee-coolers, they said. Go get a job and pay for your meals.

Well that was just exactly what he was trying to do now, wasn't it?

He wasn't some beggar. He acted polite and respectful and offered to work for his keep. That didn't matter to the prissy, tight-lipped folk in the houses he knocked at. Get on

your way, bum, they'd say, get off this property right quick
or they'd have the law on him.

It was only a meal that he wanted, dang it, not their
daughters' beds. Well, not until after his belly was full
anyhow, Aaron admitted to himself with what sense of good
cheer he had left. Not until after he'd eaten, thank you.

He sighed and put one aching foot ahead of the other.
Again. A fellow had to keep a move on around here, it
seemed, or some nebby-nosed so-and-so was sure to come
around asking questions or else outright warning one to
move on or suffer the consequences.

Aaron didn't know what it was about this town that
had folks so scared of strangers. But then he'd never before
spent any appreciable amount of time in an actual city and
in fact had little experience himself with strangers. Other
than being one his own self for the past half year or so.

Well, he was learning. And what he was learning was
not all that much to his liking.

Being around folks he knew, even folks that he didn't
much care for, seemed a whole heap better than being a
stranger in a city that was overrun with strangers and hobos
and young runaways in search of livelihood.

People in St. Louis seemed to take it for granted that a
stranger was a thief and a ne'er-do-well and acted toward
him as if he were those things and worse as well. Always
before in Aaron's experience a stranger would be viewed as
someone you hadn't met yet. But basically as a good and
honest person until or unless the stranger himself proved
otherwise.

But this up-front and completely open suspicion? No,
that was new to him. And not to his liking.

With a sigh in his throat and an empty rumbling in his
belly, Aaron gave up looking for lunch and commenced to
thinking about a supper. And while he was contemplating
what to do about that small difficulty he figured he would
pull off his boots—well, Letty's pap's boots they used to
be—and rest himself under the shade of a tree with the
bright, pale green of spring leaves peeping out on its gray

branches. He figured that would be just the ticket he needed
to get to feeling better.

He spread his capote on the ground and with a groan
that he didn't even try to contain settled down onto it for
a nap.

IV

Something hit the bottom of Aaron's boot so hard the
impact ran clean up his spine and set his neck to hurting. He
came awake in half a heartbeat and was already sitting
upright before he had time to figure out that he wasn't
asleep any longer.

The same something thumped into his sole a second
time, and he blinked, kind of hoping this whole thing was a
bad dream. But it wasn't.

The man standing over him ready to deliver a third
kick was huge. Beefy, red faced, bewhiskered . . . and
wearing a dinky little silver badge about the size of a half-
dollar to show that he was the Law.

Oh, Lordy, the damned Law. Aaron had visions of . . .
of courts and trials and prison and humiliation and he didn't
know what all else.

Letty's damned old pap must have put out warrants on
him. Or else the boys, damned old Barney and damned old
James, had caught up with him and swore out complaints.
What all could they charge him with? Rape? Letty would
swear against him, he was sure of that after the way she'd
acted when her mam walked in on them. Damned old girl.
Couldn't trust none of them. Aaron knew that now. But then
"now" was somewhat too late.

What was the old saying? We get too soon old and too
late smart. And it was true.

Rape if they wanted to push it that far, then, or theft.
The old man could claim Aaron stole the capote and the boots.
Likely a court wouldn't listen to the right and the wrong of
things, wouldn't care that Aaron was owed wages and all he

was doing was taking what he rightfully deserved. For sure wouldn't pay any mind to the fact that he'd left the cash behind.

"Up," the Law ordered in a no-nonsense tone. Kind of high pitched and squeaky sounding for so big a fella, but there was no mistaking that tone regardless of the unimpressive voice that delivered the message. "On your feet, boy."

"Mister, I ain't done nothing, I—"

"Up," the Law repeated. And kicked him on the foot again.

"Ow!"

The Law drew his boot back for another go, and Aaron scrambled to his knees and quickly—if a mite unsteadily as he was still woozy from being so sound asleep—onto his feet.

Aaron was fairly tall if lanky built. But the Law was a good head taller and put together like a breeding bull, all neck and shoulders with one layer of muscle piled atop another. Aaron had the idea, probably correct, that if this fellow wanted he could pick Aaron up, tuck him under one arm, and tote him off to prison without ever raising a sweat.

"Yes, sir," Aaron said, just as meek and respectful as he knew how.

"We don't allow vagrants here."

"What's one of them?" Aaron asked. He thought it a reasonable enough question.

"You are."

"Yes, sir." He still wasn't sure what a vagrant was, but the Law was acting like this was not a good time to pursue enlightenment any further.

"You damn bums and wanderers sleeping under bushes and in any empty corner you can find, that don't look good to the good people of this community."

"No, sir," Aaron agreed.

"There's a city ordinance against vagrancy."

"Yes, sir."

"You can pay a fine or spend your time in jail."

"I don't have any money, sir."

"Then let's go see the judge, boy. The sooner you get your sentence the sooner you start serving it out."

"Yes, sir." Aaron still wasn't entirely certain sure that this whole thing was not a dream. A bad dream. But he kind of suspected that it was real. He just wished he'd been able to find work enough to earn himself a meal before they hauled him off.

Still, there were things to be grateful for if he wanted to look at it like that. For instance that there was no mention, at least not yet there wasn't, about Letty or the capote. That much was sure to the good.

"If you want to run, boy, it's only fair to tell you that I'm too old and fat and slow to chase after you."

Aaron raised an eyebrow. The Law didn't look old nor fat nor even especially slow, not to Aaron's mind he didn't.

"So instead of running after you I'll let these here do my running for me." He pulled his coat open a bit to show the butts of a pair of horse pistols stuffed behind his belt there, one to either side of a big brass buckle. "Up to you to decide how good a shot you think I am."

Aaron swallowed. Hard. "I wasn't going to run anyhow." And perhaps that wasn't a lie. He hadn't even got around to thinking should he try it or shouldn't he. It was clear there wasn't any thinking that needed to be done on the subject now.

The Law snorted and kind of half smiled. "I believe you, boy. I surely do. Now come along nice and slow. And don't worry about getting lost. I will show you the way."

Aaron bobbed his head in quick and complete agreement and started off in the direction the Law indicated. Nice and slow.

V

"I swear, boy, I don't know should I think you're making fun of me or are you serious."

"Sir?"

"Potatoes, boy, potatoes. I never seen any human person could eat so many. And not even complain about it."

"You won't find me complaining," Aaron said with a grin. "Not about this." He reached for another of the boiled spuds and bit into it like you would an apple. The only utensil allowed inside the cell was a spoon. No butter knives or forks or any dangerous weapons of that sort. Not that anything but a spoon was needed. The Law fed cheap here—Aaron understood that reasoning—basically boiled redjackets, thin soups made from whatever greens were coming up in the garden, and for the occasional treat a bowl of oat porridge. None of those required much in the way of cutting or trimming.

"You aren't such a bad kid, Jenks."

Aaron bobbed his head and smiled and made as if he gave a fat damn what the Law thought.

"You want a break, boy?"

"Break out, you mean?" He shook his head. "Not even if you unload them pistols to give me a running start."

"That isn't the kind of break I meant. The thing is . . ." The Law pursed his lips and fingered his chin and tried to look kind of shy and innocent. Which was pushing things more than a little, but Aaron was willing to give credit for the effort if not the result. "The thing is, Jenks, I have this friend who's looking for hired help."

"Yeah? So?"

"So if I was to recommend you to this friend, see, I think he'd be willing to pay your fine and get you outa here in time for him to leave."

"He's leaving Saint Louie?" That right there was enough to capture Aaron's interest. Particularly so since he himself had been captured, so to speak, and wouldn't have a snowball's chance if a legal want order showed up here sworn out by Letty's father or maybe one of those damned cousins of hers.

"Tomorrow morning he means to pull out. But he's shorthanded. He, uh, mentioned to me that he could use some help."

"I got—what? eight days left?"

"That's right, boy. Eight days of boiled potatoes without salt."

"I like taters with or without the salt."

"You know what I mean, boy. This friend of mine, he could pay your fine and you'd be free. Just that quick."

Aaron yawned. It was something of an effort but he managed it. "Ah, eight days ain't so much. Besides, I bet this fella would deduct the fine from my wage. What profit would there be in that, huh? I expect I'm content to keep on eating potatoes for a spell."

The Law frowned, convincing Aaron that his first notion had been correct. Likely the Law was intending to collect a little fee, over and above his piece of the court fine, if Aaron went to work for this so-called friend.

"You don't want out, boy?"

"Oh, I'd ruther be out than in if that's what you're asking. But if your friend wants free labor let him buy a nigger."

"That isn't . . . look, d'you want me to talk to this friend of mine or not?"

"Talk if you like, but my terms are plain. Whatever he pays to you, for a fine or whatever, that's his choice. I won't have it taken outa my wage."

"Contrary, aren't you?" the Law asked.

Aaron grinned at him.

"All right. He pays the fine and you collect a full wage. Half a hand, though. You ain't old enough or experienced enough to earn a grown man's wage."

Aaron suspected he was being chivied out of the fine money by a side door. But in truth he was plenty tired of this jail cell—damn place had bugs crawling all over the floor and the walls, and at night he always felt like there were critters too small to see inside the blankets with him—and would be glad of a change in location even if he were genuinely satisfied with the way they fed here. "All right."

The Law rattled the cell door to make sure it was locked, then turned away. "I'll be back in a little while. Gotta find my friend and get the money in hand before I let you out. Gotta make sure all the paperwork is in order, you know?"

"One thing before you go," Aaron said.

"Yes?"

"This work I'll be doing."

"Uh-huh?"'

"What is it?"

"You'll be helping my friend haul a load of freight to Santa Fe."

"Where's that?"

"You never heard of Santa Fe, boy?"

"No, sir. Not until right this minute."

The Law grinned at him. "It's just down the road a piece," he said. "Over in that direction." He pointed, but Aaron had no idea what direction that was.

"Santa Fe. Saint Louie. You sure got religious names for places in this part of the country."

"Yeah, don't we just," the Law mused as he reached for his hat and wandered outside, leaving Aaron alone in the dang jail.

_____ Chapter _____
Seven

I

Talks To Ghosts hunkered in the shade of his lodge and observed Sleeping Fawn as she squatted over the slab of soft wood that was her fire-starting wood. She leaned down upon the flat stone that capped her hardwood spinning stick and patiently sawed back and forth with the fire bow, its loose string of buffalo sinew twirling the pointed end of the stick back and forth in the tiny notch cut into the fire starter. With persistence and a modicum of skill the heat generated by the spinning hardwood rubbing against the softer wood would result in an ember. Then several. And then Sleeping Fawn would bend low to breathe life into the embers and create fire in the bits of dry tinder lying beneath the flat fire starter.

Talks To Ghosts was content. There was food in the lodge, and Horse Camp rang to the sounds of fat, laughing children. What could be better than this?

He felt so fine on this most excellent afternoon that he very nearly succumbed so far as to experience a fondness for Sleeping Fawn.

He observed the way the antelope skin skirt pulled

tight over her thighs and buttocks as she bent over the fire stick, and he felt a gathering of juices low in his belly.

Sleeping Fawn was not the most beautiful of women, but she was sturdy. Her legs were like young tree trunks, and her back was broad and powerful. She could lift burdens that her husband could scarcely budge and carry loads of water or firewood that would stagger many a pony from the herd.

Talks To Ghosts felt a most unusual flush of interest. Even affection. Almost a tenderness. Why, he thought, this woman to whom he was married was . . .

"Did I tell you that Hand gave his wife a burning glass? Yes, even Hand, and he is the next poorest hunter in the whole clan, next only to you, neh? Hand's wife does not have to labor with stick and bow to start her fire like I do. I think I probably am the only woman left in the band who does not have her own burning glass, neh?"

Sleeping Fawn tossed the words over her shoulder without bothering to look up from her work.

The complaint should not have surprised him, Talks To Ghosts decided. After all, the lodge was full of food and there was a fresh buffalo hide staked out drying in the sunshine ready for tanning. They were at Horse Camp where life was always good.

Things did not get any better than this, and that was a truth. So what choice did poor Sleeping Fawn have but to complain about not having a burning glass?

She had to have something to complain about, didn't she?

And if it was not entirely accurate that she was the only woman who lacked a glass to start her fires—Talks To Ghosts guessed that fewer than half the women in the band had burning glasses of their own—no matter. Sleeping Fawn would not be happy if she could not find something to worry over like a pup with a knucklebone too large to get its mouth around.

"Hand's wife is very fortunate," Talks To Ghosts agreed calmly, in too fine a mood this day to rise to the bait and allow an argument to ensue.

"I should have a burning glass of my own," Sleeping Fawn grumbled.

"Yes," Talks To Ghosts said in a pleasant tone, "you should."

Sleeping Fawn gave him a suspicious look but could find nothing in Talks To Ghosts' bland expression that she could take offense at. "Do you mean that?" she demanded.

"Yes, quite."

"You will get me a burning glass of my own, Talks To Ghosts?"

"Oh my, yes."

"When?"

He shrugged. "When it is possible."

Sleeping Fawn grunted. And frowned. She was trapped and she knew it. Talks To Ghosts had given in. And he had not. The worst part of it was that he had taken her grounds for complaint away from her. He had promised to get her a burning glass and so she knew that he would, someday. When it became possible. Whenever that was. Talks To Ghosts was not one to go back on a pledge once given, nor was he one to forget a promise. But he was not a man to hurry to fulfill a promise like this one either. Talks To Ghosts had beaten her at the game she herself initiated, bested her fair and square.

Talks To Ghosts could see the conflict of emotions in Sleeping Fawn's stony, thin-lipped face. She was beaten and yet she had no chance to bemoan her loss because it was a loss clothed within a seeming victory and a victory on her own terms at that.

"I will go visit with Black Otter now," Talks To Ghosts said, rising to his feet and starting quickly away before Sleeping Fawn had time to think of some new cause for unhappiness.

His scowling wife went back to her fire stick and bow.

II

The men sat in a loose, rather ragged circle at the center of which was a cold fire pit and a small tripod made of carefully trimmed and polished cedar shafts. A bundle, wrapped in antelope leather and marten fur, dangled from the tripod. The bundle was decorated with feathers and magic drawings. Only old Laughing Wolf knew what the bundle contained, if anyone did. It was a matter Laughing Wolf never actually discussed, although he may have chosen to add to the bundle over the years if he wished to do so. It was most unlikely that he would have found reason to subtract anything from this powerful representation of the people's medicine.

Talks To Ghosts listened politely while Big Stones, Runs Far, and Hand debated whether to remain at Horse Camp a little longer or if it was time to move farther out onto the big grass in search of the huge herds of summer buffalo.

Runs Far, well known for his caution, wanted to remain here, close to the protection of the mountains. Big Stones and Hand wanted to leave soon so as to intercept the buffalo before they drifted too far south, toward the land where the Apache might come looking for meat. It was bad enough having to worry about Comanche and Kiowa without having to add the vicious and treacherous eastern-ranging bands of Apache to their concerns. Everyone, not only the people, called the Apache by whatever name in their tongue meant Enemy, for the Apache were the despised Enemy of all men.

"The spring has been gentle and the rains warm," Hand said. "By now the horse people from the far plains will have gone south to raid into Mexico for horses and slaves. At this moment we can hunt in peace and safety. But if we wait until the herds wander south in the tracks of the horse people we risk being found by horse people making their way north after their raiding or being seen by the Apache. It would be foolish to wait longer. We must go now."

"Is it true then that you know where the horse people

are, Hand?" Runs Far countered. "Have you had a dream to show you that they are in Mexico now?"

"I know this because like you, Runs Far, I know what to expect of them. Every spring their hearts turn to raiding, and they paint the battle signs on their war ponies as soon as the grass is enough to give strength to the horses. You know this, Runs Far. All men know this."

"And if this year they do not do what we expect?"

"What would you have us do, Runs Far? Should we be so afraid of the horse people that we end up fighting the Apache instead? I say we leave Horse Camp now. The buffalo . . . ," he turned and looked at Talks To Ghosts. "Tell us where to find the buffalo now, Talks To Ghosts. Are they as far south as the Red? Or only the Canadian?"

Talks To Ghosts shrugged. "Not far below the Cimarron now. Surely you know this, Hand. They move with the grass and with the rainfall to make more grass. Soon they will leave the Cimarron. Then slowly on to the Canadian. But not yet. I do not believe they have left the Cimarron yet."

"Do you know this, Talks To Ghosts?" Runs Far objected, offering the same logic that Hand had moments earlier imposed on him. "Have you flown with the eagles to see that this is so?"

"I do not know it, Runs Far. I have not seen it. I have had no dreams and sung no songs. I have not flown with the eagle. I only believe it to be so."

"Is Talks To Ghosts ever wrong about the buffalo?" Hand countered.

"This is a thing Talks To Ghosts knows," Big Stones answered. "If he says the buffalo are still on the Cimarron then this is where we can find them."

"I said we can find the buffalo there," Talks To Ghosts added, "but I said nothing about the horse people, about the Comanche and the Kiowa or even the Cheyenne. We must think about where they are too."

"Yes, and the Apache," Runs Far said.

"We are not children. We can fight," Hand said.

"Well, Talks To Ghosts?" Big Stones asked.

"Well what?"

"Do you know any reason why we should not go onto the plains at this time?"

Talks To Ghosts opened his mouth to respond . . . and could not. In truth he did not know any reason why they should stay at Horse Camp.

But there was something . . . a nagging, nebulous sense of . . . danger? No, it was not strong enough a feeling to consider it any sort of foreboding, not enough to consider it a warning of danger ahead.

But there was . . . a desire, for reasons that were not at all clear to him . . . a desire to remain here at Horse Camp. For this whole summer season perhaps.

And that, of course, was quite perfectly foolish. What would the people do for meat if they stayed here the whole summer long? The great herds were out on the open plains, not here close beneath the cool mountains. Always the people went out onto the grass to make their meat in preparation for winter. Always this was so. And this year as well.

"I know of no reason to stay," Talks To Ghosts admitted, his heart leaden with an undefined sadness even as he spoke this truth.

"Well?" Big Stones demanded, speaking to all the men of the band but in fact addressing himself primarily to Runs Far.

Runs Far shook his head, offering no more opposition to the plan.

A few more nights of discussion, Talks To Ghosts knew, and the decision would be formalized—it was as good as made now, but politeness required that they discuss it further, that every man be given his chance to speak and to endorse what the others had already decided upon— and in another week, two at the most, every person in the band would dismantle the lodges and pack the horses and dogs and cross the river to begin the every-summer trek out onto the grassy plains.

By the time they returned to Horse Camp this fall it would be difficult to tell that anyone ever camped here before, and the beauty of the place would be fresh and clean and once again the hearts of Talks To Ghosts and of the people would rise with the sight of this wonderful spot.

III

Talks To Ghosts came up from the river still wet from his bath. Sleeping Fawn started to say something to him, then stopped. Talks To Ghosts looked so . . . distant. His eyes looked like they were focused on things that were not of this world. Sleeping Fawn had seen Talks To Ghosts like this before, and the truth was that it frightened her. She mumbled a quick incantation and ignored her husband, who began rolling up the walls of their lodge even though normal movement through the camp kept the air filled with dust and if the walls were raised the dust would soon get onto and into everything they owned.

Normally Sleeping Fawn would have scolded her thoughtless husband about this. But not when he looked as he did now. She frowned but kept her lips clamped hard together.

Talks To Ghosts finished tying the wall skins high off the ground, then motioned to the first person who walked by. It happened to be Three Ears, who wore the dried-up ear of a long-ago vanquished Osage on a thong around his neck and took his name from this victory of battle.

"Three Ears, my friend," Talks to Ghosts called in an unusually loud voice. His choice of greeting would have been enough to capture Sleeping Fawn's attention even if she were not already alert to Talks To Ghosts' odd mood, for Three Ears was as close to being an enemy as Talks To Ghosts had in the band. Three Ears had taken a dislike to Talks To Ghosts when Talks To Ghosts was but a stripling and Three Ears a mature warrior, and that feeling had never changed over all the years. Talks To Ghosts swore he did not know what he had done to make Three Ears despise him, but Sleeping Fawn suspected her husband was avoiding the truth when he said that. In any event she found it most odd that Talks To Ghosts would greet Three Ears in such a friendly fashion this morning.

"Come here, Three Ears. Eat with me." Talks To Ghosts gestured toward the stewpot that contained what was supposed to be their midday meal. Well, no matter about that, Sleeping Fawn thought. There was enough for one more. There was meat in the lodge after the first successful hunt of the season, and if Talks To Ghosts wanted to boast of that success by inviting an enemy to share in the bounty, there was no real harm done.

Three Ears, acting as surprised as Sleeping Fawn, entered Talks To Ghosts' lodge and seated himself, accepting a carved aspenwood bowl of the half-cooked but rich stew that Talks To Ghosts personally dipped up for him and placed into his hands.

"Thank you, my friend," Three Ears said.

"You honor me to sit at my fire," Talks To Ghosts said. Never mind that the fire had been built outdoors to avoid overheating the lodge on these fine early-summer days. The meaning had little to do with such trivialities as bald fact. "Would Three Ears do me the further honor to accept a small gift?" Talks To Ghosts continued.

"A gift, friend Talks To Ghosts?"

Talks To Ghosts went to one of the lodgepoles at the head of the sleeping robes and lifted down a fine, braided horsehair hackamore that he had spent many nights making during the past winter. Even Sleeping Fawn had to admit that the hackamore was especially well crafted. When it was done she marveled that so silly a man as her husband had made it. Now he placed the elegant device into Three Ears's hands.

"Take this, please, and my red-and-white horse. You know the one I mean. I have seen you look at him with wide eyes in the past."

Sleeping Fawn could hardly believe what she heard. They only owned four horses. And now Talks To Ghosts had gone and given one of them away.

"Would you do me this honor, Three Ears? I would count it a great kindness if you would accept."

"I do, Talks To Ghosts."

"Thank you, friend Three Ears. Thank you. Now eat. Please. There is more in the pot if you are still hungry." Talks To Ghosts glanced outside and saw Spotted Pony walking by.

"Spotted Pony. Join us."

"What is it, Talks To Ghosts? You aren't going to shoot me again, are you?"

"No, but I need you to drop your loincloth so Three Ears and I can look for divinations and magic signs in the powder burns there."

Spotted Pony laughed, but altered his course and came nearer to the lodge. "What is it you really want of me, Talks To Ghosts?"

"I want you to eat with me, my friend, and I would be honored if you were to accept some presents from me too."

Sleeping Fawn understood then.

For some reason, for whatever reason, probably for a mystical spirit reason, it had come over Talks To Ghosts to give away the few things they owned. Very likely he would end up giving away virtually all of their things. By nightfall they no doubt would be destitute.

Well, that was all right. Talks To Ghosts was no great prize as a husband, but this would bring great honor to him and therefore to Sleeping Fawn too.

It was nice to know that he could do some things right.

Sleeping Fawn went back to scraping dried fat from the buffalo hide that had been staked out on the ground ever since the hunt. She hoped she would have time to finish the scraping before Talks To Ghosts gave the green robe away. And just think. Now she would not have to go through the laborious and painful process of tanning the flinty hide.

She began to hum a small chant under her breath as she worked.

IV

It was the last night of the council and everyone knew what decision would be reached. Tonight the youngest and least experienced warriors in the band were allowed to have their say. Not that anyone paid serious attention to them, but every man has the right to speak and to be heard.

The young man Hits Hard, who did not really live up to the name he had given himself, although no one ever was so impolite as to mention this disparity to him, finished telling the men of the band what a fine hunter he was and how many buffalo he would bring to ground, then concluded by saying that in his opinion they should leave Horse Camp and begin the summer hunt come first light on the morrow.

"Is there another who would speak?" Big Stones asked. "Yes, Talks To Ghosts?" Big Stones seemed surprised. Talks To Ghosts normally should have given his thoughts on the second night of the discussion at the latest. But of course there were no rules as to who should speak when, merely custom. Talks To Ghosts, or for that matter any other, was free to speak when and as he wished.

Talks To Ghosts stood, looked shyly around the men who encircled the fire pit, cleared his throat, and hesitantly said, "I feel we should wait. Three weeks more. Perhaps four. Then we can go ahead on our hunt."

"And will the buffalo still be in the north in three weeks or four, Talks To Ghosts?"

"No, Tall Man. By then they will be moving south."

"Close to the Canadian, down where the Apache are sometimes found," Tall Man said.

"That is true, yes."

"But you say we should wait so long regardless?" Talks To Ghosts' true friend Black Otter said.

"This is what I say, yes."

"Have you had a dream then, Talks to Ghosts? Have you had a vision?"

"I have had no dream and no vision. It is a feeling that I have. Here." He touched his belly.

"But you say you have no vision. Have you sought one?"

"You know that I have, Black Otter. Did I not give away all the things that I owned? Have I not spent the days and the nights since then fasting and seeking a vision? You know that I have. I sought the dream but it has not come to me. Only this feeling in my belly that we should wait."

"It is dangerous to wait longer," Big Stones said. "Better to find the herd in the north if we can, now while the Comanche are raiding in Mexico so they will not find us out on the open grass where they have the advantage, now before the buffalo move south to where the Apache and the Kiowa-Apache hunt. You know all this, Talks To Ghosts. And you have no vision to tell to us."

"Perhaps," Three Ears injected, "this feeling in your belly is indigestion brought on by fasting."

Talks To Ghosts sighed. They were not hearing him. They listened but they did not hear.

Well, he had expected no more. Without a dream, without a vision . . .

"I am done now," he said solemnly, folding his arms and resuming his seat at the back of the group of men who gathered in council.

V

It was convenient having so little to pack and to carry, Talks To Ghosts told himself.

The biggest load, the buffalo-hide lodge, was gone along with all the heavy lodgepoles. Instead they had a bundle of willow withes and some tattered, lightweight deerskins that generous clansmen had given to them. Those were enough for Sleeping Fawn to build a low, loaf-shaped shelter. That would do until they could gather new buffalo skins during this hunt and, when they returned to the mountains come autumn, new lodgepoles of fine, straight pine.

Sleeping Fawn had been given some dogs capable of

pulling small travois. They were enough to transport their few possessions.

As for the horses, well, Talks To Ghosts never had been all that much of a horseman. He was hardly better a horseman than he was a marksman, and everyone knew how poorly he did in that regard.

The truth was that he was at least a little bit afraid of horses. He never knew quite what to expect one would do next, and his balance was not so good that he could count on adjusting to their motions in time to avoid falling to the ground so that everyone would laugh at him. And anyway Talks To Ghosts enjoyed walking. It was good for a man to walk. Walking gave him time to think.

Sleeping Fawn, on the other hand . . . he had to give her credit. One of the few things she had not complained about lately was his impulse to dispose of their possessions. She hadn't uttered one word of disparagement about that. Thank goodness.

The band of the people stumbled and rambled into motion, bringing a sort of slow and sleepy order out of seeming chaos, and Talks To Ghosts lingered behind, enjoying these last moments at his beloved Horse Camp.

They would be back again in a few months, of course. But it was always a joy to him to reach Horse Camp and always a regretful thing when he had to leave it again.

He trailed behind the rest of the band, wanting to be the last to leave this pleasant, shady grove beside the best ford on this stretch of the little river.

He waited and finally he walked along in the wake of the slowly moving band. And when he turned to look back one last time he saw—he was quite positive that he saw—a thin plume of white smoke rising above the treetops.

That was not possible, of course. Talks To Ghosts himself, as almost everyone, had personally checked to make sure the fires were extinguished so that no harm could come to Horse Camp. Every pit was cold, the embers long since dead and the ashes dry. No fire remained. Talks To Ghosts was sure of that.

And yet he saw the smoke. As he had on his arrival here those weeks earlier.

A cold spot developed low in the middle of his back and raced lightly up his spine, chilling him in spite of the sun-heat that was already warming the new day.

Talks To Ghosts turned away from the smoke-without-fire and, chanting softly under his breath, hurried to catch up with the tail of the moving procession.

All of a sudden he did not want to be alone.

Chapter Eight

I

If this was a highway, then Emilio was a raven and could fly across these accursed mountains without pause.

If this was a highway, then Emilio Escavara was a sorcerer and would lay the path flat by way of an incantation.

If this was a highway, then the former Hernan Eduardo was a fish and might easily support himself by swimming in the sweat of his labors.

If this was a highway . . .

"Consuela good wife, we are coming to another place of great steepness," he called over his shoulder to the slim and no doubt weary girl who, like him using a staff to lean upon as she walked, followed close behind the sheep to keep the lazy ones from straggling.

"I see, Emilio."

"They will have to let the wagons down by block and tackle here. Would you mind . . . ?"

"Go ahead, Emilio. Help our neighbors. I can take the flock around. There is a path. Do you see it? There. No, to the left. It swings out past these boulders and reappears below. Do you see? I will take the sheep there and meet all of you below the boulders."

Emilio nodded. The footpath, probably many generations older than this accursed set of ruts that passed for a highway in this forsaken country in these forsaken mountains, the footpath could be easily negotiated by a person afoot or by a sheep. Or for that matter by a deer, an elk, by any of the shy creatures of the wilderness. But not by wagons.

Emilio was more pleased than ever that his belongings and Consuela's were carried on the backs of burros, for the burros could walk wherever a man or a sheep might go and there was no need to use ropes and pulleys to cozen them up or down the many ledges and drop-offs that the so-called highway traversed on its sweat-sopping journey across the high pass called Raton.

Miserable, benighted, ill-conceived excuse for a pathway, it was. And they called it a highway. Bah! Emilio turned his head and spat to emphasize, if only to himself, his feelings toward this trail of great difficulty. Highway indeed. He spat a second time.

Then, catching sight of the wagon before him as it reached the next drop-step down—a matter as he soon saw of only five or so feet and yet a great, straining, gut-wrenching impossibility of an obstacle for a wagon with its fragile wheels—he waved a quick good-bye to Consuela and hurried ahead to lend assistance to their new friend and good neighbor Hector Martine.

He reached the side of the Martine wagon three steps ahead of that overbearing show-off Corporal Delucca, and Emilio felt a small—in truth a petty—sense of triumph to be able to make the offer of assistance before Delucca could do the same.

"My compliments, señor. It would be my pleasure to help if you would be so kind as to accept, eh?"

"There is a place to tie off. Up there, do you see?" Martine returned, pointing. "And yes, friend Emilio, we thank you."

"And . . . ?"

"Yes, and you as well, Corporal. Both of you. Your help is greatly appreciated, thank you."

Emilio hurried to the back of the wagon and reached over the tailgate to drag out the heavy, cumbersome tackle.

His eyes caught, as he had hoped of course, those of Martine's daughter Serafina.

Ah, Serafina. A vision. A loveliness. So pretty. Sixteen now, or soon to be. Certainly of an age to be courted. As perfect and as innocent, as pure and as delicate, as a lily at Easter.

And that damnable Delucca. Everyone knows how soldiers are. Delucca was surely no better than he had to be. Emilio was sure Delucca was the sort who would pluck a flower, savor its fragrance for the briefest of moments, and then discard the limp and dying blossom as quickly as the first sweet scents began to fade.

Serafina Martine deserved better. Emilio wished there was some way he could help her to see what sort of crude person the corporal truly was.

Not that this was the time for it, no.

He hauled the tackle out of the wagon, gave the free end of the line to Delucca, and lugged the rest of the contraption uphill to the thick tree stump Hector had pointed out to him as a likely anchor point.

Emilio could see from the many scars and gouges on the bark of the old stump that it had been put to this same purpose many and many a time before.

Slowly, having to first make sense of the tangle of ropes and pulleys, he began preparing to lower the wagon down the sheer rock face to the passable road surface below while other hands labored to unhitch the team and begin walking them around on the same pathway Consuela and the sheep were now taking.

While his hands were busy with that task, he had the pleasure of seeing Serafina climb down from the bed of her father's wagon.

She was slim as a Toledo blade and as vibrant as a harp string. Yes, and more beautiful than a sunrise.

Ah, such a beauty. The man who gained that one would gain the world, no?

"Escavara!"

"*Si?*"

"Are you tied off yet?"

"A moment more, no longer than that." Emilio's attention, momentarily diverted into silly reverie, returned to the task at hand. "All right," he called down the hill. "This end is secure. You can start letting the wagon down now."

Half a dozen men sprang into position to help, and the first of the wagons that had to be so carefully lowered began inching downward to the precipice—the granite lip scarred white with scrape marks where iron tires had passed before—and slowly, carefully over the edge.

Emilio lost sight of Serafina Martine while he and the others were so occupied. But no matter. Even when the girl was not in his sight she remained in his mind. And especially so at night, he was finding of late. Ah, so beautiful she was, so beautiful.

As beautiful as his own dear Maria Magdalena? Well, yes, as a matter of fact. Of late Serafina seemed quite as lovely and desirable to him as Maria Magdalena once did. And was that not a most remarkable thing, although perhaps a thing best left unremarked, eh?

Emilio passed a forearm across his forehead to wipe some of the sweat away and gave his attention to the work that was at hand. There would be time enough—too much time indeed—for the torments of imagination later.

II

"Ah!" A splinter gouged deep into Emilio's palm when his hand slipped on the sweat-slickened wood of the wheel spoke. He cried out and jerked his hand back, and the wheel, suddenly freed of his steadying hold, banged hard onto a stone, jarring the wagon and making an amazingly loud thump. If nothing broke it was a miracle, no less.

Emilio caught the look of sharp annoyance, a hair-breadth short of anger, that flickered over the dark face of Hector Martine. Serafina's father was in a foul humor this day. And no wonder. This was—what?—the fourth time they had had to let the wagons down by rope and pulley since starting out in the morning. And it was not yet time for the midday halt. Man and beast alike would be worn out when this day came at last to a merciful end.

Emilio gave Serafina's father a shrug and reached to resume his hold on the wheel. He was interrupted in this effort by a piercing shriek from somewhere behind. The cry was of alarm. And of fear.

And it came from Elena . . . no, Consuela . . . at the moment it did not matter in the least what his beloved sister was called. She was afraid and she was alone tending to their sheep when Hernan . . . that is to say Emilio. . . . He spun away from Hector Martine's wagon, allowing it once more to bang and thump alarmingly against the stones of the rugged mountain trail while above soldiers and fellow travelers hauled and pulled and cursed at the ropes and the tackle.

Emilio turned and began a headlong dash toward the sound of the continued screaming. He ran without thought and without hesitation. Off toward the footpath where the sheep and the burros and all those who were not occupied with the wagons were traveling.

A hundred yards, he ran. Two. Consuela continued to shout, her voice not quite so terrified now but just as loud as before. Defiant now. Angry. And fearful too.

Emilio found the beaten red earth of the footpath. His sandals skittered and slid on loose gravel.

He could see the first of the sheep now. Passed by the leaders. His lungs burned and his chest heaved as he gulped for the nourishment of air at this high, thin elevation. His knees felt weak and sweat ran into his eyes, but he plunged on toward the source of Consuela's cries.

He caught a glimpse of her. There. Just past that sharply angled switchback in the trail from above, she stood brandishing a four-foot length of broken pine limb.

She stood between the sheep, their precious stupid sheep, and a furry brown bear that held its head low, black velvet nose almost to the ground, and shifted uncertainly from one foot to the other, rocking side to side, blinking, snuffling, capable of charging but obviously unsure of what to make of the noisy thing that was between it and the delicate flavor of lamb.

Emilio ran up behind Consuela and elbowed her aside. That was a foolish thing to do. It was not necessary. There was more than enough room for him go around her. He might have knocked her down. Might have injured the child she carried.

For half an instant, even in the urgency of the moment, he wondered if his lapse was unknowingly cruel and deliberate . . . if perhaps somewhere deep inside he resented the child she bore and wished to do the babe harm . . . but there was no time to ponder such foolishness as that.

He pushed past his wife, his sister, his beloved Consuela/Elena and stooped even before he stopped running so that he sprawled forward onto hands and knees, grabbed up a pair of stones, one in each fist, and bounded onto his feet again.

"Damn you!" The first stone soared wide of the confused bear. A second grazed the beast's right ear and ricocheted to the ground behind it. Emilio bent, snatched up another pair of fist-sized stones, and threw them at the bear while his voice joined Consuela's in shouting deprecations and disparagement at the dumb beast of the forest.

A stone hit the bear on the shoulder, almost lost in the density of the fur. Another struck it on the snout.

The bear shook its head in response to the blow on the relatively sensitive nose. It blinked all the harder, raised its muzzle, and made a sound that was not really a growl, more like a breathy, puffy "whuff."

And then, praise Jesus, Mary, Joseph, and all the saints in heaven, the animal turned its back on the flock, and on the people, and began moving back along the spine of the mountainside from which it had come.

"Elena?"

"Hern'ardo."

Brother and sister collapsed into each other's arms, sobbing and exhausted, clinging fiercely to one another.

Emilio had a moment in which to hope no one overheard their lapse into former identities. And then it no longer seemed to truly matter. The important thing was that Consuela was safe. She had come to no harm. She had been so brave.

"You are so brave," Consuela said to him.

And Emilio, hearing his own thoughts echoed aloud, began to laugh helplessly as he clung tighter and ever tighter to his brave and small and increasingly pregnant loved one.

III

"Señor Escavara. Do you have a moment?"

"For you, Señor Martine, I always have a moment," Emilio said politely. And a trifle cautiously. Hector was being so formal this evening. And his expression was so dour.

Martine took Emilio by the elbow and guided him away from the communal fire where all the women were chattering and sharing the secrets of their cooking and of their gossip.

"This way," Hector said. "I do not wish anyone to overhear."

Emilio nodded and followed the older man away from the comforting presence of the firelight and off into the shadows beneath a stand of tall pine trees.

They stopped and Hector looked carefully around to assure himself that no one stood close enough to hear. Then he leaned so near that Emilio could smell the scent of tobacco on his breath along with the warmer, sharper odor of alcohol of some sort. Hector Martine was no drunkard, though. Emilio was sure of that.

"I am not of your family, Señor Escavara."

"No, señor, you are not," Emilio agreed.

"I have no reason to love you but none to hate you either, is this not true?"

"This is true. So far as I know you have no reason to feel anything toward me but the friendship of someone who will be your neighbor when we establish our homes in the north."

"Exactly," Martine said. "And it is as a neighbor that I speak to you now. And as a substitute, shall we say, for those male relatives who are not with you now."

"Yes, señor? Have I done something to offend?" For surely that or something very like it must be the purpose of this awkward, halting discussion.

"Not yet, Señor Escavara. Not exactly. But you . . . approach insult. Better to say something now than to allow a blood feud later. Is this not so?"

Emilio felt a sickness in his belly, an empty sensation that brought sweat to his forehead and a sourness to his stomach. "What have I done, señor?"

"As I say, my young friend, you have not yet crossed over the bounds of propriety. But you come very close, like a hummingbird dipping and swooping all about the flower while not yet, not quite, dipping its beak into the nectar, eh? Do you understand me now?"

"Of a truth, señor, I do not. Hummingbirds? Nectar? I am confused."

"Nor are you yet a father, señor, although my wife tells me you are well on the way toward that most blessed of events."

"Your wife tells you the truth then. My Consuela is indeed with child."

Martine cleared his throat. Stared into the branches overhead and beyond them to the flickering fire-points of starlight. After a bit he shrugged and looked Emilio in the eyes.

"I have seen the way you look at my Serafina," Martine said in a gruff, husky voice. "The girl is beautiful, and your wife's belly is swollen. But you are a married man, señor, and in a community as small as ours there can be no room for depravity and the sins of the flesh. You have been blessed with a most beautiful wife, señor. One who carries your firstborn already within her. Do not disgrace her, or yourself, by seeking more than is yours to take." Martine scowled. "Do not come near to my daughter again, señor. Do not look upon her with lust in your eyes. I do not know how to make myself more clear than this. Consider yourself . . . warned." Martine emphasized his words by placing his fists together and making a gesture like the wringing of a chicken's neck.

"Your meaning is clear, señor," Emilio said.

And so it was.

Serafina. Serafina. Sweet, sweet Serafina. Impossibly distant. As was Maria Magdalena as well.

Emilio drew himself stiffly erect and bowed low to Serafina's justly concerned papa. "My apologies, señor, if I seem to have overstepped decency and honor. This I did not mean to do. This I shall not do again. Not by word and not by deed. Not ever."

"Thank you, señor. I accept your word as that of a gentleman, and we will not speak of this again. Nor will I say anything of it to anyone else."

"You are most kind, señor. Thank you." Emilio bowed a second time to Serafina's father and took half a step backward before turning and breaking away with a sob caught somewhere deep inside his throat and a weight like lead sheathing constricting the heart that beat so solemnly within his breast.

IV

Emilio turned over, the blankets riding up at his back so that he felt a chill. At this elevation the nights were cold and empty even so late in the season. At home there would be flowers blooming in the carefully tended pots and on the fruit trees there would be sweet smelling blossoms.

Except . . . except of course he *had* no home. Not any longer. Nor did his beloved Consuela. They had no home and perhaps they never would. Not in any true sense.

Hector Martine made clear to him earlier a truth that Emilio had known before but which he had not truly understood. Not, at any rate, in so vivid and unpleasant a manner.

Consuela/Elena was his beloved sister and, so far as the world about them could know, was his wife and helpmeet as well. And indeed, Emilio loved her deeply and truly.

But in order for her and her child to be accepted by society it was necessary that she be known to be the wife of a respectable man. Was this not so? Of course it was. And this was a thing Emilio could give her.

But the price *he* was required to pay in order to do this thing . . . ah, that price was a terrible one.

Maria Magdalena was but a memory to him. Indeed, the boy who once loved her, and who was loved by her in return, no longer even existed. And in the place of Hernan Eduardo there now was Emilio Escavara.

But Emilio Escavara was married and respectable. And it was not permitted for him to think sweet and loving thoughts about maidens such as Serafina Martine no matter how pure those thoughts. Or, worse, no matter the exciting impurity of them. For the truth was that Serafina and all other young lovelies were now and would remain forbidden to him. Forever.

Emilio Escavara, a husband who did not have the comfort of a wife's embrace, turned his face into the bundle of clothes that served him as a pillow. He turned his face into the hiding place of the night, and soundlessly he wept.

Chapter Nine

I

Talks To Ghosts remembered this place. They found buffalo here several times before, on the hills toward the morning sun, east of this tiny, often dry creek bed where the leaves on the willows were pale and small.

It was at this place, he was sure, where Sleeping Fawn gave birth to Talks To Ghosts' brother's first child. His brother's only child too, of course, but they had not known that at the time. A boy-child it had been. But not whole, not healthy. Its head was misshapen and deformed. People said Sleeping Fawn must have done something truly horrible and ugly to have caused her baby to be born like that.

Talks To Ghosts' brother had already begun the songs of celebration and had started making presents to the other men in the band before they told him.

The women who helped with the birthing took the child before allowing it to suck and carried it away over the hill—from where he stood Talks To Ghosts could see the hill and could remember the sight of those women, grieving, their heads covered with shawls and pieces of torn blanket, the sounds of their wailing small but clear even over a great distance, disappearing over the crest of the hilltop that late afternoon years before—and left it somewhere far from people, left it to live or die on its own.

No one knew what became of the baby. At least that was what everyone pretended to believe. No one spoke of it. No one ever actually said, or acknowledged, that the child was given to the carrion birds and to the coyotes.

The pretense was that some kind and caring spirit could have come along and taken the child to raise as its own. That was the pretense.

The truth . . . sometimes it was better not to think about the truth.

Talks To Ghosts wondered if Sleeping Fawn remembered this place too. He wondered if she missed the boy-child that came from her body. He did not know if she watched the women depart that day or if she knew where the child was laid down beyond that hill. Or if she even knew which hill it was that the women marched across on their errand of mercy, their duty to the people.

If Sleeping Fawn had memories of that day, they were not memories that she shared with Talks To Ghosts. She had never mentioned to him anything from that time. Not about the baby nor about its father, neither one.

Both Sleeping Fawn and Talks To Ghosts did what was necessary after Talks To Ghosts' brother died.

But afterward neither chose to speak aloud about the past.

Talks To Ghosts supposed that was a good thing. But there were times when he might have had it otherwise had the choice been his.

He stood, the fatigue a dull but somehow satisfying ache in the powerful muscles of his thighs and in his calves, and watched the people stream through the lush grasses that grew in the bottom of this hidden swale.

From his vantage point on a hillside above and behind them he turned slowly, scanning the horizon in all directions. Far, far to the east there was a thin, misty pallor in the air that he knew to be the dust of a massive buffalo herd, and that was good.

Behind him and even farther away he thought for one

brief instant . . . no, that was not possible. It was much too far, days and days distant now, and there was no way he could possibly see a plume of smoke-without-fire from Horse Camp even if there was one, which was equally impossible.

That was sheer imagination.

No, the horizon was clear in all directions save for the faraway dust that clouded the air to the east. And this dust and the cause for the dust he had quite fully expected.

The buffalo were where they should be. Funny, though. This knowledge gave no satisfaction to Talks To Ghosts. For reasons he could neither comprehend nor shed he found no pleasure this day in knowing he had been right about where to find the life-giving buffalo.

Frowning, holding on to a cedar walking stick, he walked along in the wake of the moving band, his heart inexplicably uneasy now.

II

It was dark inside the lodge, and the hour was yet early. Or late, depending on how one wanted to look at it. Talks To Ghosts knew little time had passed since he lay down to sleep. The fire had died down but there was still a bright, cherry glow from the coals and a strong scent of smoke hanging in the air. He doubted it was much past halfway between the time the burning sun buried itself beyond the far mountains and the time it came, renewed, to life once more over the great open prairie.

He sat upright, allowing the light antelope skin that was his warm-weather covering to fall to his waist.

To his left, in the direction that was below his feet when he lay on his pallet at the rear of the lodge, he could hear the soft, wet soughing of Sleeping Fawn and the faint rustling of the grasses that filled her rabbit-skin pallet. She was restless in her sleep, another sure sign that the hour was yet early, for Sleeping Fawn had not been asleep very long.

Talks To Ghosts' wife slept apart from him—this had been
their habit as long as they were together—but he was
familiar with the routines and the patterns of her existence
and knew that she must not have been in her bed more than
an hour or so.

He judged he himself must have gotten perhaps as
much as three hours of sleep. It would be enough.

He felt around on the swept earth that constituted the
floor of the low-roofed makeshift lodge—the old lodge,
much larger and properly constructed to include a floor of
tanned and carefully sewn hides, had been given away along
with all their other possessions—and found a few sprigs of
dry grass stem.

Talks To Ghosts leaned forward and dropped the grass
onto the coals of the previous night's fire. There was red
light enough for him to see a wisp of smoke curl up from the
grass, and then the stems burst into bright, brief flame.

By that light Talks To Ghosts gathered the few things
he needed. A breechclout. Moccasins. The chipped and
stained bit of clay pipe, its stem long since broken and gone,
that had belonged to Talks To Ghosts' maternal uncle. A
flake of partially worked flint half the size of a grown man's
palm. The flint would serve as knife or fire starter if either
was needed.

Those were all the things he would take with him. No
blanket or hide for warmth. Above all there would be no
metal, nothing whatsoever that came from the men with the
wide hats who lived to the south nor from the bearded
voyageurs, of whom Talks To Ghosts heard much, although
he himself had only once caught a glimpse of two such
humans, and they at the time had been busily paddling a
canoe, already with a quarter-mile head start and frantic to
preserve their lives. That had been, what, three summers
back? Four? On the Arkansas it was. The voyageurs got
away that time, which the people thought a great shame, as
had the men been slower there would have been opportunity
to trade for whatever it was that made the canoe ride so
heavy in the water.

Trade, Talks To Ghosts conceded, or perhaps a little

plunder, depending on who reached the visitors first and how the voyageurs reacted.

No matter, though. It was said the bearded men were coming onto the plains and into the mountains like the locusts preceding a swarm. A few only at first. Then more and more. And still more yet until there were numbers beyond counting. The Pawnee, the Otoes, the Mandans, and others all claimed this. Or so it was said around the council fires at night.

Talks To Ghosts had no opinion on the subject himself, as he had never yet seen any of these swarms for himself. But this matter of the wide hats and the black robes and the men with the pale beards was part of what troubled him these days. This and the even more troublesome vision of smoke where there was no fire.

Talks To Ghosts felt a heaviness in his chest when he pondered these things, and now even the presence of the buffalo where he expected them to be was not enough to bring lightness to his step.

He dressed quickly in the darkness that filled the tiny lodge once the grass stems were reduced to ash, tucked the pipe and flint into the leather pouch formed by his breech-clout, and let himself out into the cool of the night air without disturbing Sleeping Fawn.

In the morning she would notice that he was not there. Probably. And if she did not, well, he would mention it to her when he returned.

Talks To Ghosts stood, stretching as fully upright as he could manage, enjoying the fresh feel of clean air deep inside his lungs. He stretched, yawned, and then set out into the star-filled night, his steps carrying him in roughly the same direction the women once took when they carried his nephew away to be exposed to fate.

III

The earth spun crazily, eerily round and round and round again as Talks To Ghosts, faint from hunger after four days of fasting, tried to sit upright and became dizzy.

Some time ago ... yesterday? He was no longer sure of inconsequential things such as the passage of mere time ... he had crawled—or possibly floated—out of the glare of sunshine and into the cool, shadowy protection of a rocky overhang.

He blinked, only vaguely aware that he was no longer sitting up but had fallen back onto the loose gravel beneath the stone shelf, and noticed the dark plaque collected on the ceiling above him.

The stain was shiny with age, as if it had been lacquered, but the patina was caused not by a deliberate coating with tree saps but by the passage of years. More years than Talks To Ghosts could begin to comprehend. More years than he could count or imagine. This place, he saw, had been used by someone, quite possibly by his very own people, for more generations than Talks To Ghosts had years.

Since the beginning of time the people had come here in search of buffalo, and for much of that time this rude shelter must have provided protection from the elements. People came here to hunt, came here to escape hunger and cold, enemies and rainstorms. Generation after generation sheltered here, huddled close together here, slept and mated here, ate and drank and celebrated here. And for all those many years the people who came here lighted their fires, warmed their bodies, and cooked their meat, and slowly, gradually, one small bit of soot at a time, the thick, dark plaque built up upon the coarse stone until now the rock itself seemed smooth and slick to his touch.

Was he touching it? Or did he only imagine the feel of it? Talks To Ghosts was not entirely sure what was real. But he knew what was true, and that was more important than knowing what was real, was it not so? Yes, this was so. Yes, it was a truth that he saw and felt and somehow knew.

The sight of the dark smoke stains filled Talks To Ghosts with a sense of Time and People, the passage of time and the ages-long continuity of the people. People labored here, loved here, triumphed and wept here. For all the years of time there had been people here.

Talks To Ghosts shuddered and felt a deep sadness overwhelm him. The past was clear in his eyes. He could see it, feel it, here in this shelter that was not even a cave yet was a place that had given comfort to his people forever.

The future . . . his senses whirled and twisted when he thought about the unknown and unknowable.

And he did not for one moment think that he was still dizzy.

He had come here to seek a vision. What he found was only a memory. And a confusion of emptiness when he tried to find his way into the future.

Was that the vision? Was it? Talks To Ghosts' lips fluttered as he lifted a soundless chant into the sky where the spirits might chance upon his plea. Was this emptiness his vision?

He hoped, he begged, that this not be so.

IV

Ah, he was hungry. So hungry. Too weak to hunt now. No weapons to hunt with even if he were not weak. He should have thought . . . too late. And anyway it would not have been the same. To bring food for afterward would have been to try to cheat the spirits. And the spirits would know, was this not true? Of course it was true. Mere man cannot fool the spirits. He cheats only himself when he tries. But, oh, he was hungry.

His belly did not ache. That had passed two days gone. Now there was only a sense of emptiness in his gut, a sort of hollow feeling that needed some source of energy to draw upon if he was to put this disorientation and dizziness behind and get back to the camp among the willows.

Talks To Ghosts crawled slowly, haphazardly along the hard ground, his knees bruised and oozing blood from the repeated abrasions of the crawling.

He was in no hurry. And in little pain. There was a gentle fog in his mind that protected him from pain. The spirits were kind.

He knew, more or less, where he was bound. He supposed that eventually he would get there. It hardly seemed to matter anymore how long the journey would take.

He saw a small, dust-colored lizard and tried to catch it, but the quick-skittering creature was too fast for him, and his grabs became more comical—even to himself—than useful, and after a bit he gave up trying and moved on.

He came to an anthill and that was much better. He scuffed the surface lightly with his fingertips so as to arouse the ants to rebuilding efforts, then dug two fingers into the soft, warm soil.

A swarm of fat black ants quickly climbed onto his fingers, and Talks To Ghosts greedily licked the ants off and stabbed his fingers back into the anthill for more. The ants crunched when he ate them and left a sharply biting acid taste behind. They were not exactly good food. But they were edible, they were food, and that was to the good.

The juices in his belly made short work of the ants, and his stomach churned and rumbled in unhappy protest. But there was also a spurt of energy, small but enough that he could feel a thin beginning of the strength returning to his flesh.

He gathered and ate ants until his stomach would accept no more of the bitter, acidic intrusion, and he knew if he tried to eat more he would throw up and lose what little nourishment he had gained thus far.

He crawled on, a little clearer in the head now, and found the trickle of water that he knew he could expect at this time of year.

He lay down on the sparse grass at the side of the occasional creek and pressed his cheek onto the sweet-smelling green sprigs, then wriggled forward and plunged his face ear deep into the cold water, splashing the weariness from his mind and cleansing his spirit for a moment before drinking deeply of the clean, chill water so as to cleanse his throat and fill his belly.

The life-giving water flowed into his stomach and thence into his soul, and he felt clear of mind and joyous after the fasting.

The ants, now the water, between them they were enough to revive him and give him the strength and the determination to stand upright as a man should and to return to his people.

And if the vision was a failure—a failure that he feared was his own due to an inability to understand the message contained within the vision, not a failure to achieve a message—so be it.

He tried. A man could do no more.

He lay beside the bit of water awhile longer—minutes, days, the time did not matter, and so he made no attempt to keep track of its passage—and then stood, coming shaking and wobbly onto his feet again for the first time in several days.

Then, in no hurry, he began the placement of one careful foot before another, the act of walking a conscious and determined thing in his weakened but no longer woozy state.

Talks To Ghosts commenced the journey back to his people.

V

It was well with the people. From the top of the last rise Talks To Ghosts could see that there was meat in the camp. Since he left several days past—he did not know how many the days had been—they seemed to have made a good start on the season's kill.

Racks had been skillfully built with the thin, whippy willow withes available along the wet bottomland, and now the women of the band were busily, happily slicing fresh

buffalo meat into thin strips to be dried in the bright sunshine on those racks and stored for winter use.

The ground all around the encampment was littered with
the pegged-down hides of buffalo, the skins staked out with
the wool side downward so the flesh could be dried and
removed and the hides tanned and turned into the leather that
supplied so many, so very many, of the people's needs.

Ah, this was a good time of year, a fine time for all the
people, and Talks To Ghosts' heart lifted at the sight, never
mind that he returned from his vision quest without the
knowledge he sought. A fine time of year indeed.

In the evenings so long as the fresh meat lasted there
would be feasting on the livers, tongues, and other portions
not so easily preserved. There would be fresh gall to sprinkle
on the raw liver, giving it that piquant, rather spicy flavor
so beloved by Talks To Ghosts and his people. There would
be intestines to stuff and roast as boudins. There would be
hump meat to cook over hot coals and sweetbreads to boil
and marrow to suck from roasted bones and there would
be . . . Talks To Ghosts smiled gently to himself, recognizing
where his thoughts had become so firmly fixed. Could it be
that those days of fasting made him most unnaturally interested in foods? Despite the eminent satisfaction of a recent
meal replete with black ants and cold water? Hard to satisfy
him lately, eh? He laughed aloud as he descended the rocky
slope and came near to the willows, bright green in their
cloak of springtime growth.

He laughed and something rattled in the brush nearby.

A small animal startled by his unexpected approach, no
doubt.

Idly he wondered what it was he had managed to creep
up upon, for normally he was the most clumsy and inept of
hunters. Perhaps that was the trick. He needed to hunt
without intending to do so. Perhaps in that way he could be
as silent and as stealthy as all the others.

Grinning, pleased to be coming back, and especially
pleased to be coming back to a camp full of food, he looked
into the willows in an effort to see what made the small
rustling noise in response to his laughter.

He looked into the brush and his eyes went wide. A dark form, big as a fully grown bear and as fearsome as a demonic spirit, painted, horrible, deadly, bearing a club studded with brass tack heads—he had time to see that, the brass bits shining in the sunlight, had time to see and to despair—the demon was rising up from the greenery.

The brass-studded club lashed out. Smashed solidly onto his forehead.

A bitter blackness closed over Talks To Ghosts, and the last thing he heard was the hollow, melon-thump sound of a war club striking hard onto his skull.

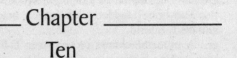

Chapter
Ten

I

"What stinks?"

"Indians, that's what. Stinking damn Indians."

Aaron looked around. They were coming down into the bottom of another of the ten thousand and one shallow coulees that rumpled the only seemingly flat plains here, and so the horizon was not particularly far. Inside the circle of his vision, however, he was quite positive that there were no Indians, never mind what Mr. Matthewson told him.

The only things Aaron could see in any direction were sky and pale, wispy clouds above, willows, and a glint of sunlight sparkling on water ahead. And grass. In every direction grass. Miles of grass, days of grass, weeks and even months of grass to cross. He hadn't thought there could *be* so much grass. At times it seemed there was more grass out here than sky to cover it all. And still the wagons passed through an endless vista of grass and yet more grass.

It was wonderful. It was also somewhat frightening. Intimidating. The plains here were as empty and as broad as Aaron had always heard the oceans to be.

Ever since they pulled out of St. Jo and left the trees behind they were surrounded by grass. The ox-drawn wagons labored day after day and week after week through grass.

Over one hillock and thence onto another and always, eternally, on the other side they would find . . . more grass. Sometimes buffalo too, of course. Skittish, shyly inquisitive antelope. Soaring hawks and quick-booming prairie chickens rising without warning from tufts of—what else?—grass. But essentially there was only . . . grass.

Scarcely a tree to be found. This was no country for dogs, Aaron sometimes thought. Poor dang dog out here would puff up and die, just swell up bigger and bigger until it blew up and busted clean apart. No, this here country was not at all meant to be inhabited by dogs.

He had his doubts about its usefulness for humans too, for that matter.

Day after day it was always the same. Rise before dawn to help start the breakfast fire, then go out to haze in the herd of dull, plodding oxen. Eat quickly whilst on the run, then help segregate the oxen into the proper pairs—oh, hadn't Mr. Matthewson bellowed and hollered the first week or so until Aaron learned which ox was to be put with which other and on which side of the yoke—and help muscle the heavy, hickory yokes into place. And finally prod and pull and cuss the dumb beasts into place ahead of the loaded, canvas-covered freight wagons and big trailers till the chains could be hooked up and the day's travel begun.

The fire would be kicked apart and the lead wagon in motion within minutes of dawn's breaking.

The train would lumber ahead at a snail's pace for five hours, never less and rarely any more, until the noon halt. Then it was Aaron help build the fire, boy help break those hitches, kid lay the damn yokes where they won't be trompled on. Sometimes Aaron thought there wouldn't have been a lick of work accomplished by a single member of the whole damn train if they hadn't brought him along to do it all.

They nooned close to water if they could find it, otherwise stopped wherever Mr. Matthewson took the notion. Aaron seldom could see what there was about one particular spot that the wagon master, the eldest and meanest partner in the firm of Matthewson, Matthewson, and Roberts, saw to recommend over any other. Mostly it all looked like just more grass to him. But then Mr. Matthewson knew what he was about. Or so Aaron supposed. After all, the man had made . . . what? This was his ninth crossing of the road they'd opened a few years back and called the Santa Fe Trail.

Matthewson's ninth crossing it was. Over and back twice each year for the past two years and now on his way over to Mexico yet again for the first crossing of this third year in business. Five trading ventures to Mexico—welcome ventures now that the Papist Spaniards were no longer there to throw honest American traders into the . . . what did the men say they called it? *Calabeza?* That or something close to it, jail being what it meant but a particularly disgusting and bug-ridden sort of jail from the way the men spoke of it—and after those first four trips people were talking about how rich Matthewson, Matthewson, and Roberts surely was.

Aaron couldn't help but think that maybe someday he just might want to make his own venture into trading. There wasn't a thing wrong with honest business, no sir. Wasn't a whole lot to be said against the idea of being rich either, for that matter. But all of that would have to wait until he knew what he was about. As for now, well, there were sights to see and experiences to experience and señoritas to, uh, dance with—or so all the men claimed—and other things as well.

But no Indians.

Not yet, by damn, and never mind what Mr. Matthewson said about the smell down in this coulee being the stink of Indians. Aaron looked, and he couldn't see a single Indian. Not anyplace. He could see some offal where buffalo must have been killed, and he could see where there'd been fires laid here not so awful long ago.

But there sure as certain wasn't a single Indian in sight. No sir, there dang sure was not.

"We'll noon here," Mr. Matthewson bawled, holding his arm extended toward the heavens so the men back along the train could see the signal and know that this was where they'd stop.

Aaron wrinkled his nose, and Mr. Matthewson must have seen.

"It stinks," the rich boss man agreed, "but this is the only water I know of for a good ways more. We'll stop here until tomorrow morning and fill our barrels before we drive on straight west. Cut acrost to the little river that heads up over toward the Spanish Peaks."

Aaron nodded, not understanding much of the reasoning but willing to accept Matthewson's decisions if only because the boss was the boss and therefore entitled to decide. All Aaron had been told was that they were taking a shortcut route that would cut the journey short by a good two, maybe three weeks.

There was said to be an even shorter route that would cut twice as much time or even more, but that one was plagued by a chronic lack of water at the best of times. And Mr. Matthewson was known to be prudent in his decisions. He liked to use this route for his first trip each year, early enough that he could pretty well count on finding water. The men said that unlike some train masters Mr. Matthewson never took the much more risky dry route around the eastern shoulder of the mountains.

All of which Aaron found somewhat suspicious at this point. The men talked about mountains. What dang mountains? All he could see, about all he had seen ever since they left the States behind, was grass. And then some more grass.

No sir, near as he could figure it the fellows were teasing him about there being mountains anywhere in this huge, empty country. They were just pulling his leg, that's what it was. They were . . .

"Boy."

"Yes, Mr. Matthewson?"

"Take this yoke and lay it out over there."

"Yes, sir."

"Then you can lead this pair to water. I'll finish breaking the hitch and taking the yokes off while you water the stock. Oh, and boy."

"Yes, sir?"

"Mind you help Mr. Thompson with the fire. If you see any wood or dry chips while you're watering the animals, make sure you carry in enough for our fire."

"Yes, sir. Sir?"

"Yes?"

"Are there really . . . I mean to say . . ."

"Indians?"

Aaron nodded.

"It's really the stink of Indians that you smell, but there aren't any of the black-hearted bastards here any longer. You see over there?"

"Uh-huh."

"Those stone circles are where they put up their tents. Like inverted cones, their tents are. And over there you can see where they made meat. Staked out the hides for tanning, put up drying racks for the meat, like that. After the chores are done, if you like I'll walk across the creek with you and point things out to you."

"I'd like that, thank you."

Matthewson shrugged. "Now get along, boy. Take this pair and water them."

"Yes, sir." Aaron gathered up the lines that dangled from the nose rings of Mr. Matthewson's pair of lead oxen—the boss always had first call on the services of the train's hey-boy—and led the pale, cream-and-yellow oxen toward a cattail-rimmed pond in the creek bed.

II

"Help! Help!" Aaron stood rooted in place, one lead string in each hand, so immobilized by fear that he was actually, absolutely, honest and true too scared to turn and run away.

"Indians. Help!"

He wasn't able to flee but he was managing to scream for help very nicely. He drew a deep, shuddering breath and screeched again. Louder.

"Help."

Mr. Matthewson came running with a pistol in his hand, and close on his heels were Owen Joiner and Carl Adams carrying shotguns that they must have snatched from under the seats of their wagons.

"What is it, boy, where's the damn Injuns?" Matthewson puffed and panted. The wagon master waved his pistol at the reeds but was looking at Aaron, probably trying to figure out where Aaron's fear-stricken gaze was directed.

Despite having been able to yell, Aaron suddenly lost the use of his tongue. But regained a modicum of movement. He lifted one arm and pointed, his outstretched finger shaking.

"Where, there? Oh, yes, I see it." Matthewson frowned and motioned his armed drivers to follow. "Well I'll be damned," he exclaimed a moment later. "Damned if it ain't an Injun for certain sure." He inched forward, stopped, peered closer at the form lying still in the mud beside the water. "You thought this'un was laying in ambush didn't you, Aaron, but he ain't. Dead Injun, this one is."

"One of them good Indians," Joiner snickered, letting the hammer of his shotgun down to the safe-cock position and visibly relaxing.

"This your first wild Injun?" Matthewson asked.

Aaron nodded. He felt . . . foolish. Dumb. Just as much the kid tenderfoot everybody in the train teased him about being. Dammit. Spooked and scared all spitless by a dead Indian.

"Come take a closer look," the boss invited. "Son of a bitch isn't but half a heartbeat away from being an animal," he said with a contemptuous glance at the body.

The Indian was lying on the far side of a small spit of water, surrounded by cattail reeds and thick young willow shoots so that it was difficult to see him clearly. All Aaron had seen when he first approached was a hand and arm and part of the dead man's torso. And yes, it was quite true that he'd thought the Indian was alive and in hiding ready to spring out and brain him. Or something.

Now that he was closer Aaron could see that someone else had already done that favor to the Indian, for the man's scalp was split wide open and covered with dried blood and a mass of flies. Damn flies. Aaron hated flies almost as much as he hated mosquitoes.

It was flies that were crawling all over the Indian's face though. Or what was left of the Indian's face. The mask of blood was so thick that it was hard to tell what he must have looked like in life.

"Is it all right if I go closer?" he asked, not sure why he did so but finding the idea of permission comfortable nonetheless.

"Sure, kid, go ahead. He won't mind." The two wagon drivers laughed at their boss's wit. "Hell, take his scalp for a souvenir if you want. I see nobody else went and lifted it, though I don't know why that would be so. Funny thing, come to think of it. Mostly you'd expect a kilt Injun to be scalped too." Matthewson shrugged. "Oh, well. Anyhow, boy, you go ahead an' look it over. Then finish watering the stock, mind."

"Yes, sir."

Joiner and Adams went back to their work, and Mr. Matthewson paused where he was to begin the rather serious process of getting his pipe tobacco properly tamped and ready for lighting. He produced a magnifying glass and focused sun rays onto the surface of the tobacco. Aaron dropped the lead lines of the oxen and pushed his way through the thick reeds, avoiding walking into the water, to the side of the dead man.

He had seen dead men before, of course. But . . . not like this. And never a wild Indian. He wondered what tribe this Indian belonged to. Whatever tribe it was, Mr. Matthewson was right about one thing. They were an almighty primitive people. Why, this man wasn't hardly wearing any clothes. He had a breechcloth made out of some sort of small, soft animals' skins and a pair of shoes, also made of crude skins that, unlike the fancily beaded or quill-worked things sold at trading posts back in Missouri, had no decoration on them whatsoever. The shoes—moccasins, he thought they were called—were no better than skin pouches big enough to put a foot into and tied at the ankle.

The Indian's hair was chopped short, not worn long and plaited into braids like they always showed in newspaper illustrations whenever there was a report about an Indian raid or else an Indian treaty. Those Indians always wore their hair either real long like that or once in a while would be depicted showing their scalps shaved save for a tall, broomlike projection of decorated hair.

Well, the truth as shown by this particular Indian wasn't a bit like those illustrations. And this Indian wasn't wearing any other sort of ornamentation either. Not that Aaron could see while the body was lying face-down. He wondered . . . oh, why not. The Indian wouldn't mind.

Aaron hooked a toe under the nearest shoulder and lifted, shoving the body onto its side, and from there its own weight flopped it over onto its back.

In this new position Aaron could see that he'd been right. The Indian wore no decorations or ornaments or paint or anything like that.

Which was interesting.

What was kind of distressing was that now Aaron could get a better look at the wound that had killed the man. It was a nasty thing, it was. A real hard whack on the head and the left side of the face. There was blood caked thick all over that side of the man's head. It was practically enough to sicken a body.

Aaron shook his head.

And no, he wasn't going to take the dead man's scalp. Not hardly. Even if he'd wanted the thing, which he did not, he wouldn't have wanted a scalp bad enough to bend down and actually touch the dead flesh. The skin would be cold,

Aaron was sure, and slimy to feel. Just thinking about it
made him shiver.

And besides, there were all those flies, buzzing and flit-
ting and crawling all about. The damned despicable flies
crawled into the Indian's mouth and into his nose and all
over his eyes. They swarmed over his eyelashes and . . .

Aaron gasped. Recoiled back a couple paces without
thinking and stepped into the mud and cold water behind him.

"Help! Help!"

III

"Jesus Christ, boy, what is it this time?" Matthewson
came tramping through the reeds trailing a stream of white
smoke, his expression sour and his jaw set. He looked,
Aaron thought, more than a little disgusted with his hey-boy
and sometime protégé, young Mr. Jenks, late of Pennsylvania. "What's spooked you this time, eh?"

"The Indian, sir. He's alive!"

"Made a sound when you turned him over, did he?"
Matthewson shook his head in quick annoyance. "You got a
lot t' learn, son. It's just gas. The rot bloats the belly, see,
and when you move them, or sometime just while they're
laying there, the gases seep out and make a sound, like
they're alive and gasping or passing wind or like that. But
they aren't really alive, kid, they're just—"

"No, sir, that isn't what I meant at all. I mean, there
wasn't any sound. It wasn't gas or something. The flies . . .
that is to say . . . the flies are crawling on the face and I was
looking close and I saw . . . sir, he blinked his eyes. A fly
crawled on his eyelashes, and he blinked. He's alive, sir.
Honestly."

"Bull," Matthewson suggested.

"No, sir. Honest. Look for yourself."

Frowning, Matthewson bent down and touched the
Indian's eyelash. And was rewarded with a blink. It wasn't

much. But the supposedly dead man did most assuredly blink.

"Well, I'll be a son of a bitch," Matthewson said around the stem of his pipe. "I will be a double-dipped red-dog son of a bitch. Damn if he ain't alive after all."

Mr. Matthewson straightened upright, shrugged, and pulled out the pistol he had shoved into his waistband when he went to filling his pipe. He checked the priming powder, snapped the frizzen back into place, and dragged the hammer back to full cock.

"Sir?" Aaron asked.

Matthewson did not bother to answer. He lowered the muzzle of the big horse pistol and aimed it at the Indian's forehead.

IV

Aaron pushed Matthewson's hand aside just as the big pistol fired. A lead ball the size of a quail's egg splashed into the mud less than a foot away from the Indian's head, sending a small geyser into the air but doing no harm.

Matthewson gave Aaron a dirty look and an equally unpleasant cussing. "What in hell 'd you do that for, boy?"

"You can't kill him, sir. That would be murder."

"Murder hell, boy. You can't murder an Injun. Just kill 'em. It's only murder if you kill a white man."

"But, sir—"

"He's dying anyhow, kid. You can see that. Really it'd be a kindness to put the poor thing out of his misery." The wagon master fumbled inside a pouch on his belt and produced a paper cartridge with powder and ball wrapped inside it. He bit the tail end off the cartridge and first poured a small amount of the fine-grain gunpowder into the priming pan of the pistol, then dropped the frizzen in place to hold it there. The remainder of the powder he poured down the barrel of the gun, then stuffed the paper in on top of the powder as wadding, the lead ball still wrapped in what was left of the cartridge. He pulled a short steel rod from its cradle beneath the barrel and used that to ram the ball down firmly onto the powder charge, completing the loading process.

"Don't spoil my aim this time," he warned.

"Sir, I can't let you kill this man."

"And why the hell not?"

"It wouldn't be . . . it wouldn't be Christian, sir. It wouldn't be right."

"Boy, you got an awful lot to learn. Out here you go trying to act Christian and you'll get your scalp lifted. By just such a one as that Injun bastard lying right there." Matthewson gestured toward the nearly naked, blood-caked Indian lying at his feet, and Aaron tensed ready to jump if his boss should ear back the hammer on his pistol.

"By God, I see you mean it, don't you? You'd come after me, wouldn't you, and me a head taller and fifty pounds to the better of you."

"I expect I'd do that, yes, sir. With respect."

Matthewson laughed. "You'd tear into me, but with respect, is that it?"

Aaron smiled. "Yes, sir, that's about it all right."

"How come this Indian means so damn much to you, boy?"

"It's just . . . dammit, sir, he's a human being and he's hurt, and I just can't see letting him lie here and die. Or, worse, finishing the job of killing him."

"Well, we can't take him with us."

Aaron looked down at the Indian and then up at his employer. "Why not?"

"Hell, we just can't, that's all."

"I'd take care of him."

"He's dying anyway, boy."

"All right, then I'll take care of him until he dies, and then I'll give him a decent burial."

"Won't do a damn bit of good, son."

"I'll do it in my free time, sir. I won't let my work slide. And if he recovers enough to eat anything, why, I'll pay for what he eats out of my wages."

"I don't think—"

"Sir, you let Kestermann keep that ugly feist dog in the box of his wagon. If he can have a pet, why can't I?"

Matthewson threw back his head and roared. "Keep a stinking damn Injun for a pet. Now I expect I've heard everything."

"Can I keep him?"

The boss was still chuckling. With a final guffaw he stuffed his pistol back into his waistband. "When he dies you gotta bury him, mind. Unless, that is, you know somebody that can stuff and mount him." Which idea sent Matthewson back into a paroxysm of laughter. "Stuff and mount him," he snorted. "What a thought. Stuff and mount an Indian." A fresh gale of mirth overtook him. "Now an Injun woman, maybe so. Ugly damn wenches most of 'em. But the young ones, well, there's always some good to be found in a young female, never mind what they look like. Or would you be too young to know about that, boy? Aye, I expect you would be. Too young to know what I'm talking about there, eh? Ha! Stuff and mount. Wouldn't that be something." And, still chuckling, Matthewson turned and started back toward the wagons while Aaron knelt beside the wounded and quite probably dying Indian.

It occurred to him only then to wonder what, now that he had this Indian, just what in hell he was going to do with him.

With a sigh of resignation, having talked himself into this situation without really thinking it through, Aaron tore a piece off the tail of his shirt and dipped it into the water. Carefully and as gently as he could manage he began bathing the crusted blood on the Indian's face.

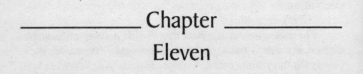

Chapter
Eleven

I

It reminded him—he hoped it was no sacrilege—of what it must have looked like when Moses led his people out of Egypt to the Promised Land.

The column was strung out beyond all proportion to the in truth rather small number of people. There were flocks of sheep and of long-haired goats. There were high-wheeled carts carrying crates of chickens and small pigs. There were wagons piled heavy with household possessions. Mules, burros, and donkeys bore ungainly packs and swayed to and fro with each shifting step forward. People bearing staffs like the patriarchs of old walked beside the flocks, and a few, a very few, rode on horseback like overseers.

Deliberately Emilio hung back as the long, dusty column began its last descent from the mountainside. He was enjoying this opportunity to see the entire assembly strung out before him to be viewed all in one wondering glance.

And far far below, out beyond the rather idyllic sight of the slowly moving procession of new settlers, he could see what was their own promised land. In this case a land promised not by the Lord Almighty but by the somewhat timid—and oh so very distant—government of Mexico.

At the base of the foothills the settlers were now about to leave he could see a broad, rolling expanse of bright and verdant green. Grass enough to feed thousands upon thousands of sheep and goats.

Beyond that in the middle distance was the much darker and quite starkly drawn watercourse. That would be *El Rio de Las Animas Perdidas en Purgatorio*. The River of Souls Lost in Purgatory. This was the water that, despite the foreboding of its name, gave life and beauty to this most wonderful and lovely land.

The riverbanks here were thick with cottonwoods and other excellent growth so that someone settling close by the water would never have to venture very far to gather the wood for building or for fuel.

And far away, stretching for miles and miles upon miles and miles, there was the dry, pale brown prairie grass that extended north and east to the horizons and beyond.

Behind them to the south, of course, were the mountains. Stark and difficult but, with effort, passable.

And to the west, ah, to the west was a magnificence indeed. More mountains. Mountains even higher and more awe-inspiring than the ones the settlers were able to conquer, and commanding this great wall of mountain were a pair of supreme mountains, the tallest and most magnificent mountains Emilio had ever seen, perhaps the tallest and finest mountains to be found anywhere on the face of the earth.

Both were high and conical but rounded at the tips and softened there with twin mantles of white where the snows of the winter past lay deep. The Breasts of the World, some said they were, and Emilio was in no position to dispute the claim now that he could see them clearly.

Still, it was nearer than those mountains that his gaze remained fixed.

It was to the river, to what was most often referred to nowadays simply as the Purgatory, that his attention mostly focused. For it was here, along the banks of this most beautiful stream, where Emilio's destiny would be played out. His and Consuela's. And that of the child she carried within her bulging belly.

Emilio thought of his sister and of her baby, and it was all he could do to keep from breaking into tears. He had done the right and loving thing, had he not?

Aye, of course he had. So why then did he have this empty, sinking feeling in his gut? Selfishness, he supposed. But . . . it seemed so unfair. Did his love for Consuela, who no longer was Elena, did this have to mean that he was doomed forever to exist without a woman's love? Did it mean that he would never feel a woman's arms, a woman's lips, a woman's warmth beside him in a bed of love? Did it mean . . . ?

Emilio took a stern and angry grip on his thoughts and on his emotions and forced his attentions once more onto the river, onto the future.

It was unimportant what the future held for him, after all. What truly mattered was the future of Consuela and of her infant child. Was this not so?

Emilio did not trust himself to venture an answer to that last question. Better to leave it strictly rhetorical in nature. Better not to dwell upon that or things like it.

He took a fresh grip on his staff and moved down the mountainside in the wake of the long emigrant procession.

II

Ah, she was beautiful, his Magdalena. Her skin was as flawless as the finest porcelain and her eyes as deep as the Wells of Moctezuma and her heart as pure as that of the Virgin.

He touched her hand—the fingertips only—and bowed. Held himself handsomely upright and glided around her first in one direction, then in the other. Dipping, turning, floating in time to the music of the strings.

The orchestra was heard but unseen, and the other dancers—were there other dancers? Oh, but of course there surely must be other dancers—moved half seen as if in a fog, encircling Magdalena and her adoring swain Hernan Eduardo, gliding, floating, briefly appearing and then once more withdrawing into the mists and into the haunting strains of the minuet.

The music changed into that of a slow reel, and Magdalena whirled closer. Closer. Her cheek within inches of his, her lips so full and moist coming near, near. Then, tantalizing yet never quite touching, never quite meeting the unspoken promise, she swept gaily away again, leaving behind the scent of her powder and the memory of her beauty.

She glided away, away, toward the fog.

There were no other dancers now. No music. Only mist and silence.

Emilio cried out.

He found himself sitting upright on the hard soil that was his bed, the rough, scratchy woolen blanket fallen to his waist. No matter. He did not need its warmth. He was drenched with sweat and his heart was pounding.

"Emilio? Are you all right?"

Consuela's voice came from her pallet on the side of the fire opposite his.

"I'm fine. Truly. Go back to sleep now."

Emilio lay back, trying to arrange more comfortably the lump of cloths under his neck that served in the place of a proper pillow.

He'd been dreaming. He was fairly sure of that although he could no longer remember anything of the dream. All he could recapture was a sense of loneliness and loss. Better, he thought, not to remember a dream that would lead to such feelings.

He closed his eyes once more and tried to relax his aching muscles. He needed his sleep, for tomorrow would be another day of unremitting labor and if he did not complete the tasks at hand there would be no servants to perform them for him. There were no peons here to serve him. The responsibilities were his and his alone.

That knowledge should please him, he supposed. There was dignity in labor and all that. There was worth in toil.

Ha! Those sentiments, he more than half suspected, were but a sop for the masses. A means of imparting patience. If you cannot cure the pain then try instead to make the pain tolerable by making the sufferer believe that pain itself is noble.

The truth was that Emilio would have preferred to lie abed while someone else dignified and ennobled himself with the pain of common labor. But then Hernan Eduardo was able to accomplish that without so much as bothering to think about it. Emilio Escavara, never.

Emilio Escavara closed his eyes and tried to will himself to sleep.

III

With a groan of purest relief Emilio set the basket upon the ground and began lifting out the flat stones he had brought, piling them carefully one by one.

It might have seemed more efficient to simply upend the basket and dump its burden onto the ground, but rude experience had taught him better. Consuela was no more adept at hard work than he, and the thick, clumsy baskets she was able to weave came quickly apart if the wear he put upon them was excessive. He had learned to treat them with some degree of tenderness.

Even so, his supply of stones was coming along nicely. In time—ah, they did have time now, did they not?—there would be enough and he could start the construction of a proper house for Consuela, for himself, for the child.

They already had a jacal, like everyone else in the new settlement. Those had taken only a few days to build, for they were simple in the extreme. The walls consisted of nothing more complicated than a ditch dug a few feet into the soil and a row of saplings set butt end down into the ditch. Willow withes were woven loosely through the sapling framework, and the whole quickly erected slab was plastered over inside and out with thick mud. The roofs were more saplings overlaid with a thin layer of sod, a layer of dried grass, and then another of sod. Once the mud of the walls was dry and the roof settled, such a jacal would turn the coldest wind or the harshest sun-heat.

And most of the settlers seemed to feel that such a structure was all they could desire. They were content to remain in their jacales as permanent homes. Emilio, on the other hand, wanted more for his tiny family. He was determined to build a house of stone.

He did not know how to build such a house. Exactly. But then, how difficult could it be? And a mere lack of knowledge was not enough to affect his determination on the subject. And so, while the other men of the settlement fished and hunted and pondered which of the native flora might best be converted to pulque or some reasonable substitute, Emilio laboriously picked, carried, and piled all the flat stones he could find.

He paused now, sharp pain slicing into the broad muscles of his back and a dull ache in his shoulders where the sacking-wrapped ropes he employed as carrying straps bit into soft flesh.

Closer to the river he could see Consuela, cheerful and every bit as determined as he to make a fine home for their little family. Despite her now very visible condition, she was diligently preparing a large garden patch ready for the seed she had brought.

Emilio had cut and carved a sharp-ended digging stick to her specifications, and with it she broke the soil and turned it, then went to her knees and with her soft, bare hands broke up the clods to make a bed for the seeds she would soon plant and water, bringing one heavy bucket after another from the river.

The work was hard but the rewards would be great. They had brought seed to grow maize, several varieties of squash, pumpkin, beans. And chilies. Of course chilies, again in multiple varieties.

This fall and for all the years to come they would benefit from Consuela's labors in her garden patch just as next year and for all the years afterward they would enjoy the shelter of Emilio's stone house.

And in the meantime, well, in the meantime they would live in a jacal like all the others and tend to their flocks and hope for the best.

Enough of wasting time in rest, though. Emilio picked up the empty basket and went off in search of more flat stones, one eye on the sheep grazing on the pasture close by the land he had chosen and the other kept on Consuela lest she in her delicate condition be in need of him.

IV

They acted like it was a celebration, but Emilio's feeling, kept carefully to himself, was that there was anything but a cause for rejoicing here. Sadness and sorrow would have been more appropriate, for early on the morrow the soldiers would leave the settlers behind and return alone to the civilized comforts of Santa Fe.

For reasons that remained quite beyond Emilio's comprehension, though, everyone else seemed quite excited by the departure.

Perhaps they felt that this was some sort of affirmation of the permanence and high quality of the newborn settlement. If that was their reasoning, Emilio thought, then they were most easily persuaded.

The settlement, as such, barely existed. Sixteen jacales had been built, scattered with no particular pattern along the south bank of the little river, situated there only because the wood grew the thickest on that side of the river.

There had not yet even been time enough for footpaths to be worn into the grass that blanketed the ground. Paths, to say nothing of roads, would develop over time. But settlement here was so new that the area had more the impression of a well-developed encampment than the town all swore it was destined to become. Town indeed. There was no church, no priest, no alcalde, no judge, not even a store or cantina to boast of.

And come morning there would be no law either. Once the handful of soldiers who escorted the settlers here took their leave there would be no law north of Raton Pass save that of self-restraint. Emilio had scant faith in the effectiveness of self-control.

What if someone went mad? What if smoldering passions burst into flame? What if some small insult festered until it erupted into violence?

What if? A useless question, to be sure. But an inescapable one.

Emilio stood amongst those who would be his neighbors quite probably for the remainder of his life and said nothing while everyone else joined together in toasting the soldiers, thanking the young men for their help, offering prayers of Godspeed, asking that letters or messages be delivered upon the soldiers' return to the provincial capital. Well-wishes and assurances of continued good health many of those messages would be. Also pleas for tools or supplies found to be needed now that actual experience was taking the place of planning and foresight, Emilio suspected.

There were things he might have asked for too, if he and Consuela had anyone behind them of whom a favor might be requested.

But there was no one. No one to ask for assistance. No one to greet. No one to care if they yet lived or died.

This night Emilio felt more alone, more lonely, than he ever would have thought possible, for on this night the soldiers prepared to return over the mountains and their departure served as a cruel reminder that Emilio and his pregnant "wife" had no family to receive any messages.

Emilio would eagerly have gotten drunk this night. Except he did not have liquor for the purpose. What he had, all he had, were Consuela, her unborn infant, and all the responsibilities attendant upon them. What he had, Emilio acknowledged, was a plate brimming full with self-pity.

He grunted softly to himself, not especially pleased to recognize this.

"Corporal Delucca."

"*Si*, señor?"

Emilio motioned the soldier closer to him and dropped his voice to a whisper. "A moment ago I noticed Serafina Martine leave the group. She must fetch something, I think, from her father's house. I did not hear what it was she was sent after. But it is dark, no? And there might be dangerous animals hiding in the trees. It would be a kindness, I think, if you were to follow after her. For her own protection, eh?"

The corporal looked startled. Then he smiled. "Thank you, señor. I thank you most heartily." With a quick grin he touched the brim of his kepi, then whirled and hurried off into the night, not having to so much as pause to think about which direction he should choose in order to find the Martine house and the route Serafina would have taken to reach it.

Emilio watched Delucca trot off, then turned back to pay attention to the others.

It was a small atonement, perhaps. But it made Emilio feel at least a little better than he had.

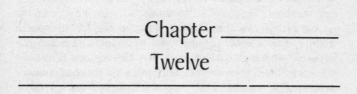
I

The ironbound wagon wheel rolled onto a rock, tilting the huge rig ever so slightly, then slammed hard onto the baked earth on the other side of the obstruction. Behind him Aaron heard a short, sharp cry. He turned but saw that the Indian was still unconscious.

It had been three days now and the Indian had yet to regain his senses. Morning and evening Aaron bathed the man's wounds and tried to get some liquids down his throat, water each time without fail and sometimes a thin broth made of the fatty juices taken from whatever happened to be in the cooking pot at the time.

But never did the Indian respond. Not really. Oh, whenever a fluid was forced into him his throat would respond by reflex, but Aaron was never sure if he actually swallowed anything, for most of whatever was poured in trickled right back out the sides of the man's slack mouth. Still, he must have retained some of it else he would not have lived.

If, that is, this could be considered life.

Mr. Matthewson insisted that the Indian was as good as

dead and would certainly soon die regardless of Aaron's best intentions. "Best to leave the son of a bitch on a rock so's he can die in peace, boy," the wagon boss advised on more than one occasion. "He'll croak anyhow, and what would we do if a bunch of damned Injun bucks come along and see him. They're like to think we stole him from his people or that we done this to him. Get the whole train in trouble, that would, for the sake of a Injun that's dying anyway. And hell, kid, it isn't like he'd mind. Injuns do the same their own selves. Old folks or the bad sick or deformed or whatever, Injuns got no compassion for them, son. They do it to their own people. Just lay them out in the sun somewhere and walk away. If they survive somehow then that's supposed to be a sign from the spirits or some such as that. Same thing if they die, of course. Which everybody knows they will do. And which you oughta do now to this poor SOB. Let him out of his misery, for this sure as hell ain't living, boy. Leave the poor SOB be."

Matthewson's advice was probably sensible. After three days Aaron had come to more or less accept that. But he couldn't bring himself to take the advice. Not yet. Not while there still might be some shred of a chance that the man would come around again.

Lordy, Lordy, though, it was awfully hard to see the Indian's pain, and now to hear his hurting too, and know there wasn't one single thing more he could do to make any of that the less.

The wagon lurched and thumped again, this time rolling over a half-buried log that lay in the unmarked trail, and once more the Indian's agony was expressed by way of a groan as the pain sliced through the anesthetic fog of unconsciousness.

Aaron winced, as good as feeling the hurt himself, and stifled an impulse to ask Buck Deeley to be more careful of his driving. Buck had a short temper and was already peevish with Aaron for bothering him about that so much. Besides, Aaron was fairly sure that the wagon driver had no regard for Indians and didn't much care if this one hurt or died or whatever. So Aaron bit his lip and tried to think of some other way he might be able to comfort the dying Indian. The truth, though, was that he couldn't think of a single thing more he could do, which was small comfort to him and none at all to the Indian.

II

Half a dozen rigs ahead the lead wagon came to a halt and Mr. Matthewson raised an arm high into the air signaling all the rest to stop as well. He made the gesture in silence, though, instead of calling out a voice command as well. And that was not usual for him.

Deeley leaned out to the side to spit a stream of yellow juice onto a clump of pale, dusty soapweed, then straightened on the pillow that served him as a seat and said, "Go see what this's about, kid."

"Yes, sir." Aaron glanced into the back of the wagon on his way over the sideboards but knew better than to waste time seeing to "his" Indian when Buck gave an order.

He dropped onto the ground and trotted forward past the other rigs. He noticed that all up and down the train the other apprentices and hey-boys and camp helpers—not that there were so very many of them—were doing the same thing. The drivers who lacked helpers mostly stood in their boxes, driving lines in hand, with worried expressions.

As soon as Aaron reached Mr. Matthewson's wagon he could see why they stopped.

For the first time since they left Missouri Aaron could see smoke in front of them.

Not dust. They'd seen plenty of dust before, nearly always raised by buffalo herds that they'd later approached, occasionally clouds of dust sent up by the presence of animals, people, or unknown forces that they never had identified.

But this, this was smoke. No doubt about it. Three, four, maybe half a dozen different plumes of smoke, in fact, all rising from within or very close by a dense thicket of dark green trees, the sort that Aaron had lately come to recognize as cottonwoods.

"Indians?" someone asked.

Mr. Matthewson, who had the advantage of elevation as he was standing on the seat of his wagon, which itself was situated near the crest of a small rise, frowned in deep consideration as he pondered the question before answering.

"Don't think so," he said after a few moments. His voice was slow and thoughtful. "Spread out too far to be an Injun camp, I'd say. They bunch up more'n that. Put their tents close t'gether, generally."

"There's nobody but Indians live around here, though," another voice put in.

"Wasn't last fall when we came back from Santa Fe. That doesn't mean there couldn't be somebody there now."

"A new trading post? Somebody competing with Bent up on Fountain Creek?" Bent's post, Aaron already knew from listening in on countless campfire conversations, was on the north side of the Arkansas and therefore in American territory. This down here was in what they were lately calling Mexico, although it used to be under Spanish rule.

"Could be," Matthewson acknowledged. But the skepticism in his voice clearly said he doubted the likelihood of that possibility.

"What do you think then?"

"Damn if I know what to expect. I'll tell you what I hope, though. I hope this isn't some new army post set here to keep us out o' their damn country."

"Would they do that?"

"How the hell would I know? The Spanish did. They wanted to force the people in the north country to do all their trading with the gentry down in Mexico City. Didn't want us Americanos coming in and taking any of the profits back to the States with us. Last few years the Mexes have looked at things different. But who the hell knows what their mood is this year? They coulda put a new government in down south since we was here last or something else mighta happened." Matthewson paused for a moment to stare out across the brown, rolling hills that separated the train from the source of those smoke plumes. Then he shrugged. "Whatever it is out there it ain't Injuns. An' we won't learn no more sitting here jawing about it an' trying to outguess whatever the truth is. Get on back to your rigs, boys, and let's go pay a call on whoever is over there."

III

Mr. Matthewson had a few words of Spanish and a couple of the drivers were fluent in the language. Aaron didn't understand a word of it. Well, hardly a word. Some of the fellows had been willing to teach him a few selected cuss words and dirty expressions. He learned them by rote, though, and wasn't entirely sure what all of them meant. The one thing he was positive about was that he shouldn't risk saying anything he learned from the freighters whenever there was a pretty girl in sight.

And as for pretty girls, well, Aaron hadn't seen so much beauty in such a small sampling of femininity since . . . once he got to thinking on it he had to accept the fact that he hadn't *ever* seen such a truly remarkable collection of beauty in any such group. Not ever in his whole life.

These Spanish—that is to say, these Mexican—girls were just . . . gorgeous. There wasn't any other way to put it.

There were only a dozen or so of them. But Aaron could have lost his heart to almost any one of the dozen.

Oh, there were a couple who weren't especially to his taste. One plump girl had pimples and a flat nose and dark hair on her upper lip. Another wore a habitual expression sour enough to curdle milk. He supposed he would have had to think twice before bedding either one of those. Not that he would've been unwilling, of course. Just that he would have hesitated half a moment beforehand.

As for the others . . . well there would be no hesitation. Not so much as a heartbeat.

They were so pretty it like to took his breath clean away. Black shiny hair. Black sparkling eyes. Skin the color of honey and every bit as smooth. Waists tiny. Bosoms full. And legs. Lordy, Lordy, those gorgeous legs. *Bare* legs. That was the thing about their legs. They wore skirts so short that anyone, absolutely anyone at all, could see their limbs. And not just some fleeting peep at an ankle either but most all the way up their calves to their dimpled knees. Which he knew were dimpled because whenever they turned sharply their skirts swirled and floated and he could see all the way up to their knees sometimes.

Never, not in all his wildest imaginings, had he ever so much as contemplated a sight like this. Bare limbs. Tiny waists. Sleek shiny hair. Proud bosoms. And such lips. Incredible!

He could see more of these beautiful . . . what was it they were called? Senritas? Something like that . . . he could see more of them standing right here in public than most American girls allowed him to see in a hayloft or a bed of ferns. Most girls in Aaron's past experience kept themselves covered up, kept their limbs and certainly their more private parts hidden even when they were busy doing the most delightfully remarkable things with a fellow.

It was enough to put a sweat on Aaron's brow. And no small amount of discomfort into certain other portions of his anatomy as well. Aaron was afraid if he spent very much time around these lovely Mexican girls he would embarrass himself aplenty.

But if he stayed sensibly away from them . . . well, he had no real desire to do that. No sir, he did not. It would be a pleasure just to look at them. Just to smell the air when one of them walked by. Just to be able to admire the shapely turn of a calf or the delicacy of an ankle. Oh, yes it would.

And one of the most wonderful things about it was that they were all so beautiful. They really were. All of them, even the fat girl with the mustache and the sour-faced girl, even they had something about them that was beautiful sort of, in its own way. Beauty enough for Aaron's starved tastes anyway. Oh, my, yes.

He stood there sweating and squirming and thoroughly enjoying himself and then he saw a girl—young, she was, and shy—standing at the back of the crowd of jabbering Mexicans that had come to gather round the wagons and the American visitors.

He saw her and his heart turned over inside his chest and of a sudden he was having difficulty breathing, for this was without question the most wonderfully beautiful girl Aaron ever in his whole life saw.

Her eyes were as soft and luminous as those of a doe come to water at eventide, and her smile—she smiled when she caught him staring at her through the crowd—her smile was more radiant than a lantern's powerful light.

She was tiny. He doubted the top of her head would reach to his shoulders. That was why it took him so long to spot her, he supposed. She hung to the back of the crowd and did not try to push herself forward. He hadn't been able to see her at all until some of the Mexicans moved closer to Mr. Matthewson's lead wagon, their mouths running all the while in that strange foreign tongue.

Except of course here it was God's given English that would be considered foreign. How odd, Aaron thought. It was something he hadn't realized nor thought about before this moment, and now it jolted him just a little. If he spoke to the girl over there, that most beautiful girl in all creation, if he should speak to her it would be his language that would be out of place and likely she would not know what it was he wished to say to her.

And oh, there was so very much that he wanted to say. To ask.

But then . . . perhaps words were not really necessary. Perhaps he could get across quite nicely the most important parts of the things he would say and the things he would ask.

A touch. A smile. A kiss. Surely those things would be language enough. Surely he could . . .

"Kid. Boy! Aaron, dammit." He felt a tug at his sleeve and reluctantly turned his attention away from the most beautiful girl in all the world. "What d'you want?"

"Fetch one of those small bales from the trailer behind

Devereaux's wagon, will you. One of them with the tinker's goods."

"The beads and like that?"

"No, those are the Injun trade goods. The boss wants some needles, scissors, small whetstones . . . like that."

Aaron nodded. He remembered now the bales they wanted. It seemed the train was not only welcome here, they were finding their first customers here as well. Fine. Maybe that meant they would stay awhile and do some business.

And if they did that, well, surely that meant he would have time to visit with the girl. A few moments. That was all he asked. Just time enough to look into those haunting dark eyes and she would know all that was in his heart. That was all Aaron wanted.

He turned, thinking to speak to her with his gaze. But she was gone. In the few seconds his attention was diverted the girl had disappeared.

He looked frantically from face to face, but she was nowhere to be seen. Nowhere.

"Dammit, boy, move!"

"Yes, sir." But still he hesitated.

"Now, Aaron. Right damn now."

"Yes, sir." Unhappily he turned away and went off down the train of wagons in search of Devereaux's wagon and trailer. He found the trailer and he found the bale Mr. Matthewson wanted. But throughout, all Aaron could see in front of him was the delicate beauty of that one small face.

IV

"Aaron."

"Yes, sir?"

"Tomorra morning I want you to ride in Tom Milius's rig. He needs a helper with that damn bad-wheel trailer of his. Damn thing hasn't been right ever since he hit that rock when we was crossing the Pawnee Fork. And we got some extra bad rocks to crawl over in those mountains just ahead.

Places there we'll have to unhitch the stock and haul the vehicles up by block and tackle. Milius will need you more'n Buck does."

"What will I do with the Indian then, Mr. Matthewson? There isn't any room for him in Tom's wagon, and I'm pretty sure Buck wouldn't want to bother looking after him. Buck fusses about him being there as it is, and without me to watch out for him . . ."

"I been meaning to say something to you about that anyway, Aaron." Matthewson pulled out his pipe and focused his attention on it while he spoke, his big hands continually caressing the briar and fiddling with the stem and tamping the cut tobacco already loaded in the bowl ready to be lighted.

"Yes, sir?"

"Deeley tells me the stinking Injun isn't a lick better than the day you loaded him onto that rig."

"I don't know as you could say that, sir. Why just this morn—"

"Never mind this morning, dammit." The man's voice was sharp, impatient.

"Yes, sir." Aaron knew when to close his yap. Sometimes. This most definitely seemed one of those times when good sense should prevail.

"I've talked to the Mexes here about your Injun."

"They'll look after him, sir?"

"They've agreed to bury the son of a bitch."

Aaron frowned. "He ain't dead yet, dammit, sir."

"He will be."

"You're going to do what you said before? You're going to just lay him out on a rock someplace and wait for him to die so he can be buried. Ain't you."

Matthewson's eyes lifted and met Aaron's square on. The boss's expression was cold. "Yes, dammit, that is exactly what we're going to do. The red bastard isn't but a nuisance, and he'll die regardless. Hell, boy, it's a kindness to him to let him lay in peace to get his dying over with. If we was to carry him on in the wagons he'd be pounded most to pieces by the thumping and jarring we're fixing to get into. Buck tells me the poor SOB moans and cries something awful just from the little jostling he's been getting so far. And that ain't nothing to what's fixing to come once we start climbing up into those mountains. Damn Injun would be begging you to kill him before we ever reached the top if we was cruel enough to carry him on. Better to let him die here in peace than make him suffer all the more and then die anyhow. More to the point, boy, I've thought it over and set my mind on the subject. I let you keep your damned pet this long but no longer. The Injun stays whether you like it or not, and the Mexes will bury him once we're gone. And that, as they say, is that." Matthewson bent to find a sprig of dry grass on the ground, ignited it from the campfire, and used it to light his pipe.

The conversation seemed to be over. And that, as they did indeed say, seemed to be that.

Aaron was not happy with it. But there, like it or not, it dang well was. The Indian would not travel any farther. At the very least, Aaron decided, he could make sure the dying man was given a comfortable place in which to live out his last few hours.

It was coming dusk, and soon the light would not allow good vision, so while he yet had time Aaron went to Buck Deeley's big wagon and let the tailgate down.

The Indian was unconscious, as he had been ever since they found him. Aaron careful tucked in the trade blanket Mr. Matthewson days earlier told him he could use for the Indian. The man hadn't mentioned wanting the blanket back—hadn't thought to, obviously—and Aaron certainly was not going to remind him about it. Instead he tucked the edges of the blanket tight around the desperately injured man and then tugged on the coarse, thick wool to drag the Indian to the edge of the wagon bed so Aaron could lift the dead weight—poor choice of words that, Aaron realized and amended the thought to that of lifting an awkward burden—gently in his arms.

As Aaron tugged and grunted with the effort, the Indian's head waggled back and forth, virtually unsupported by slack neck muscles.

"Sorry," Aaron mumbled.

The Indian groaned. And his eyes briefly fluttered.

The man's eyes were dark, Aaron saw. And bright. There was the clarity of life and intelligence held within those eyes. Life, yes. And intelligence. And this was a man, a human being, they would drop onto a slab of rock and walk away from. A kindness, Mr. Matthewson said, to let him die in peace.

Bullshit, Aaron thought. There's no such damn thing as death being a kindness. No matter how Mr. Matthewson wanted to rationalize it there just wasn't no such a thing as that.

The Indian's eyes fluttered only for a moment and then they closed again.

But Aaron saw what he saw and knew if he lived another hundred years he wouldn't forget what he'd seen there. He'd seen life in those eyes. Life condemned now to a kind and peaceful death. Kind? Peaceful? Bullshit, Aaron repeated silently to himself.

He hefted the Indian's weight, trying to get a better grip so he wouldn't drop the poor SOB and complete the job of killing him any quicker than had to be. Then, his steps wobbling and staggering under the weight of the grown man he was carrying, Aaron set off upriver from the wagon camp in search of a place where he could lay the Indian down in comfort and solitude.

Kind and peaceful, he muttered under his breath over and over as he walked. Kind and peaceful. Bullshit, kind and peaceful.

Chapter Thirteen

I

Talks To Ghosts' visions swam through mists as insubstantial as quicksand. Spirits talked to him as kindly as if he were a beloved nephew, and animals shared with him the wisdom they and their kind had learned through the generations. Talks To Ghosts was in a place he had never been before. Whatever this place was, he liked it and wanted to enjoy more of it. It was quiet here and comfortable.

Comfortable except for an annoying, nagging, niggling dryness in his throat and an occasional deep, burning ache in his head.

It was the dryness that bothered him the most, interrupting the pleasure of his visits with Coyote and Owl and Otter so that he could not concentrate on the many wondrous things they attempted to tell him.

Talks To Ghosts tried to swallow the dryness from his throat but that only seemed to make it worse. Still, it was all he could do, and so he tried again and again to swallow away the discomfort.

And in time his efforts were rewarded. He felt the press

of something hard and cold on his lip and then the sweet, refreshing flow of moisture flooding his mouth and trickling into his throat.

Gratefully he swallowed, allowing the sweet water into his parched, empty belly. More cool water came and he swallowed that too. He felt the spread of it cold and soothing inside his body, and it was good.

He opened his eyes and was comforted to see that one of the spirits was there with him.

The spirit would have frightened him under other circumstances, but not now. Would have frightened him because of its unnatural look. But now he had no fear of it, for he knew it was but a spirit and a kindly spirit at that, and it gave him water to drink when he was thirsty.

The spirit was unlike anything he had ever seen before, although of course that was only right and proper, for as often as he had dreamed in the past he had never before had such an immediate and compelling encounter with anyone or anything from the spirit world, and so of course he accepted this spirit as it was and would not have been so rude as to question or complain about its outward look.

In truth, though, Talks To Ghosts was curious about this spirit that had come to him. So odd it was. So different from the people.

The spirit had something of the look of a man about it. More or less.

Men have smooth skin on their faces. This spirit was furred about the face as an animal is furred. Its nose was bare, of course, as all noses are bare of hair. There were also patches bare of hair on the spirit's upper cheeks and above the eyes.

The eyes were of a most curious color. Not dark as man's eyes are dark but pale, a light and translucent appearance much like the small bright stones found on the mountain to the north of the ancient trail between the north plains and the wintering ground high in the shining mountains where . . . of course! It was long known by the people that the mountain where the bright stones were found was a spirit mountain. Talks To Ghosts—no one—had ever fully understood before. Now he did. This spirit came from just such a source. Perhaps from that precise source, for the eyes of the spirit were the same blue-green hue as some of the clear stones gathered on that far mountain. Now Talks To Ghosts knew, and he was grateful to the spirit for allowing him knowledge and understanding.

The eyes were a clear and liquid blue-green, and the fur—it was incredible yet undeniably true—the mantle of fur this spirit wore was red. Not a garishly artificial vermilion red such as the women traded for and used in their hair but a bright and clean and perfect red lightly tinged with gold, the same sort of gold so cherished by the traders and the big hats and the black robes. The same sort of gold, Talks To Ghosts remembered, that was found sometimes in the very same white-bubbling streams where the colored stones could be found. On the same magic mountain to the north. Another proof of where the spirit sprang from.

Talks To Ghosts was pleased with his knowledge.

But tired. So tired.

He drank deeply of the water the spirit gave to him—magic water? No doubt—and let his eyes sag closed once more as he was no longer able to hold them open.

He felt himself drifting light and happy as if upon a cloud, and after mere seconds he drifted away from the spirit to a place of soft and gentle peace.

II

Talks To Ghosts was having a nightmare. It was strange, but even at the time he was having it he understood what the experience was.

In his dream he saw a man—a Kiowa this man appeared to be and like all Kiowa whether living or in dreams very ugly of face and limb—rise up from among a cluster of reeds growing beside water.

The Kiowa warrior came out of hiding as if startled. He held something in one hand. A club, Talks To Ghosts thought this thing was. A length of polished root, knurled and knobbed at one end and sparkling in the sunlight where the heads of decorative brass tacks appeared. The club was awesome to look upon, awesome and fear-giving. And so was the huge warrior who wielded the ugly weapon.

The Kiowa—Talks To Ghosts was sure now that it was a Kiowa that he saw in his dream—sprang into sight. Swung the club.

In his dream Talks To Ghosts heard the hollow, ugly thump of the club striking hard upon its living target, and then there was a time of disorientation.

The eyes of his dream spun and whirled for this time and then steadied once more.

Talks To Ghosts dreamt he was upright. Perhaps seated on the ground. Immobile. Unable to move his limbs but maintaining the power to see. Unable to give warning or help but forced to watch.

It was a raid, he saw in his dream. An assault upon his own village, his own people, by the fearsome Kiowa. The raiders came leaping and shouting from the reeds to descend upon the people.

Where were the warriors who should have been in camp? Hunting buffalo? Perhaps so. Wherever they were, where they were not was in their own lodges, in their own camp. Where they were not was where they were needed.

Talks To Ghosts would have closed his eyes to avoid seeing that which in his dream he was forced to see, except of course in a dream a man's spirit cannot control his eyes, cannot keep himself from seeing whatever it is that the dream wishes to show him. He was forced to watch as the shrieking, whooping Kiowa poured from the reeds like quail breaking cover.

His mind "saw" clubs rise and knives flash.

He dreamed the sight of dust rising underfoot as terrified children and women and old men—Carries Water, in his dream Talks To Ghosts was sure he could see old Carries Water try to hobble to safety on legs that had not functioned properly since the time twenty winters past when a pony fell on him and crushed both his knees—in this dream he watched helplessly as the people tried to flee and the Kiowa stabbed and battered and one by one cut them down.

Carries Water fell to the club of a warrior scarcely old enough to swing a grown man's weapon. The child, as if unsure of his strength and his power, continued to batter the old man's head long after Carries Water was dead.

Woman Who Waits was stabbed and stabbed and stabbed until her skirt was heavy with blood, and she fell to her knees and died there looking into the eyes of the man who killed her, the last sounds in her ears those of the Kiowa warrior's victory cries.

Talks To Ghosts saw a short, stocky Kiowa with black paint on his cheeks and yellow on his forehead shoot an arrow into the belly of a child. The child in this dream looked exactly like Otter Tail, who was the second son of Tall Man. It was really quite uncanny how very much like Otter Tail this dream child appeared. In the dream the boy stopped in his flight and turned to shout defiance at the invaders of his home, and in the dream the stocky Kiowa with the blackened cheeks shot the boy in his belly and then kicked the fallen child in the forehead as he ran past to grab Otter Tail's mother—no, that was wrong; to grab the mother of the dream boy who had the appearance of Otter Tail—to take this woman by the hair and fling her to the earth with a shout of triumph.

In the dream as in real life the conquering warrior had the choice to gain honor by killing such a woman or to gain riches by possessing her for a slave. The dream Kiowa chose to keep the woman for a slave, Talks To Ghosts observed. The dream warrior knelt between the woman's widespread legs and used her with swift, brutal contempt, then stood and dragged her upright by her hair.

Others of the Kiowa were as busy—grabbing, hacking, laying about with lance and knife and club.

Lodges were trampled and meat racks overturned.

Dust rose in the air. In other places there was blood upon the ground to settle the dust that might have lifted.

Blood and flame were everywhere as the Kiowa killed whoever they could capture or bound the few they would take as slaves, as they wantonly broke open parfleches, taking what they would choose to keep and dumping all else onto fires that had been built by hands other than their own.

The Kiowa destroyed and destroyed and destroyed, and Talks To Ghosts hated this dream just as he hated the ugly Kiowa who were in it.

His eyes began to leak bitter tears as the dream unfolded within his mind.

He felt the fluid hot on parched flesh. Felt the trickle of its passage over a fevered cheek. Tasted the salt of it as a thin runnel of tear-water wandered into the corner of his mouth.

And it was then, only then when the flavor of real tears jolted and jarred his senses, that Talks To Ghosts remembered. It was only then that he knew with a sense of aching, wrenching horror that this dream was not a nightmare but a memory.

Talks To Ghosts' spirit was shattered and his heart became heavy and soon his weeping was beyond all control, for he knew then that his people had been killed by the marauding Kiowa and he along with them.

Talks To Ghosts regained control over his sobbing and willed himself to become calm.

He lay silent and still and told his spirit to fly away from his body because his people were all dead and he had no more wish to live without them.

And with that, mercifully, the dream went away along with his spirit, and he knew no more.

I

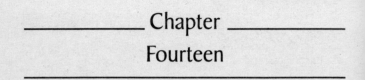

The juniper berries were much too young, at this early stage hard, tiny, waxy white balls that looked much like freshwater pearls but were even more useless. In time, when the berries of the juniper ripened, they could be dried and crushed and steeped in boiling water to make a quite credible sort of tea. Which in fact was what he wanted today. But not juniper berry. Not so early in the season.

Emilio ambled along with the handle of a basket draped over his arm. The sheep were moving in a group, their motions as undirected and lazy as were his own. They came to the mouth of a small . . . Emilio was not sure just what to call an opening in the hillside of this size. It was too large and broad to be considered an arroyo, really. Too small to be a canyon. A gulch, perhaps, or a gully. Whatever, the flock of mixed rams and ewes seemed to find it of interest. The lead ewe turned into it and the rest dutifully followed. And so did Emilio.

He supposed the gathering of herbs or bark for tea ~~̣~~ be considered a woman's work, but Consuela was ~~̣~~ stomach most of the time of late and did not leave the jacal unless there was good reason, and so it was left to Emilio to do all the things necessary, including such as this.

The truth, though, was that he really did not mind it, and the picking of ingredients for tea was something he in fact quite enjoyed.

When he returned home during the afternoon and shut the sheep into the brush pen he had erected, he would then have to do Consuela's work in the garden. And that was another matter indeed. Emilio did not like poking and prodding the ground with sticks, did not like bending to pluck weeds, did not at all enjoy carrying water from the river to the eternally sun-dry soil. It had to be done, of course, but it was something he could not help but regard as a peon's toil. And despite the common status he and Consuela had so cheerfully adopted for themselves and for her child to come, Emilio could not yet accept the thought of himself as a peon. His blood was rich and his honor strong, and if he could not claim to be an hidalgo he at least could forswear the label peon.

He checked briefly on the sheep—it seemed unlikely even an animal so stupid as a sheep could manage to get into trouble within the enclosed walls of this narrow defile—and turned momentarily aside to investigate a cluster of piñons. Pine nuts from the piñon make an excellent beverage and, when roasted, an even better snack. Not that there should be many left from the previous autumn's crop. But one never knows. The wild creatures might have overlooked a few.

Emilio shouldered his way in among the dark, furry-needled branches and began hopefully inspecting both the limbs of the plants and the ground underfoot.

He bent to closer inspect the deep litter of old grasses and countless years of fallen needles. And froze in place at the sound of a gunshot from somewhere farther inside the gulch where his sheep were grazing.

II

Emilio was frightened. He admitted that to himself. So frightened that his legs had no strength and the small muscles in his cheeks and around his lips trembled and quivered.

A gunshot. That could only mean trouble. Very probably serious trouble. He was sure the shot was fired by no man from the settlement.

The members of the community had only two firearms among them, a pair of old but serviceable muskets left behind by the soldiers so the people could hunt or defend themselves. The idea was that any member of the community could make use of the muskets, borrowing them when and as needed and then returning them to their proprietor afterward.

One of the muskets was quite naturally held by Luis Del Garza, for it was Del Garza who was mayordomo and captain of the pioneers.

The other, just as naturally, was in the possession of Hector Martine. For the choice of distribution was made by the corporal whose eye had been so firmly caught by Serafina Martine, and who would such a one choose to toady to but the father of the maiden he hoped to impress?

Emilio regretted now the impulse that had led him to send the damnable corporal after the girl at the baile that night. Regretted and could not help being nearly consumed by jealous curiosity as he wondered just what transpired that night away from the light of the fires and the gaiety of good fellowship.

But the muskets, the muskets, he was almost certain no one had taken one of them hunting this day. Surely it would have been mentioned when the men gathered last evening. After all, there was so little of true interest or importance to talk about that any thought or plan, no matter how insignificant, was not only brought up, it was apt to be debated to the point of—at least in Emilio's private opinion—nausea. The men gabbled and gossiped worse than a pack of ancient crones.

But the muskets, he was sure no one had taken one of the muskets away from the settlement to hunt today, and . . .

It occurred to Emilio that what he was doing here was finding excuses to continue hiding inside this thicket of piñons. Meanderings about Corporal Delucca and Serafina and whatever else . . . all that was but the fabrication of reasons why he did not yet move. But move he surely must.

It was unnatural for there to be a gunshot in this empty place, and Emilio had many reasons to inquire as to the source of the noise. He had his sheep to protect. Consuela. Indeed, the whole community of pioneers.

If the gunshot was fired, God forbid, by wild Indians . . .

There were said to be Indians who frequented this country, yes. The soldiers assured everyone that there was no chance of danger, that all the Indians were of a peaceable and friendly disposition. But the Americans who traveled through had other advice to give. The Americans spoke of hostile raiders who traveled far and wide, killing and marauding wherever they went.

And had they not been carrying a dying Indian with them? That one, they claimed, was slaughtered by his own kind, one tribe warring with another as savages were said inescapably to do in their wild and uncontrollable state.

Emilio had seen the dying Indian himself and knew that Luis Del Garza gave a solemn promise that the men of the settlement would give the man a civilized burial as soon as he breathed his last.

So the shot could well have been fired by hostile Indians. And if there were in fact savages in a position to attack the settlement, surely it was Emilio's duty to ascertain this and to give warning to his neighbors.

It was most assuredly his duty to protect his neighbors, to protect Consuela, to protect if possible the sheep upon which his and Consuela's future and fortune revolved. It was his duty. . . .

He was doing it again, wasn't he, Emilio recognized.

He crouched low within the screening branches of the pinyons and gave himself over to logic and deep thought while somewhere very close by there was a man or a group of men who fired that single gunshot.

Emilio felt a chill sweat bead on his forehead, and his legs began to shake as he forced himself to stand erect, his head and eyes protruding above the dark green branches. He could see nothing inside the gully save the dirty white fleeces of his sheep as the flock grazed deeper and ever deeper into what might well be a trap.

Reluctantly, fearfully, Emilio crept out of the pinyons and began making his way slowly and silently into the gully. Like it or not—and he very much did not—he had to find out who fired that shot and why.

III

The sheep, he found, were actually a big help. The sounds of their rustling about in the undergrowth and of their feet crunching onto the gravelly soil covered whatever sounds his own footsteps made, enabling him to creep through the grazing flock and ahead of them.

He kept as close to the brush as he could manage, pushing into and through the scrub oak, pinyon, and, underfoot, the spreading juniper. Afraid that he was closing in on a band of wild savages, Emilio was almost disappointed to learn that he could as easily have walked up the gully while banging a drum. No one would have cared.

The shot, he soon discovered, had been fired by the crazy American. This was the first Emilio had seen of the man. But not, of course, the first he had heard about this one.

For the first few days after the Yankee freight train passed through, the talk at night had been about little else than this somewhat mad Americano.

Mad, they said, because the fellow ran away from his employer and his companions out here in the midst of the wilderness, with no one and nothing to turn to for help should he need it.

The *jefe* of the Americans, it was said, was livid in his

fury that morning when he discovered his helper missing. That was all the worse, it was said, because the helper was a bond servant who owed the *jefe* labor in exchange for securing his release from a prison back in the distant land that the Americans always seemed so eager to escape. Emilio suspected that the Estados Unidos must be a terrible place indeed if so many of its people were willing to risk journeys into the unknown in order to escape it. And if the country was so terrible, how much worse would its prisons be. Emilio shuddered a little at the thought.

He had never heard just what offense this particular Yankee was supposed to have committed in order to find himself in prison. Surely, Emilio reasoned, the crime could not have been of too extreme a nature else the young man—which Emilio could now see that he was—would not have been released into the custody of an employer. Even an employer who was about to leave the country. Or so Emilio now fervently hoped. For he was quite fully committed at this point to meeting the Yankee.

Not that the Americano was paying any great amount of attention to his surroundings. Far from it. But by now the sheep had caught up with Emilio and were pushing past him in their search for grasses to eat. A few minutes more and they would surround the Yankee too, and even one so pre-occupied and unobservant as this would surely notice being bumped and jostled by some hundreds of woolly ewes and musky rams.

In the meantime, however, the Yankee seemed quite oblivious to all that was about him, and even one so un-skilled as Emilio could sneak up on him without fear.

The Americano, Emilio saw, had a gun much like the elderly Spanish muskets the soldiers left for the settlers to use except the Yankee's gun looked even older and more crude. If that was possible.

Still, the gun was powerful and accurate enough to bring down a fat doe deer that the red-haired American was now trying—rather awkwardly—to butcher. He knelt on the ground ripping and sawing with a dull knife at the doe's relatively thin hide. Emilio, who knew nothing about the arts of butchering, knew enough to realize that the Yankee's efforts lay somewhere between the extremes of laughable and pathetic.

"Can I help you?" Emilio offered courteously by way of an introduction.

The Yankee, who seemed not to have yet noticed the approach either of Emilio or of the sheep, jumped half out of his own skin, never mind the skin of the dead deer, and grabbed for his rifle. Which Emilio knew just enough to recognize was unloaded and harmless, as the frizzen was displaced and the priming pan empty.

The Yankee said something back to him in that incomprehensibly barbarian tongue that the English invented for the torment of all mankind. Emilio could speak not a word of English, and the men of the settlement had been quite clear that the strange Yankee who ran away from the wagons could speak no Spanish.

The young fellow—he was not a bad-looking sort, tall and with bright red hair and wide, trusting eyes—glanced down at his unloaded gun and had good grace enough to blush in quick embarrassment. He put the gun down, propping its barrel on the haunch of the deer he was butchering so badly, and wiped the blood from his hands before standing and offering to shake.

His smile, Emilio saw then, was gay and truly friendly. When the lad—Emilio suspected this American was even younger than himself—smiled like that, it would have been difficult indeed to dislike or to fear him.

Emilio smiled back—he could not have helped himself had he wanted to—and accepted the handshake. "Welcome," he said.

The Yankee answered but of course in words that Emilio could not comprehend.

"Are you lost?"

The Yankee merely grinned and shrugged. He pointed to the deer, then to his knife, which Emilio could now see was but a small folding knife and not a very good one to begin with.

"I have here a knife of some quality," Emilio said,

reaching inside his sash and withdrawing the slim dirk that had been his birthday present when he completed his sixteenth year.

The American recoiled as if he expected Emilio to strike with the blade. Then, blushing again, accepted and began to admire it.

"Go ahead. Please." Emilio added to the spoken offer with gestures, pointing from the finely tempered and superbly wrought Toledo blade to the doe that lay at the American's feet.

The Yankee grinned and said something, then quickly knelt and began once more to hack and slice at the deer.

This time, however, he was able to make good progress. The skin was quickly opened from breastplate to pelvis and the guts dumped out. The Yankee sorted through the squishy, smelly mess to locate and extract the liver, then began cutting away the feet, tail, and head. Carefully slicing here and tugging with bloody hands there, he began to remove the hide.

Emilio did not know much more about this process than the Yankee seemed to, but he knelt beside the crazy American and helped as much as he could.

The two worked together like that for twenty minutes or so, by which time the carcass of the doe was naked—if somewhat fouled with dirt and loose hairs—and had the appearance not so much of a dead animal as a supply of most desirable fresh meat.

Emilio had not had fresh meat since . . . ah, it was of no matter how long it had been. This meat was not his to claim. Consuela would surely have enjoyed . . . no, it was not proper for him to think in such a manner, not at all.

The Yankee used Emilio's fine knife to slice the haunches away for easy carrying. Cut off the shoulders and breast. Carefully trimmed out the tenderloin and some strips of rib meat. Finally he took the previously discarded hide and cut it in two, then in each resulting piece wrapped half of the delectable and delicate liver.

Emilio watched in some confusion as the American set

aside one share of the liver, one haunch, one shoulder, and roughly half of the other strips of meat.

Then the man wiped Emilio's knife clean as best he could and handed it back, saying something as he did so and motioning toward the two piles of meat and hide. His meaning was clear. One of those piles was Emilio's to take. And the visitor was welcome to pick whichever one he preferred. The Yankee said something more and smiled.

Emilio could hardly believe ... but it was true. The crazy American was a young man who repaid small debts in large measure. It was a kindness Emilio could never have anticipated, and the generosity of it touched him.

He said as much. Over and over again. But of course the Yankee could not understand him. Not a word. Still, it was good to say the things that were in his heart, whether he be understood or not, and so Emilio told the uncomprehending Yankee how much he and Consuela both would enjoy the bounty the American gave them.

He said it in words, then he laid one hand—a still bloody hand as it turned out; Consuela would no doubt be annoyed with the extra washing she would be required to do now—over his heart while he smiled and pointed first to the bundle of meat and then to the friendly, grinning Americano. "Thank you. Thank you, my newfound friend," he told the crazy American, wishing that the young man could understand his Spanish but knowing he could not.

The American said something back, still grinning, then bent and began gathering up his things, including the dull pocket knife and empty rifle and weighty package of fresh, tasty venison.

Emilio watched the American make his way over the ridge toward the west, then he too began preparing to go back. The sheep had been at the grazing long enough for the moment. And besides, he wanted to take this meat back to Consuela so she too could enjoy this wonderful good fortune.

Chapter
Fifteen

I

Fat, that was what was needed. And what was mostly lacking. Venison was a fine meat but with too little fat. The Indian needed fats in his diet in order to recover some strength and speed the healing process. Aaron did the best he could, stripping bits of fat wherever he could find them, mostly from around the heart and kidneys, and adding them to the water boiling in the lone tin pot he owned.

Not that he was complaining about having so little. In fact he felt downright well off. He had a pot, a trade fusil with two waxed boxes of ready-prepared buck-and-ball, a patent fire starter complete with charred linen tinder, and an entire bale of trade goods consisting mostly of steel knife blanks, blue beads, and burning glasses, all tidily contained inside a thick bundle of two-point wool blankets.

It had been generous of Mr. Matthewson to give Aaron all that.

Or, more accurately, it would have been generous of the gentleman to have given it had he known in advance that he was doing so.

By now, Aaron figured, the losses most likely had been discovered, calculated, and cussed about. Just about the right amounts, he thought, to comprise a reasonable wage for services rendered between St. Louis and . . . wherever the heck this place was.

The river was called the Purgatory or sometimes the Picketwire. He knew that much from listening to the experienced hands among Matthewson's freighters. But none of them knew the name of the new settlement. Or even if the place yet had a name.

Not that it really mattered. Now that he'd run off from the train Aaron felt lighthearted and free, never mind that he had no employment nor the likelihood of finding any out here so far from civilization.

Never before in all his life beyond shouting distance of other humans, Aaron was discovering a peculiar sort of pleasure in the idea that here he could stand on a hilltop and shout his fool head off and in all probability there would be no human ear close enough to hear.

He would have liked to discuss this feeling with the Indian, but that soul—not half as dead as Mr. Matthewson swore he ought to be—couldn't speak any more English than Aaron could speak the savage's gibberish.

And the same, sadly, was true of the Spaniards hereabout. No, dagnabbit, the Mexicans, Aaron reminded himself. These folk were Mexican now, not Spanish. He needed to keep that in mind should any authorities come around and question his right to squat here.

Aaron had no one, absolutely no one, he could talk to. That made for something of a lonely feeling but one he could alleviate at least to some extent by the time-honored method of talking to himself. And to the Indian who understood not a word of what Aaron was saying.

"Ah, it won't be long now," Aaron assured his drowsing, sleepy-eyed patient. "We'll make this broth good and rich, we will, and then we'll cool it a mite so's it doesn't burn your lips. No sense piling hurt on hurt, right?" He smiled at the Indian, who stared back at him without expression.

"Aye, I'd say you're looking stronger today, Pocahontas." Aaron knew Pocahontas was supposed to be the name of an Indian woman and from a tribe that lived practically a continent distant. But it was the only Indian name he could think of, and he'd wanted to be able to call his Indian guest by name, even a wrong name. And anyway, since it was Indian in origin the name Pocahontas was surely more appropriate than calling the fellow George or Daniel or Ebeneezer or any such good American name.

Besides, the Indian didn't know what the English words meant nor the Indian name among them and so wouldn't take offense no matter what Aaron told him or called him.

It was all sort of like talking to a puppy, satisfying in that the intention was good and no one expected there to be a response from the passive listener.

"Just let me set . . . this . . . aside . . . there!" Aaron managed to get the pot balanced over a pair of flat stones to begin cooling. He did it without burning himself or spilling any of the rich broth and so felt inordinately proud of himself for the achievement.

He grinned at the Indian and thought he saw a small flicker of acknowledgment deep behind the Indian's unwavering stare.

"Are you hungry, Pocahontas? Aye, bound to be, aren't you? Well, you'll eat quick as this cools. And while you're eating, my friend, I'll cook me some dinner too."

He used his knife—cursing his lack of a whetstone as always—to hack the deer's heart apart, then pierced the dark, tough meat with a pointed stick and propped it over the coals of his fire to begin roasting. Nothing, absolutely nothing, could compare to the flavor of roast heart, Aaron believed. Nothing, that is, save the taste of a roasted potato. He hadn't had so much as a sniff of a potato since he left that St. Louis jail months back and would cheerfully have sold his soul for a peck of russets. Or if not for a peck then certainly for a bushel. Or two. He grinned at the Indian and gave the savage a wink, then dipped a fingertip into the broth to check the temperature.

"Ouch." He sucked on the wounded finger and blew cool air onto it, then said, "Give it a couple more minutes. Then you can eat, Pocahontas." Aaron mimed feeding broth to the fellow, and the Indian slowly, solemnly nodded.

"Yessir," Aaron said cheerfully, "you sure are fun company for a fella. Plenty of laughs with you around." He grinned again. "Tell you what. Pocahontas really don't fit. What d'you say from now on I call you Plenty Laughs. That sound all right to you, does it? Eh, Plenty Laughs?"

Aaron pointed to his own chest and, too loudly, said, "Aaron. Aaron Jenks." He pointed to the Indian and said, "You, Plenty Laughs." He pointed at himself again. "Aaron." Then at the Indian. "Plenty Laughs. Okay?"

The Indian closed his eyes and began softly to snore.

"Yeah," Aaron said. "I kind of thought you'd like it."

He looked at the broth, then at the sleeping Indian. Finally, with a shrug, he turned the deer heart on its stick to begin roasting the other side. What the heck. There would be time enough to feed Plenty Laughs later.

II

Aaron came up out of the shady spot where he'd been napping and grabbed for the fusil lying nearby. Had he reloaded the musket after he shot it last? He couldn't remember. Too late to do so now if those footsteps meant danger, dammit. He could hear someone approaching but couldn't yet see who it was. His best hope was that it was one of the Mexicans from the settlement, lost or hunting or whatever else might have brought him so far upriver.

That was the best it could be. The worst . . . Aaron wasn't sure which would be worse, wild Indians like the one he'd been tending lately or someone from the wagon train come to cart him off in manacles because of the stuff he stole when he took the Indian and ran away.

Whichever it was he . . . aw, dagnabbit, there was no powder in the priming pan of the fusil's flintlock and so there more than likely wasn't any charge or ball in the barrel either. He must have clean forgotten to load the thing after he shot that deer . . . what? . . . two days ago? He thought that was when it had been. Time had a way of getting away from a fellow out here, he'd noticed. Just didn't seem very important anymore. He'd completely lost track of days and dates and such. He thought it should be July. But he wasn't positive even about that. It could as easy be late August.

Was it important for a man to know the date of his own death? Probably not.

Aaron gripped the fusil and wondered—if it was indeed some wild Indians he heard tramping through the dry leaves and underbrush—if a bluff would work as good as a bullet.

After a few more moments he realized he wouldn't have to answer that question. It was a Mexican who came into view, peering left and right and obviously not quite sure of where he was going.

Aaron recognized the fellow. It was the same smallish, handsome young Mexican he'd given the venison to those couple days before.

Aaron laid down the fusil—no need threatening anybody, especially with an unloaded gun—and stepped out from behind the bush he'd been standing behind. "Hello."

The Mexican smiled and said something in Spanish. To Aaron the words sounded pretty much the same as the babbling a toddler makes before it learns how to talk. Aaron nodded politely and said, "And the same to you, Joe."

The Mexican approached, then slowed when he saw the wounded Indian lying on his pallet of blankets. He stopped beside the Indian and said something more. Asking questions, Aaron guessed. Not that Aaron understood a lick of it, nor could he answer even if he could figure out what the questions were. He shrugged by way of an apology and said, pointing, "Sit down and make yourself to home."

Aaron sat cross-legged beside the Indian and gestured for the Mexican to take a seat on the flat rock Aaron normally perched on when he was visiting with the Indian.

The Mexican nodded, spoke, sat where he was told. He

smiled and said something that took a while to get out.
Aaron was polite throughout and listened right through the
whole, unintelligible spiel.

"I got no coffee," he said when the Mexican eventually
ran dry of words, "but there's some herb tea I can hot up."

With grossly exaggerated hand movements so there
wouldn't be any misunderstanding what he had in mind,
Aaron built the fire higher and set his pot of tea over it. The
Mexican smiled and nodded his comprehension.

There weren't any regular cups to offer, but Aaron had
gouged the insides out of a couple chunks of dead wood to
fashion makeshift cups for the Indian and himself. He filled
the Indian's cup with tea and handed it to the Mexican and
then, partially to assure the fellow that it wasn't anything
too nasty for human consumption, poured some for himself
as well.

The Indian watched all this without a change of expression. Which was pretty much the way he accepted everything
and anything that went on around him. The Indian hardly
ever made a sound, much less a comment.

The Mexican said something that could have been a
deadly insult, for all Aaron could understand it.

"You're welcome," Aaron told him. "Drink hearty and
die." The Mexican grinned and bobbed his head.

Both men drank tea, the silence between them broken
only when the Indian began to snore.

"You'll have to excuse my partner's manners," Aaron
said. "He hasn't been very good company ever since the
president's missus refused to dance with him at the ball."

The Mexican smiled some more and nodded his
agreement.

"More?" Aaron offered the pot, and the Mexican motioned that he'd take another round. The cups didn't hold
much more than a mouthful at a time. Which was just as
well because the teas Aaron brewed tasted mostly like
they'd been drunk once or twice before already. This
Mexican was sure a polite fellow to be taking seconds.

The Mexican spoke again, and this time it was Aaron
who did the quiet smiling and head bobbing.

After a bit, when the tea was gone and all the social conventions—such as they were—fully observed, the Mexican reached inside his shirt and pulled out a small bundle wrapped in the dried leaves off cornstalks. He held it out to Aaron on both hands.

"For me? Thanks." Aaron accepted the gift—he suspected this package was the reason the Mexican had come walking out to find him today—and unwrapped it.

There were two presents inside the corn husks, he discovered.

One was a thin stack of the cornmeal pancakes that he'd seen the Mexicans eating when the wagon train was stopped at their settlement, and that was fine, for it would add to the diet he could offer to the Indian. And he expected he might even enjoy it himself for that matter.

But it was the other thing that like to took his breath away, and for that there was a rush of gratitude that he couldn't express in words but that he really and truly hoped the Mexican could see in his face.

For the little fellow with the dark eyes and the white, white smile had brought him a fist-sized, jagged and broken, small and ugly . . . and remarkably beautiful, wonderful, marvelous . . . whetstone.

Aaron didn't think he'd ever before in his life received such a fine and welcome present as this scrap of discarded whetstone brought to him by a Mexican whose name he didn't even know.

Aaron jumped up so sudden that he startled the Mexican, scaring him backward almost clean off the rock where he was seated. Then the Mexican and Aaron both began to laugh. Aaron pumped the Mexican's hand and thumped himself on the chest, loudly proclaiming his name as he did so.

"Emilio," the little Mexican returned with a finger aimed at his own chest.

Aaron and Emilio shook hands some more, each one trying to outgrin the other.

Couldn't understand a word of either Spanish or

Indian, Aaron thought, but that didn't mean it wasn't possible to make friends out here.

Laughing, he began to crumble some fresh pickings of bark and leaves and other such forest trash into the pot so as to make some more of his execrable tea, and while Aaron was busy doing that Emilio went off to fetch the water.

III

She truly was the most beautiful girl in all creation. The delicacy of her features, the perfect texture of her complexion, the depth and clarity of her eyes . . . no girl had ever been so beautiful. No one, not ever.

The room was small and dark, paneled in slabs of planed and polished wood that was of a honey-amber hue and that gleamed in the light from the single candle.

There was furniture in the room. He was sure that there was. But he could not see it, for everything save the broad, soft bed was in shadow.

The girl joined him by way of a door that opened briefly and then was seen no more, as it, as everything, receded from sight beyond the edges of the candle's dim light.

There was light enough for him to see her, however. Light enough for him to fully know the extent of her beauty. Light enough for him to see the soft love that shone within her eyes. Light enough for him to follow every motion as she disrobed, offering the sight of herself as a gift that was his and his alone.

Her hair spilled halfway down her back, glistening in the candlelight, shimmering and flowing with each small movement of her lovely head.

Ah, her features were so small and perfectly formed, so delicate and fair. Her skin so pale against the silky black of her hair and the dark depths of her eyes. Her lips so blushingly perfect, the shade that of rose petals coated lightly with the frost of an early autumn freeze. Her throat so tender and vulnerable. Her figure . . .

He could scarcely believe his own good fortune. To be offered a gift such as this was beyond belief. Greater than anything he had ever known.

Smiling, smiling, she lifted the hem of her blouse and without hesitation, yet at the same time with an appealing shyness, pulled it quickly over her head, lifting the shining sheaf of black hair and spilling it in shimmering waves down her back.

And that back. Oh, it was lovely. Her shoulder blades were prominent, her flesh without blemish, warm velvet molded as no other could ever be. He could see the ladder-work of her spine hiding beneath that marvelously textured surface. Could see the incredibly tiny span of her waist and the plump, rounded, womanly swell of her hips a hands-breadth below.

She turned, facing him full on without shame, offering him the full impact of her beauty as she stepped out of her skirt and undergarments so that all of her was revealed.

There was nothing held back from him. All was offered. All was given.

She extended her arms to him. Smiled. Said something. He did not know the words, but he was sure of the meaning and, smiling, he welcomed her onto the soft bed, welcomed her into his embrace.

The touch of her flesh was like that of no other woman he had ever known. She was softer than a handful of eiderdown, warmer than a banked stove on a cold winter's evening.

He bent, wanting more than all else in the world to taste the sweetness of her lips.

His mouth moved, actually physically moved, and Aaron came blinking and cursing awake, disgusted. Not so much disgusted with his dream as with the fact that it was but a fantasy and not a true happening.

Dream he called it, but his visions of the Mexican girl were only partially a dream, for he was more awake than asleep when his mind's eye "saw" the girl before him.

He had been somnolent but truthfully more awake than

otherwise, awake enough to guide and control the developments of his half-dream imaginings.

And they had been powerful visions indeed. Powerful enough to leave him aching with want of the girl he had so briefly glimpsed at the Mexican settlement that day. Powerful enough to tell him that for the twentieth time in his life—and for the first by all the measurements that were of real importance—Aaron Jenks was well and truly in love.

The Mexican girl—God in heaven, he didn't even know her name—had looked into his eyes and captured his heart.

She was so . . . perfect. So beautiful. So wonderful.

He had seen no more of her than her face. And yet he knew so very much about her. Knew not merely her beauty but the abiding goodness of her soul. Knew her capacity for love. And her vulnerability to hurt. Knew without question the way her voice would sound whispering tenderly in his ear. Knew the delightful gasps of pleasure she would make when someday—soon—they joined one with the other. Knew the gracious, giving generosity of her spirit.

Knew, in short, that this was the girl with whom he hoped to share his life, his body, his all.

Aaron never before felt such tenderness toward another human soul. But he did now. And his heart soared with a fierce and loving joy at the newfound purpose this sweet girl gave to him.

Shivering with excitement rather than chill, for the night air was mild and pleasant, he sat upright to check first the stars overhead, then the dull red glow of the coals from last night's fire and finally the measured breathing of the now healing Indian who slept across the fire pit from him.

All was well, and so Aaron lay down again and pulled his blanket onto his shoulders.

But he had no desire now to sleep. Better by far to return to his fantasy visions. Better by far to once more let the beautiful Mexican girl love and coddle and pamper him. And to give herself unstintingly to him.

Aaron closed his eyes, and somewhere in the dim glow of a candle's flame the gorgeous lass tugged lightly at the ribbon that held her bodice closed. Somewhere almost but not quite within reach she began to disrobe. For him. Only and ever for him and him alone.

In his half-sleep Aaron's mouth moved, kissing and suckling, and his hands gripped and then gently, so gently stroked.

In his sleep Aaron was happy.

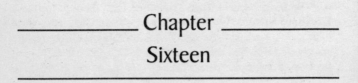

Chapter Sixteen

I

The white man seemed very odd. And in his own way caring, almost kind in the treatment he dispensed. Mostly, though, he just seemed odd.

Talks To Ghosts had never before seen a human being with red hair. He had seen a few of the dark-skinned white men from the south. He had seen one of the black-robed ones from the south and of course heard of others. And with his own eyes once he saw a pair of small voyageurs who wore the red caps and the big beards. But a red hat was certainly not the same thing as a human with red hair. Talks To Ghosts had given this much thought and deep study, and he could only conclude after all of it that this strange white man had hair that was truly red. Not only on his head either but all over his body. Talks To Ghosts had looked for himself—in considerable amazement once he realized what it was that he was seeing—and this white man indeed had red hair and, where the sun did not reach it, flesh so pale and ugly to look at that it nearly made Talks To Ghosts sick when he first saw it.

A truth is a truth, however, no matter how unusual or

disgusting, and the truth in this case was that the white man provided living proof that the world is full of mysteries that are beyond the comprehension of any one person.

Talks To Ghosts lay still, feigning sleep as he often did while he tried to work out a plan to escape.

So far he was in luck. The white man thought him still far from recovery. Well, he was partially in luck. The white man did not know how far Talks To Ghosts' healing had progressed. On the other hand, Talks To Ghosts remained far from being well enough to get away from his captivity.

Talks To Ghosts' primary fear was that the white man would too soon deem him sufficiently healed, or at least that he was far enough along in his healing, that they could move on, that Talks To Ghosts would be well enough to work by the time they got to wherever it was they were going.

Talks To Ghosts had only the most vague idea of where that might be. Somewhere far to the south, it was said. That was where the dark-skinned white men took their captives to sell.

So far as Talks To Ghosts knew no one among the people had ever been sold into slavery, but many and many times the people heard of such things happening. The dark-skinned white men traded in women, children, even some men. Arapaho sold to them by the Comanche. Comanche sold to them by the Kiowa. Kiowa-Apache sold to them by the Arapaho. The people heard of all these things.

Heard too that anyone sold away to the south never came back. Never.

It was rumored that the men were required to labor inside the earth. Why this should be so was unclear, but that was what was said.

The women, of course, had more logical and obvious purposes. As for the children, well, any tribe is always anxious to increase its numbers through the addition of children to its bands. Talks To Ghosts assumed the dark-skinned white men in the south were no different in that regard.

But if the rumors were true about the work that was required of the men ... Talks To Ghosts shuddered. The thought of being sent to live in a cave—it was said these caves were actually dug by the hand of man, although no one could give a rational explanation for why someone might wish to do such a thing—the thought of being sent to labor inside a cave, natural or otherwise, and to work and live, sleep and eat beyond the healing presence of the sun, beyond perhaps the benevolent influence of the spirits ... such a thing would be beyond endurance.

No one of the people had ever been taken into such captivity, and Talks To Ghosts had no intention of being the first of his kind to make that journey beyond the southern mountains.

He would do quite literally anything that he had to in order to escape such a fate as that.

Just as quickly as he had some small measure of strength back. The pounding in his skull and the sharp pains in his face he could manage to ignore. All that was required, really, was that he regain his strength. Not all of it even. Just enough that he could run. A few minutes only. And walk. An hour, two if possible. After that he would hide. He would crawl if he had to. He would find his people—what few of them the skulking, cowardly Kiowa left in this world—and he would escape the subterranean tortures of the dark-skinned white men.

He would. He had to. He would rather die than accept a life apart from the sun and the spirits.

And so he closed his eyes and pretended to sleep and all the while he healed. Slowly he healed.

II

It was gone. Wiped out. As if it had never been. This was a sad thing but a truth, and what man can deny the truth?

The sight in his left eye had been blurred and fuzzy ever since he first awakened from his long sleep. Now it was gone completely. The Kiowa who almost killed him succeeded in blinding him in his left eye.

Talks To Ghosts felt of the eye—it was tender, but there no longer was actual pain when he touched and probed and inquired of the healing—but the scab that he hoped to find was not there. He had hoped, fruitlessly, that his vision was obscured by dried blood or the like.

He knew better, of course. Red Beard not only fed him, his captor bathed Talks To Ghosts' wounds at least once each day and sometimes more.

But still Talks To Ghosts had hoped. . . .

He sighed, careful to keep the sound of it small so Red Beard would not hear, and accepted the truth. He no longer had even the least vestige of sight in the left eye.

He squeezed his right eye shut and peered as intently as he could toward the distant stars, but no glimmer of light reached him through the damaged left eye.

He tried again, this time with the right, and could see the stars clearly. The magic patterns were all as they should be. All in place. But with the left eye . . . nothing. No matter how hard he tried to see.

A moment of hope flickered within him as he thought, perhaps in the daytime, perhaps with a strong enough light . . .

But it was no good. He was sure of that now.

The Kiowa killed that eye with his club. It was gone and there was nothing any man could do to bring back an eye that was dead. Talks To Ghosts was sure of that.

The loss of his eye was bad. And if there was so much damage done that the eye was dead, what of the rest of him? For the first time since he wakened it occurred to Talks To Ghosts to wonder about his appearance now.

Questioning hands told him that there were whorls and ridges in his flesh where there used to be none.

What would Sleeping Fawn think of him now? Talks To Ghosts had not been a handsome man to begin with. Nor had Sleeping Fawn favored him even before this wound. What would she think of him now? Would she turn her face from the sight of him? She had given him contempt before. Would she now be disgusted by him?

Talks To Ghosts wished he could find a steel mirror or at the least a still pond where he could see.

But that would mean moving about in the daytime, and he did not want Red Beard to know how far the healing process had come. Talks To Ghosts did not want his captor to realize that the patient would soon be strong enough again to work, for that would surely lead to slavery and the underground labors from which no man ever returned.

Talks To Ghosts had adopted the habit of sleeping through the days and lying awake at night, and when Red Beard went to sleep Talks To Ghosts could sit upright and swing his arms about and prepare himself for his escape.

But tonight, tonight the last of his sight flickered and faded away and finally expired.

Tonight Talks To Ghosts found himself blind in the one eye. Was there anything else yet to go wrong? Would the Kiowa's blow kill him after all? Better that than to be kept underground like a mole, of course.

But if he had a choice . . .

Talks To Ghosts looked at Red Beard sleeping peacefully on the far side of the glowing coals left from the evening's fire. It might be wise to make his escape attempt now, quickly before anything else happened to slow his flight or make it impossible.

He could kill the white man—Red Beard did not hide his knife or gun when he went to bed; he left them in plain sight, practically within arm's length of Talks To Ghosts' bed—and be gone before the dark-skinned white man came back to visit his friend Red Beard. That very probably was the sensible thing to do, Talks To Ghosts concluded. He could do it easily. Red Beard would never hear. Never even know.

But Talks To Ghosts hesitated.

Red Beard had taken good care of him. Still was gentle and patient with him. Prepared teas and broths and lately soft bits of liver and heart to patiently feed to him one slow bite at a time.

Talks To Ghosts was sure Red Beard only did this in order to assure the value of a property. Yet even so it was

more than Talks To Ghosts could have expected from his
own wife or clansmen had they found him beside the water
back there where the Kiowa ambush was laid. Had one of
his own people found him they would have grieved for
him—as they no doubt already did—but they would have
left him to complete his dying. Oh, they might have washed
him and dressed him in his finest clothing and prepared him
for the journey beyond. But they would not have tended to
him the way Red Beard did.

It would be poor repayment now to kill Red Beard in
his sleep.

Poor payment, yes, but it was also true that in his still
weak condition Talks To Ghosts could not expect to outrun
Red Beard. If he intended to escape he would have to be
sure that Red Beard did not follow. Or wait until Talks To
Ghosts' own strength was great so that he would be able to
get away and remain ahead of Red Beard's pursuit.

Yet, Talks To Ghosts argued with himself, what if he
waited and some new thing went wrong with his battered
body? Tonight it was the eye. Tonight some other thing
might make itself known to him. If he waited he ran the risk
of never being able to get away.

He shook his head, the movement causing only a very
little pain now, and reminded himself that if much more
went wrong with this body he would only die anyway. Here
in the camp of Red Beard, somewhere out in the hills
seeking the people, on the way south toward slavery . . . if
he would die anyway it hardly should matter where the
event occurred.

So perhaps it would do no great harm for him to wait.
To continue to heal. To have patience. After all, he could
always kill Red Beard later if he had to. In the meantime
Talks To Ghosts would continue to eat and to rest and to
gather the life forces inside his belly.

Tomorrow or tomorrow or tomorrow he would make
his escape. Not tonight.

Chapter Seventeen

I

Despite the season the mornings were cool, almost chill. Emilio yawned as he left the warmth of the jacal, brushing past the deerskin drape that served as a door, and went out to the heavy crockery olla to pour clean water into the basin that sat on a flimsy willow table beside the east-facing wall.

It was not so terribly cold, really. There was no film of ice on the water in the olla. But the air that reached Emilio's bare chest felt almost cold enough anyway to foretell freezes yet to come.

He poured a pint or so of the river water into the basin and, shivering, plunged his hands and face into it. The shock of the cold water striking flesh still warm from the blankets was quite enough to complete the job of waking him. Had he needed such assistance, that is, which he most emphatically felt he did *not*.

He washed quickly—rather more quickly than he might have had there been any hot water available—and used the well-chewed tip of a willow switch to scrub his teeth, then rinsed and spat.

Among the many things he and Consuela neglected to think of when stocking up on supplies back in far-off Santa Fe was a mirror. It was an object missed perhaps more by Consuela than by Emilio, who was becoming quite accustomed to brushing and combing his hair without benefit of a mirror. As for his not-quite-always daily shaves, he resolved that problem by having Consuela attend to it for him. She proved to have a delicate touch with the razor and indeed gave him a finer shave than he could manage for himself.

That, however, would have to wait today again. Consuela remained abed, never mind that the sun had already left the horizon behind and was rising inexorably into the eastern sky.

Consuela slept so much of late that it sometimes worried Emilio, but both she and the chatterbox neighboring women assured him that this was entirely customary and that both she and the child were well. He hoped they were right.

Emilio finished his morning ablutions, wiped himself dry with a scrap of rag suspended from a peg for that purpose, and went inside to fetch his shirt.

The interior of the windowless jacal was dim, but in the shadows he could see Consuela's still and silent bulk—there was quite a bit more of her now than there used to be—lying beneath a blanket on the pallet closer to the adobe fireplace. Emilio's bed, such as it was, was laid close by the door. He always put it as far as he comfortably could from Consuela's. This was not because he feared disturbing her in the night so much as because he feared his own masculine reactions to the nearby presence of a woman. Not that Emilio was tempted by this flesh of his own flesh. He was not. Of course he was not. But at times the sight and the scent of female flesh, any such female flesh, was simply too much a reminder of what it was that he had given up, and the urges within his body became almost unbearably strong in their demands. Better, he had discovered, to remain aloof and determinedly disinterested, the same attitude of isolation

that he imagined priests and monks must learn to acquire for
their own peace of mind.

Although dry now and warm he shivered, a chill racing
madly up his spine. Emilio shook his shoulders to throw off
this unwelcome sensation, then backed silently out of the
jacal into the growing warmth of the sunshine. He did so
without disturbing Consuela in her sleep.

Later, when she awakened and was ready to start her
day, later Emilio would think of breakfast.

Now there was work to be done.

II

Gently, hesitantly, he prodded the result of last night's
labors.

He groaned and bit back an impulse to curse and rant
in anguished frustration.

The stone, the damnable irritating miserable stupid
stone, shifted position, cracking the river-bottom mud he
was using for mortar. The stone wobbled at the fingertip
touch, broke easily from its bed of dried mud, and tumbled
clattering off the rock pile that was supposed to be—but so
clearly was *not*—a fine and sturdy wall.

Emilio lifted his eyes skyward in mingled despair and
beseeching.

How was he ever to build a house of stone if he could
not manage to make one stone lie atop another? It was maddening. Worse than maddening. It was miserable. It made
Emilio miserable. It made Emilio mad. What it was doing, it
was making him crazy. Why, oh why, did his piled stones
not remain as he placed them?

He set them ever so carefully one on top of another.

He mortared them lovingly into place.

He even talked to them. Begged them to be good, to
stay where he put them.

It did no good. Nothing he tried did any good. Not
when he used river mud, not when he tried using clay, not

when . . . not with anything he knew or imagined or simply thought up to try. No matter what he tried, no matter how he experimented, his every effort to build a rock wall collapsed. Literally collapsed. Fell apart at the first slight touch.

He could just visualize what it would be like to live in a stone house built by his own inexpert hands. Huh! Sneeze indoors in such a house and the roof would come roaring down upon the occupants. If, that is, he could find anyone so foolish as to set foot inside a building built by Emilio Escavara. He himself would certainly never trust such a structure, no indeed.

He knew better.

And this knowledge was reinforced each and every morning when he came out to test the results of the previous evening's efforts.

Furious with himself and frustrated with the stones, Emilio kicked apart the tiny section of wall he had put so painfully together the evening before. It was a morning ritual that was becoming quite routine and so far represented the sole aspect of stone-house building that he could manage.

He kicked the stones somewhat harder than was required simply to move them off the sandstone slabs that he had emplaced as foundation markers, but in truth there was no real satisfaction in the show of pique.

On the contrary, he kicked one of the larger stones so hard that he felt pain jar his foot and ankle all the way into his calf.

Miserable stupid damned . . .

"Emilio."

"Yes, Consuela?"

"Would you bring in an armload of wood, please, so I can start the fire and cook your breakfast?"

"Yes, of course."

He would eat, tend to the few things that needed to be done around the house, and then take the sheep and the burros out to graze.

Later. This evening, he would try once more to teach

himself how to build a wall that would not so readily fly
apart.

Maybe if he tried mixing sand and gravel into the river
mud . . .

III

Emilio heard the greeting call and recognized the voice
if not the incomprehensible words. He looked up from his
ungainly pile of uncooperative stones and smiled as the mad
red-haired Yankee came into sight along the path.

"Hello. Welcome." He knew that Aaron had no more
Spanish than Emilio had English, but that was of no importance. Aaron was welcome here and this Aaron would
know, even without language. Emilio was sure of that.

The lanky American was carrying a bundle slung over
one shoulder. The bundle was of deer hide and contained
something that was fairly bulky. Emilio did not want to
guess what the article was. Or why Aaron might be bringing
it here. But he could not help but hope. There was no fresh
meat in the settlement. No one had enough livestock to
waste to the luxury of slaughter, but the fresh meat Aaron
gave him before had been wonderfully nourishing for Consuela. If this bundle now was . . . but he should not expect
such a thing, of course. It was rude of him even to think it.
Emilio stood, brushing the rock dust and dried mud from his
hands, and grinned at this new friend whose language he
could not comprehend. "Welcome, Aaron. Have you eaten?
Would you like some supper? We have tortillas and beans.
Very good. Very filling."

Aaron said something in return, something that assuredly
had nothing whatsoever to do with Emilio's invitation.

The American set his bundle aside unopened—perhaps,
Emilio thought, it was not a present after all; ah, it was
indeed rude of him to have made such an assumption; he
felt shame flood through his veins, felt it bring heat into his
cheeks and forehead—and said something. He smiled and

pointed to the pile of ready stones nearby, to the foundation course of flat rock and to Emilio's latest unsteady efforts at the building of a wall.

The tone of Aaron's voice made it clear that he was asking a question, but Emilio had no idea what. He smiled and shrugged broadly, then with gestures mimed the placement of a stone house at this spot close by the river and the woodlot and the garden that Consuela occasionally felt well enough to tend.

Emilio gestured toward the jacal, then showed his fingers walking from it to the stone house that was yet to be.

Aaron nodded as if he understood. The jacal was crude and in winter would be cold and was only temporary. A stone house, a proper domicile, would replace it. Someday.

Emilio said as much to his Yankee friend. Aaron nodded as if he quite understood and said something in return.

And then, quite oddly, he bent and began picking through the stock of piled stones, tossing some in one direction and throwing others away, moving through them swiftly and surely and without hesitation.

And then when he was satisfied with whatever mysterious choices were made, the red-haired American dropped to his knees with a grunt and began quickly and deftly assembling the rocks into an orderly, even a cohesive pattern.

Within minutes Emilio could see that a wall was rising. A real wall, about a foot and a half wide at the base and sturdy even without an application of mortar.

It was a miracle. Aaron knew how to make a wall. Now if only the barrier of language could be breached and he would teach Emilio how to do this most remarkable thing . . .

Chapter Eighteen

I

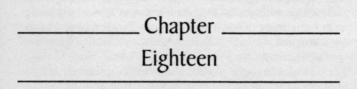

Aaron didn't think he had ever met anyone before who couldn't do something as simple as laying up a stone wall. Not that he'd known about anyway. Why, there wasn't hardly anything so simple. He had been doing it since . . . since he couldn't hardly remember when, it had been that long. You just looked at the rocks and saw what should fit where and then you put them in place, and that was that.

Back home in Pennsylvania most everybody used stone for building fences and outbuildings and the like. The stone was free and convenient and durable so it was only prudent—which is a nice way to keep from saying "cheap"—to use it.

Lately wooden gates were becoming popular for their convenience, but there were still a good many farmers, especially among the Dutchies that some called the Amish, who forswore convenience in favor of, uh, prudence. Those folk didn't want to lay out cash for hardware nor unnecessary labor for lumber and so they still built their fences and pens without gates. When you wanted a gap in the fence you simply dismantled the stone wall, moved your livestock in or out as required, and then built the wall back again behind them.

Aaron couldn't begin to count the times he had taken walls apart and laid them up again like that. Putting up a rock wall was about as difficult for him as knowing how to walk from hither to yon without mixing up his feet one from the other.

It really amused him now to see what a mess poor Emilio was making of the job, and it wouldn't do him a lick of harm to help out a bit. After all, the Indian had been sound asleep when he left to hunt. Likely he would have to wake the fellow in order to feed him when Aaron returned to . . . to what? Camp? Or home, was it?

That was a question he'd been pondering the past few weeks. Was this savage, unsettled country where he was destined to stay?

Sometimes it almost seemed like it. For sure he felt no tug of attraction, no yearnings or longings, whenever he thought about going back east to the States. But then he felt no excitement either about the prospect of moving on south into Mexican territory.

The truth was that he kind of liked it here. Liked the stillness and the expanse of it, the sight of the mountains to the west, and the clean, crisp feel in the air.

Liked too the idea that the girl was nearby. He had no idea yet what her name was. But she lived here in the settlement somewhere, and if he stayed any length of time he would inevitably run into her again. Even if she deliberately tried to avoid him—and why would she think of doing such a thing when she likely didn't so much as know that Aaron Jenks existed in this world?—even if she did that he would eventually come upon her, at one of the gatherings of the people or down along the river fetching water or some darn thing. It was just plain bound to happen sooner or later.

And the simple truth of the matter was that this was the girl who was meant for him. Aaron knew that just as surely as he knew which way was up or when his belly was empty. That Mexican girl with the soft eyes and the prettiest smile in all creation was meant to be his. Was *meant* to belong to him. He knew that. For a fact he did.

So for the time being he was content to lay up a bit of stone wall for old Emilio and think his own private thoughts and after that, well, after that who could know what might come next?

He bent, tossed aside half a dozen useless stones, and deftly continued assembling the rest into a tidily interlocking whole.

II

He was far from being tired, but he knew he shouldn't spend much more time here. Not today anyway. The Indian would be waking up soon, and he would be hungry. Aaron wanted to get back to camp and cook some broth ready for when the Indian woke. If possible he would like to get it done before dark.

He finished the course of stone he was working on at the moment and stood, brushing his hands clean of dirt so as to show Emilio that he was through for the day.

Pretty much as an afterthought—and indeed once he got to messing with the rocks he had completely forgotten the reason he came here to begin with—he picked up the bundle of raw deer hide and fresh meat and handed it to Emilio.

"For your supper," he said, knowing the Mexican couldn't understand a word he was saying but feeling a yen to talk anyhow.

That, he supposed, was the thing he missed the most out here. Not being able to talk with anybody. Oh, he could talk *to* folks often enough. He talked to the Indian much of the time whether the man was awake or asleep. And he talked to Emilio. The problem was that he couldn't understand a damn thing either one of them ever said back.

He surely did miss conversation.

Emilio said something that sounded like he was trying

to tell him about the grass hereabouts. Except that wasn't likely. Aaron was sure the strange words were a form of saying thank you and only sounded like he was talking about grass.

"It's all right," Aaron told him. "The meat would only go bad if somebody doesn't cook and eat it. Better to share it with you than let it rot, that's all." He smiled, and Emilio, who surely hadn't comprehended the least lick of that, smiled back at him.

Aaron stood there for another moment made awkward by the desire to communicate and the knowledge that he couldn't, then turned to leave.

Emilio stopped him with a light touch on the elbow. Not insistent. Just asking.

Aaron glanced at the sky. There was still a little daylight remaining. The sun hadn't quite touched the mountaintops yet, and the long, lingering twilight of the mountain country remained to go.

"Reckon I can wait another minute more if you want," he said.

Emilio smiled and bobbed his head and hurried away with the deer meat toward the pole-and-mud shanty that was nearby. Obviously that was where Emilio was living until his house was built.

At least Emilio had the gumption to try and build himself a house, Aaron thought. Most of the other Mexican settlers here didn't seem much interested in making themselves anything better than these pole affairs. Although to be fair he would have to admit that a few of them were sun drying mud bricks and building themselves mud houses. Aaron remembered one of the fellows with the freight train telling him the word for the Mexican mud buildings, but he couldn't remember what it was.

Anyway, Emilio was trying to do better than that for himself. Not that he was apt to accomplish much the way he'd been going about it before Aaron took a hand. But at least he was trying.

Emilio disappeared inside the curtain that covered his doorway and came back out less than a minute later, the deer meat left behind. This time he was carrying a corn-husk bundle that Aaron recognized with a grin.

Those thin cornmeal flapjacks were funny to look at, but there was nothing wrong with the way they tasted. And the Indian seemed to like them right well too. If Emilio wanted to swap some of them for the deer meat, that was just fine by Aaron. That was a trade he would go for any old time.

Emilio said something to him and handed him the cornshucks, and sure enough the wrapping was filled heavy with the Mexican pancakes.

"Thanks."

Emilio responded with a spray of Spanish that came out so fast it's a wonder his tongue wasn't singed from the heat of it.

Aaron thanked him a couple times more, pretty sure Emilio got the gist of what was being said if not the actual words, then once again tried to go.

And once again Emilio stopped him with a touch on the elbow.

"Yeah, Emilio, what is it?"

Emilio held up a finger in the universal gesture for "wait a minute" and turned toward the shack. "Consuela," he called, although what that meant was anybody's guess so far as Aaron could tell. He was willing to trust that it didn't mean "attack," but beyond that he wasn't placing any bets.

Emilio took him by the arm and led him toward the shanty, calling out that word again a couple times.

About the time he dragged Aaron close to the shack the curtain was pulled back just a little ways, and a pair of eyes peeped out.

Not just any pair of eyes, though. Aaron knew right from the first glimpse that this was the girl.

The girl. His girl. The girl to whom Aaron pledged his heart—and selected other parts too—every night before he slept and every sleeping in his dreams.

This right here in Emilio's hut was the girl that Aaron did intend to marry.

How could he be so lucky that his new friend knew this

one particular girl? Of all the girls in the whole wide world, it was just pure, plain, wonderful luck for him to find her here.

And Emilio, why he was practically a good friend. Good enough that if they would work out the language problem, Aaron would bet Emilio would speak to the girl on Aaron's behalf.

Hell, of course he would.

They were friends, weren't they? They'd shared meat, hadn't they?

Of course Emilio would speak to the girl for him.

Aaron smiled. Felt his heart begin to race and his chest to swell. Felt a fullness at the nape of his neck and a constriction in his chest. Felt a rush of raw desire send heat boiling through his groin. Felt . . . felt plenty damn confused when it finally occurred to him to wonder just what the girl, this girl, his girl, was doing in Emilio's damned house.

And then felt a cold, sickening emptiness as the girl, this girl, Emilio's girl, stepped from behind the curtain to join the two men outside. She came out preceded by a belly that was swollen big with child.

Aaron had only seen her face before. The rest of her had been hidden from him by the crowd of people she was in when he first saw her.

But now . . . !

She was seven, eight months along.

She was married. And to Emilio. Of all people it was Emilio she slept with every night.

Aaron mumbled something—he himself didn't know what it was that he said, and it was probably a very good thing that Emilio and the girl spoke no English or he likely would have embarrassed himself beyond the possibility of explanation—and turned to stumble away into the fading light that seeped over the distant mountain peaks.

He was almost all the way back to camp before he realized that he was still carrying the package of Mexican pancakes but had gone and left his gun behind. The fusil was still lying where he'd left it, he supposed, leaned up against Emilio's pile of smooth stones. The stones that were intended to build a house for the girl Aaron Jenks was in love with, the girl Aaron knew now he would never marry.

Dammit, dammit, *dammit*! Aaron groaned silently to himself as strong and ever stronger waves of anguished self-pity washed through him.

Chapter Nineteen

I

The time was good. It would be dark soon, and Red Beard was not yet back from his hunting. Talks To Ghosts debated, though, whether he should wait and make his escape during the night, after Red Beard fell asleep.

The advantage of waiting was that then he could steal the red-haired white man's gun to take with him. The people would be amazed if lowly Talks To Ghosts, who never was known for his skills as a warrior, returned not only alive and healed but carrying a musket too.

The disadvantage was that Red Beard might hear and, learning of Talks To Ghosts' physical abilities, not only stop him from going but tie or chain him in the future so that he would be prevented from making any fresh attempt to get away.

If he wanted to take the gun he would have to wait.

If he wanted to be sure of escaping he would have to go now.

Talks To Ghosts had been thinking of little else this whole afternoon. Now he decided. He would forget about making any foolish attempts for glory and leave now while he still had some daylight in which to find his way, now before Red Beard returned and began a pursuit.

Talks To Ghosts stood and looked carefully up and down the defile of the small gully where Red Beard had placed his camp. He heard and saw nothing save the aimless drifting overhead of a pair of black-and-white magpies who searched for carrion that would make an easy meal. If only people found things to be as simple as the magpies, Talks To Ghosts thought. Sadly, that was not the way the spirits intended things to be.

Talks To Ghosts smiled ruefully as he thought: How much more sensible things could have been had the spirits only thought to ask for the immeasurably valuable advice of Talks To Ghosts before they decided these things.

Ah, but he was procrastinating, was he not? That was foolish, perhaps as foolish as the spirits had been when they failed to consult with Talks To Ghosts.

Better to go now while he had the light and yet when it was late enough in the day to ensure that Red Beard would lack the advantage of daylight when he returned to find his property missing.

As for the other property that would be missing . . . Talks To Ghosts was still too weak to carry much with him. He took up one blanket of the many Red Beard owned and helped himself to a knife blank. The steel had not yet been sharpened nor fitted with a handle, but those things could be accomplished at leisure later on.

There was no food in the camp to take, and Talks To Ghosts knew that without a bow or a gun he would have difficulty finding food. Of course the truth was that, poor a hunter as he was, he would have had some difficulty obtaining food even if he had a bow *and* a gun.

But that was beyond his control and so not worth worrying over. He would survive. He had managed to live this long, and he had no intention of allowing himself to starve to death now.

Somehow, somewhere, he would find the people. And

he would survive long enough to do so. Of that he was quite certain.

He folded the woolen trade blanket like a serape and draped it over one shoulder, tucked the steel knife blank into his waistcloth—the metal was cold in its first contact with the flesh of his belly but quickly warmed to his body heat—and pronounced himself as ready as he was likely to be.

Without a backward glance, Talks To Ghosts began walking up the gully in the direction of the mountains.

II

Before he had gone a mile Talks To Ghosts knew he had made a mistake. His strength was not nearly so great as he had thought.

There was no problem when he was lying beside a fire and being fed by the efforts of another. But now that he was walking the energy he thought was his was quickly, much too quickly, used up and gone.

His legs felt as soft and weak as green grass stems in the early spring when the new growth was more water than fiber. They scarcely supported him as he tried to climb the gentle elevation leading deeper into the narrow gully. If he had to do any serious climbing or even something as mild as trying to get up the slopes on either side of the bottom where he now found himself, he doubted he would be able to do it.

His wind was all right, but his legs had no more substance than clay. Soft, muddy clay at that. They felt like they might give way beneath him at any moment, without so much as a twinge of warning beforehand.

Talks To Ghosts staggered, caught himself by grabbing at the trunk of a small aspen, and wobbled on a few paces more.

No good. This was no good at all. He could not continue on like this. A few hundred paces more and he would be flat on his face or reduced to crawling.

It was bad enough to think that Red Beard might—

no, not might; almost certainly would was more the truth of the matter—catch up with him again. It would have been worse to allow Red Beard to see him crawl. Talks To Ghosts had no power, but he still had his dignity. No one, not Red Beard and not the dread Kiowa, could take that away from him.

While he yet had strength enough to choose, Talks To Ghosts looked about in the fading light of the evening. This was not the day he would have chosen to die. But it would do.

He saw a place that pleased him. A smooth, slick lump of granite surrounded by aspen to the rear and with a thicket of wild raspberry nearby.

It was a place where birds and squirrels, deer and curious bears, rabbits and stealthy coyotes would all come from time to time. It was a place where Talks To Ghosts thought his own spirit could find rest and happiness. It was a place where he would be satisfied to die.

Slowly, not wanting his legs to give out while he still had need of them, he made his way to the rock, climbing onto it and making himself as comfortable there as was possible.

Then Talks To Ghosts closed his eyes and lifted his face to the clouds above. With his heart strong and the blood beating solemnly in his ears, Talks To Ghosts began lifting soundless chants into the sky where the spirits watched.

He sang his songs of entreaty, and he waited for Red Beard to come and finish what had to be done here.

Chapter Twenty

I

Poor son of a bitch must have come up here to pray, Aaron thought.

If, that is, Indians prayed. Did they? It was something he never considered before. If they did pray he supposed it wasn't to God but to ... what? A rock? A tree? Everyone knew that Indians were all godless savages. But he didn't exactly know what all that meant.

For sure it looked like this one had come up to the head of the gulch to pray. Or some dang thing.

Now the dumb savage, godless or otherwise, was sprawled out on top of a boulder sound asleep.

Aaron might have missed seeing him altogether except that he was stretched out in plain sight, and the bright green of the blanket he'd brought with him stood out against the gray of the stone and the soft, natural greens of the young aspen grove behind him. The Indian couldn't have been more obvious about where he was if he'd been beating a drum and ringing brass bells. He wasn't trying to hide, that was for sure.

Which pretty much ruled out what Aaron first thought,

and that was that the Indian was trying to run off to his own people.

Aaron had no objection to that, in fact would be glad to be shut of the responsibility for feeding and bathing the wounded man, but the Indian just wasn't strong enough to make it on his own. Not yet.

If he insisted on trying it, of course, the decision was his to make. With that in mind Aaron had brought along some of the fresh deer meat from the doe he'd killed earlier in the day. He'd intended to give that to the Indian to help him on his way if he insisted on going.

Obviously, though, that wasn't what was going on here.

Aaron assumed the prayers, if any, were ended now since the guy was sleeping. No harm, then, in taking him back to camp, he supposed. Though it seemed a shame to wake him. Still, the guy spent about all his time sleeping. A few minutes awake shouldn't hurt him all that much.

Aaron tied a rawhide thong around the bundle of meat he'd brought and slung the resulting pack, sort of a makeshift haversack, over one shoulder.

The Indian was too heavy to carry all the way back down to camp, so Aaron figured he would just have to wake the guy and drape one of the Indian's arms over his shoulders so as give him some support. But he would have to do most of the walking himself.

No harm in that, Aaron decided. If the damned Indian was well enough to walk up here he should be well enough to make it back with a little assistance.

With a sigh—dammit he was tired to begin with after putting in a full long day, and he hadn't counted on having to do this too before he could so much as think about fixing supper for the two of them—Aaron squared his shoulders, and his resolve, and went over to wake the Indian.

II

Oho, now what was this here? Dang savage hadn't gone off to pray at all, had he? No sirree bob, he hadn't. A person didn't need a knife if it was praying that he had on his mind. And that was sure enough one of the knife blanks out of the bale of trade goods that Aaron was seeing now tucked inside the waist of the Indian's breechcloth.

So the guy was thinking to steal a blanket and a knife and go back to his own. The thing that stopped him was his lousy condition. Apparently he just plain wore out before he could get the job done. But he was trying it. He surely was.

Well, there wasn't much harm in that, was there?

Aaron felt no hostility toward the Indian over it. If anything he felt a certain amount of respect that anyone so weak and hurting would up and tackle a chore that difficult. As for the blanket and the knife, those were simply things that a man needed to survive.

Again Aaron's response was more on the order of respect than resentment over the paltry items that the Indian took with him when he lit out for home. Wherever that was.

No gun or bow or anything important to his name, shucks, Aaron was in fine fettle but he wouldn't have thought of taking off alone into the mountains like this Indian was bent on doing. Even counting for the fact that savages were supposed to be at home in the wilderness, the amazement wasn't that the guy stole a couple things but that he didn't try and clean the camp out.

And if one wanted to recall that the man wasn't strong enough to carry much of anything, well, the fact remained. What he tried to do was a courageous thing, the way Aaron saw it. And there hadn't been harm done.

Aaron put the Indian back onto the pine-bough bed he'd been sleeping in and covered him over with the green blanket he'd stolen.

He did take the knife away from the Indian, though. Took it and put it back with the other crude, unfinished blanks that he intended to sharpen and fit with deer-horn handles when he got time enough.

"Look'a here, Lo," he told the poor Indian, "let me put some meat on to boil, then you and me will talk."

Aaron sliced thin slivers of deer meat into his pot, added water and some wild onion that he'd found growing in a marshy bottom, and set the pot onto the fire to boil and make a broth. A broth is easy on the stomach, but maybe, he thought now, he'd been overdoing that concern. The Indian needed strength and that meant more meat along with his broth. Aaron resolved himself to giving the Indian more in the way of solid food for however long the fellow chose to stay around until his next decision to head for home and the rest of his people. Which, Aaron guessed, would be no longer than it would take him to get a little strength back.

That time could come while Aaron was away or in the middle of some night or at any moment the fellow took a notion through his mind to stand up and walk off. There wasn't any way Aaron could stop him short of tying him up. Nor for that matter any reason why Aaron would want to. The Indian was a free man and welcome to go if he dang pleased.

Aaron got the meat to boiling and gave the weary, worn-down Indian some herb tea to suck on and took a little of the tea for himself while he was at it. Then he hunkered close by the Indian—who was pretending to sleep again although Aaron could see plain enough that he was wide awake—and said, "Lo. Hey there. Wake up, you!"

The Indian's eyes opened about halfway.

"You see this knife you took outa my pack?" He retrieved the article and held it up for the Indian to see. If the Indian had any reaction to being shown the weapon he'd tried to steal, the emotion was thoroughly hidden behind a carefully guarded expression. "It's no good. Not sharp. See?" By way of demonstration he drew the blunt edge over his arm, pressing down good and hard, managing to create a thin red line where he roughed up his own skin but certainly not coming close to drawing any blood. "No good." He shook his head. "You want something better than this thing, Lo."

Aaron tossed the knife blank onto the trade bale again

and pulled out the one knife he'd finished and was carrying for his own use.

It was a handsome enough thing, the haft made of a section of antler that he had laboriously shaped and smoothed and polished so that it looked quite appealing.

The blade was sharp too. Between the use of native rock to rough it in and the whetstone Emilio had given him, Aaron had put an edge on the cheap trade knife sharp enough to shave with. If the man doing the shaving was tough enough to stand a little agony, that is.

Still, the knife genuinely sharp. For utility purposes, that is, not shaving.

"Best for you to take this one, Lo. I'll work on the other for myself and use my old folding knife in the meantime. But you, you might be needing something sooner than that. Here." Aaron smiled at the end of the spiel, which he knew good and well the Indian couldn't understand any more than Aaron could fathom his language. Or Emilio's. "Here," he repeated, holding the handsome knife out to the wounded man.

For the first time there was a reaction, if only a very brief one, in the Indian's eyes. They widened. Just a mite, but Aaron was sure he saw them grow the least bit wider as the gesture seemed to startle the Indian.

But then when he thought about it that was probably reasonable. After all, the Indian didn't know what he was being told. All he could be sure of was that this strange white man had found him when he tried to get away, brought him back to camp . . . and then took out a knife to wave in front of him.

Likely the poor fellow thought he was being threatened, never mind the mild tone of voice.

Aaron smiled again and in broad gestures made something of a show out of reversing the knife so that he was holding it by the blade and extended the deer-horn handle out to the Indian.

"It's yours," Aaron said, offering it.

Hesitantly, as if expecting some sort of trap, the Indian

reached out. Accepted the knife. He said something in his own wildly incomprehensible tongue.

"Yeah, well, I hope what you said was friendly," Aaron responded with another smile.

And while he was on a roll he plunged on with some more gift giving, accompanying all of it with overly broad hand and arm gestures to make his intentions clear. He gave the Indian a pair of trade blankets, a magnifying glass so the poor fellow could start a fire without having to use up much of his limited strength, a handful of beads, and nearly all the meat Aaron had in camp.

"This stuff isn't so much but it's more than you had when I found you," he said and, grinning, added, "More than what you were gonna walk off with on your own too, so I don't feel so awful bad about how little it is."

The Indian said something that sounded solemn and serious, then closed his eyes. This time Aaron didn't think he was pretending about being asleep.

Chapter
Twenty-one

I

The spirits must have entered Red Beard's head and were commanding him now. Either that or the white man was daft. One or the other of those.

Whatever the reason or reasons for this madness, Talks To Ghosts was grateful for his unexpected good fortune. Imagine. A fine, handsome knife and blankets and a burning glass too. Incredible. Sleeping Fawn would be impressed. The burning glass would warm more than bits of kindling, Talks To Ghosts anticipated with a hint of smile drawing his lips tight.

Why, it was quite probable that Sleeping Fawn would be pleased to be his wife now. And not only because of the burning glass that would lighten her burdens and make it possible for her to show off among the other wives.

After all, it is not every husband who can die and yet return to his people a rich man. Well, more or less. Return anyway as a man with a burning glass and a handsome knife and meat to fill his wife's parfleche.

Talks To Ghosts sat in the warmth of the morning sun—his sleep was late this morning; he had been truly exhausted yesterday evening when he fell asleep while waiting for Red Beard to catch and kill him—and thought about the homecoming he could look forward to.

It would be good to see his people again. Those who remained alive. Surely the Kiowa did not kill them all. Most should have escaped. With luck perhaps Talks To Ghosts himself was the only one of the people who were killed by the Kiowa. That thought pleased and mightily amused him, and he hid a smile behind a blank expression as Red Beard prepared a breakfast for them both and handed Talks To Ghosts a short plank of split aspen loaded with meat roasted over coals. No weak broth this time but good, solid meat. Talks To Ghosts' belly ached for meat, and he practically snarled as he bit and chewed on the rich red deer meat.

When he could hold no more, Talks To Ghosts thanked the white man, knowing full well that Red Beard could not understand even the simplest of words but feeling impelled to speak his mind regardless.

Red Beard said something in return, the bright, fluffy beard parting in a broad grin as he did so.

Red Beard stood and—he did not know better and so Talks To Ghosts forgave him—touched Talks To Ghosts lightly on the shoulder, then lifted the offending hand in a small gesture and turned away, taking his musket and walking off up the defile in the same direction Talks To Ghosts had tried to flee.

Hunting, Talks To Ghosts concluded. Red Beard had given virtually all the food away and now he was going hunting for more.

It would be no great thing for him to bring down another deer. After all, Red Beard had the musket. With the gun a man could kill all the meat he wished.

Talks To Ghosts watched Red Beard out of sight and then, his belly warm and heavy with food for the first time since the Kiowa killed him, stood and began preparations to leave. He would go. But not until he felt strong enough. In the meantime there was much to do. Red Beard gave him the better part of a yearling buck to take with him, and the meat would spoil unless Talks To Ghosts did something to prevent that.

Using the sharp knife Red Beard gave him, Talks To Ghosts began paring the deer meat into thin strips for drying.

He cut the meat thin and draped it over the outer branches of the scrub oak that grew thick along the slopes of the gully where Red Beard chose to camp. If the sun was bright enough and the air dry enough, one day in the sunlight would be enough to preserve the meat and keep it safe from rot.

And if Red Beard brought more meat into camp later, Talks To Ghosts would show him how to dry that too. That seemed a small enough repayment for bringing Talks To Ghosts back to life again.

Talks To Ghosts kept himself busy in that manner for the remainder of the morning, and while he worked a low, muted chant ran through his mind and rumbled deep inside his chest.

The chant, he surprised himself to notice, was one of contentment.

II

Talks To Ghosts stood and looked around with—it took him a moment to correctly identify the unusual emotion—with something approaching sadness. A reluctance at the very least.

It had been—what?—ten, twelve days since he tried to escape from Red Beard. During that time Talks To Ghosts had done little but eat, sleep, and dream of what it would be like to be back with his people.

Now he was rested and stronger than he had any right to expect. Now he felt up to leaving again. But this time he would leave with dignity. This time he would pack what he thought he could carry and walk away without fear.

The white man he called Red Beard was odd. So very

strange. But not cruel and not greedy. That perhaps more than anything else was a source of amazement to Talks To Ghosts. It was always his understanding that white men were by their nature both cruel and greedy. And perhaps most of them were. But not Red Beard.

Talks To Ghosts knew now that he had nothing to fear from this strange white man and so he could return to his people from death itself and tell them his amazing stories about Red Beard and about the dark-skinned white men from the south who now were so busy destroying Horse Camp with their foul buildings made of mud and about the other marvels Talks To Ghosts saw and dreamed while he was yet dead. Ah, there was much to tell.

Yet anxious though he was to return to his own, Talks To Ghosts felt almost sad to be leaving this place. These past few days, once he realized Red Beard did not wish to sell him away from sunlight, he had been happy here.

Red Beard fed and cared for him, and all Talks To Ghosts had to do these past days was eat and allow his body to heal and listen to the soft whisperings of the spirits. These days had been good ones, and he suspected he might never know such idle luxury again. Still, he felt strong now and the time was come for him to seek his own.

It would be good to sit with Black Otter or share a pipe with Short Knife or invite his neighbors to eat from the kettle of food Sleeping Fawn would prepare for Talks To Ghosts and his guests.

Sleeping Fawn. Talks To Ghosts wondered how it would be with her now that he was no longer dead. Had she taken another husband already? That was possible. After all, without Talks To Ghosts she had no one to bring meat for her to cook. Not that Talks To Ghosts had ever brought in so very much for the pot.

The truth, he supposed, was that Sleeping Fawn likely was glad to be shut of him when the Kiowa killed him. He wondered what her reaction would be when she looked up from her fire and saw Talks To Ghosts approaching.

It might, he thought, be very funny indeed to see the expression on Sleeping Fawn's face at that moment. Oh, he was looking forward to it. He smiled, anticipating the quiet deliciousness of the thought.

And smiled again at another thought almost equally funny to him. Red Beard. Ha! It seemed hardly possible, but Talks To Ghosts almost would have sworn that Red Beard never saw anyone dry meat before.

The white man seemed amazed by the ancient, simple process and observed Talks To Ghosts closely that first day, then began hunting at a feverish pace that he maintained ever since. These past few days whenever Red Beard was not hunting he was busy cutting meat and drying it, even going so far as to build drying racks—under Talks To Ghosts' direction for the first few—after they ran out of space on the bushes to lay out the strips of fresh meat.

Talks To Ghosts had no idea why Red Beard would want so much. After all, fresh meat tastes so very much better than dried. And with a musket to shoot game with Red Beard need not fear running out of fresh meat for his pot.

Still, who can understand the ways of a white man? Even, or especially, one so unusual as Red Beard? Talks To Ghosts was not going to worry about the aberrations of the white man who had befriended him or . . .

Befriended? Was that a reasonable way to think of what Red Beard had done for him? Well, perhaps it was. In a manner of speaking. Certainly Red Beard went far beyond simple kindness to a stranger. Perhaps in a way what he did for Talks To Ghosts was indeed a sort of friendship.

Talks To Ghosts shrugged and picked up the bundle of possessions that were now his. He had a willow withe basket loaded with dried meat, his two blankets, his handsome knife, and, wonder of wonders, the treasured burning glass that Red Beard so casually gave to him. Talks To Ghosts felt positively rich for the first time in his life. When he returned to his people, he thought, he would have to give a feast for his many friends. The meat would go for that purpose. As for the burning glass, well, it remained to be seen whether he would give that to Sleeping Fawn. If Sleeping Fawn proved no longer to be his wife, then it would be foolish to give the burning glass to her. And wouldn't she squirm and grumble if she spurned him only to discover too late that Talks To Ghosts finally had the burning glass that she had coveted for so long. Ah, such an irony that would be.

Not that Talks To Ghosts hoped that such a thing would come to be. But if it did, well, it would be funny. That was all.

With a sigh, Talks To Ghosts shouldered his bundle and his basket and looked about him for one last time.

Red Beard was, as usual, off somewhere hunting more meat to dry. Even if the white man had been here there were no words between them that Talks To Ghosts could have used to express his ... what? ... gratitude? It would have been difficult for Talks To Ghosts to say the things that should be said even if there were words. And since there were not ... this way was perhaps the easier.

Talks To Ghosts took up his things and as a final gesture broke off a cedar branch and laid it beside the fire pit to point out the path he would take. He hoped Red Beard might understand the implied trust that lay behind that volunteered information. And if not, no harm was done anyway. After all, it was unlikely that Talks To Ghosts would ever again see Red Beard.

Talks To Ghosts grunted something that might have been taken for a good-bye of sorts, then began the long walk in search of his own kind.

Chapter
Twenty-two

I

Emilio was peeved. He was sweaty and tired and his feet hurt. Two of the lambs—stupid creatures sheep are and so very aggravating—got lost from the rest of the flock in the late morning and he spent practically the entire remainder of the day looking for the foolish little beasts. And when he found them what happened? The bigger of the two acted like the whole thing was his fault—imagine—and butted him right in the belly. The spot was still sore and it had been the better part of an hour ago that it happened. Bah! Damned sheep. Stupid damned sheep.

He hazed the flock inside the scantling fence he and Consuela had worked together to build, he with the thought of keeping the sheep safely enclosed, she with the thought of keeping the miserable cantankerous stupid things out of her garden.

Emilio was halfway to the house, the fine stone house that had been built largely through the kind assistance of the yanqui Aaron, before he realized that the burros were also in the corral.

That is, he realized to begin with that they were *there*.

The burros were supposed to be gone. Aaron came and borrowed them, what? A week ago? Week and a half? Something like that. Now they were back. One does not so easily hide half a dozen good-sized burros in a bare enclosure of such small size. But the fact had not particularly registered until now.

Emilio reversed direction and went back to the corral to check on the furry-eared creatures. So much more pleasant to have around than sheep, eh? So much nicer and easier to get along with. Sheep are incredibly stupid. Burros as pleasant as sheep are dumb.

Ah, they were all there and all in good flesh. No harm had come to them. Emilio worried about them when they were away. Not that he did not trust Aaron. Of course he did. And how could he deny such a small request after Aaron virtually constructed the fine stone house that Emilio and Consuela now shared. But even so Emilio had been concerned. A little bit.

Now he felt much better from knowing the friendly little gray beasts of burden were safely home. That, of course, meant that Aaron was back too. And that in turn meant that tonight there would be fresh meat.

Aaron for some odd reason that was perhaps understood only in the strange thought processes of yanquis—all of whom seemed to be at least a little bit daft what with their frantic bursts of energy and their legendary impatience— Aaron for whatever reasons of his own had lately taken to killing vast numbers of whatever game he could put beneath the muzzle of his musket.

The local deer were not enough for him, and so he had begun ranging far out and shooting buffalo too. Or elk or antelope or anything else of sufficient size that he could get within range of his buck and ball.

That was why he needed the use of Emilio's burros, to carry back all the meat and hides that he took.

The hides were staked out to dry and then piled inside the jacal that used to be Emilio and Consuela's house. The meat was cut into thin strips and jerked on frames that were sturdy enough to remain permanently in place.

It was all very strange to Emilio, and he often wished that he and Aaron shared a language so some small measure of understanding might be achieved.

Even without that, however, there was no question that the loan should be cheerfully made. After all, he and Consuela were getting the better of the bargain. Not only did Aaron assume responsibility for the burros while he had them, meaning that neither Emilio nor Consuela had to feed or water the burros as part of the daily regimen, whenever Aaron returned he brought fresh meat with him, hump and loin and hams to jerk, tongue and ribs and brains to cook fresh. Whenever Aaron returned there was a virtual feast. Consuela did the cooking while Emilio and Aaron provided the appetites. How could any man resist such a bargain as that?

Emilio looked only briefly at the burros and then, satisfied that all was well with them, he hurried to his house, where Consuela even now should be busy preparing a huge meal for the three of them.

Already his mouth was watering at the thought of fresh tongue and of ribs roasted over a bed of coals. Emilio increased his pace, practically trotting the last little distance.

II

Emilio's belly was full, warm and full, filled with fresh buffalo tongue sliced thin and then braised over the coals of hard pinyon. Could anything be better? Of a certainty nothing could. Well, nothing of food, that is. And for Emilio these days the only pleasure available to him was food, it seemed.

Not that he was complaining. Much. For what would be the point when there was no one to listen save Consuela, and any complaint directed toward her would only serve to make her feel worse than she already did. And she, large as an elephant was said to be or perhaps somewhat larger, surely had enough to fret about as things already were.

Emilio belched loudly and gave a wink and a grin in

return for Consuela's corrective glare. She only glared the harder, but Emilio continued to grin at her and after a moment she relented, the harshness of her expression melting into a smile to match his.

"Ah, little one, it is good to see you smile again," he told her.

"I smile often," she said.

"No. But you once did. I hope you shall again."

Consuela frowned. Then shrugged. "It will not be long now, I think."

"The baby?"

She nodded.

"You aren't . . ."

Consuela laughed. "No, silly, not now. But I think, oh, another few weeks. Then we shall see."

Emilio smiled. That would be good. The waiting, the worrying, they would end then. Once the child was born . . . he did not know exactly how their lives would be changed by the coming of the small one. But he was sure there would be changes. And changes must surely be for the better, no? It was to be hoped so. Always it was to be so hoped.

He stood, carrying his soiled utensils to the bucket on the sideboard and piling them in to be washed later. He belched again, careful to avoid being so noisy about it this time, and reached for his sombrero.

"You are going out?"

"Do you mind?"

"Of course not. One thing only."

"Yes?"

"Bring in a pail of water before you go, would you?"

"One only?"

"Two then."

"Two only?"

"Stop now or I shall want four, eight, who knows how many."

"Two," he said quickly lest she make good on such a burdensome threat.

"You will not gamble tonight, will you?" Consuela asked.

"Not much. Enough to double our flock but no more."

Her expression became quickly solemn. "Hern ... Emilio!"

"Don't worry. I will not gamble. Not even a little. I promise." He knew what she was thinking. Poor Adolfo Gomez had a run of bad luck—combined with obstinate stupidity—and in one night managed to lose everything he owned. In that single evening he was reduced to hauling water and wood in exchange for whatever scraps might come his way. His wife and his two small children were little more than beggars now. It was a thing that terrified Consuela and probably every other woman in the community.

Satisfied with Emilio's assurances, Consuela was able to venture a lighthearted parting. "If you do gamble tonight, win. And if you win, bring me diamonds."

"One for each ear," he pledged.

"And a huge one for my bosom."

"For your bosom I can manage, but do not ask me to find a diamond suitable for your belly. I doubt I could find a melon big enough to be noticed on such a mountain as that."

Consuela made a face, and Emilio went out into the night.

III

He found the men, a surprisingly large percentage of them, gathered in a grove close to the ford where the road crossed the river. Someone had built a fire. Someone else brought a bucket of pulque made from the local cactus. Emilio contributed some tidbits of grilled tongue that Consuela had ready for him by the time her water buckets were filled. It was a congenial group who gathered virtually every night, not every man in the community coming on every evening but everyone making an appearance sooner or later.

"Emilio! *Hola, amigo*."

"*Hola*, Rodrigo. Hector. Juan." He upended a short chunk of sawed cottonwood log and used it for a stool, squeezing in between Diego Torreon and Rodrigo Hernandez.

"Pulque?"

"Thank you." A dipper made from dried gourd floated in the milky liquid. Emilio drank deep of it. The beverage had a smoky, musty flavor. And a kick that spread a sort of heat through his belly that was quite unlike the kind given by the very warmest or best of foods. "Ah!"

"Have some more."

"*Gracias*. I believe I shall." And so he did.

"You want to play the dice tonight, Emilio?"

"We shall see, Rodrigo. We shall see." He helped himself to another dipper of the pulque.

The bucket passed to other hands, and the slow, muted conversations flowed like honey oozing smooth and sweet from the comb. Emilio closed his eyes and let the pleasure of the night spread through him.

"The eagles were back today. Did you see them?"

"Eagles. Bah. The devil's own fowl, they should all burn in hell."

"They took a lamb from Del Garza's flock and tried to steal another from Martine."

"Tried only?"

"He threw a rock and made the bird miss its strike. The lamb was cut on the head but not carried off."

"Lucky man."

"Huh. Not in all things."

There was the sound of soft laughter. "Lucky for the rest of us, though. Is that not so, Diego?"

Again there was laughter. Emilio opened his eyes and raised an eyebrow.

"You know, Emilio," Torreon said with a wink and a dig of his elbow into Emilio's ribs.

"Not Emilio. He has a young and pretty wife of his own, no? Emilio does not need the same things that we do."

"Don't tell me that. Emilio's lady is pretty indeed. But she is ... what is it now, Emilio? Ten months due with child? Eleven? Long enough that you must be tired of your bed being cold, no?"

Emilio felt a flush of embarrassment bring heat into his cheeks. That was foolish and all the more embarrassing, but he could not help it. The reaction was quite beyond his control.

"See? Did I tell you?" Diego's voice was triumphant. "But do not worry, friend Emilio. If you have need of relief, see Martine's pretty daughter. A small present is all she asks."

"A small present now or the promise of one some time later on," another voice put in gaily.

"And you don't even have to worry about knocking her up," Rodrigo advised. "She is already carrying a little bastard."

"A soldier's brat, it is said."

"She has no shame, that one."

"Luckily for us."

The men laughed loudly at that one.

"We should invite her here some night, eh? Give her a little pulque and we can all have some of that."

"But soon. Before her belly becomes too big for us to enjoy her."

Emilio felt sick.

Serafina. Beautiful, gentle, sweet Serafina. What went so terribly wrong that she would become soiled goods to be passed like dirty linen among the menfolk here?

Emilio stood, his head swimming just a little from the effects of the pulque.

"Where are you going, Emilio? You can't leave so soon."

"Hey, we haven't even brought out the dice yet. Won't you try your luck tonight?"

Emilio shook his head mutely. His luck? Ha! He had no luck. Not in love. Not in anything. Not, at least, in anything that was of worth.

He turned away, ignoring the jibes of the other men,

and walked blindly into the darkness. And he paid no attention, he would have sworn that he did not, to the fact that his feet carried him unconsciously not toward his own stone house but toward the jacal of Hector Martine.

In any event he was too blinded by misery to care where he went. Or why.

Chapter
Twenty-three

I

Talks To Ghosts squirmed and twisted. There was something sharp digging into the pad of soft muscle between his hip and his ribs, and no matter how he turned or wriggled the object continued to annoy.

If he did not know better he would think the thing followed after him. He would find a new position, a comfortable position, and try to sleep. Then a few breaths later he would begin to feel the intrusion. Only a little at first. The very smallest of discomforts. A bump. A pebble. No more than that. But that was to begin. The object grew as if in size and sharpness alike, and soon the tiny intrusion became a jagged spearpoint presence that dug into his flesh and gouged away at his peace of mind and after more minutes passed he could think of, and feel, very little else.

It was maddening.

He knew what he had to do. He just didn't want to go to the trouble of doing it. He was too sleepy to want to be awakened so completely as would be necessary if he set out to remove the unknown, unseen, too thoroughly felt dagger. Or whatever the cursed thing was.

Still, it was inevitable that soon or late he would have to sit up, shift his bedding, and remove the miserable object. Either that or find an entirely new place to sleep. And that he did not at all want to do. This shelter was ideal, the best he had found in days, and he did not want to give it up.

So, reluctant but resigned, he pushed away the blanket Red Beard gave him and sat upright, careful to avoid cracking his skull—that portion of his body had sustained quite enough damage lately—on the dark, angled slab of rock that lay over top of his bed.

He pulled away that blanket and then its twin, the one he was using to cover the pine tips from which his bed was fashioned.

It was amazing, he thought, that he could feel anything through all of that. But he could. Oh, he most certainly could. He made a sour face and felt around amongst the pine cuttings first, thinking perhaps it was a bit of stubborn bough that bothered him. But all the stems were soft and tender and he could find none that wandered into an upright position and so dig into his flesh.

He could find nothing in the bed itself, and so piece by piece as he examined the bedding in the offending spot he removed it all and laid everything aside until he was down to bare and—or so he thought earlier—quite innocent sand.

There! With a grunt of most unexpected effort he uprooted the sharp . . . sharp what? He had no idea. It was sharp-tipped, yes, but it felt too smooth and rounded elsewhere to be the stray rock he might have expected, much less the flint spearhead his sore flesh swore to.

It was too dark to examine the thing immediately, so Talks To Ghosts took some of his bedding and with it stirred the coals of his evening's supper fire to create a quick, bright blaze as the oily pine took fire. The sudden blaze gave off good light. And smelled nice too. There is very little, Talks To Ghosts thought, that smells quite so good as fresh pine burning.

He looked at the thing he was holding and scowled. It was a piece of broken pot, the sort of thing small amounts of grain might be carried in. Or water. Whatever.

That was not so unusual. Pots are fragile and often broken. And he knew when he chose this place that he was far from the first to visit here. The stone roof at the edge of the protecting overhang was black with the smoke of countless past fires, so many and so old that a heavy, varnishlike patina had built up over the years and now lay like a hard, thin skin over the rock itself. So no, he was certainly not the first to take shelter here, merely the latest in a chain of visitors who spread through many generations of people. It was no surprise to him at all that some of those may have left behind a forgotten arrowhead here or a bit of broken pottery there.

No, the thing that surprised him now was the appearance of the pot itself. It was unlike any he had seen before. It was . . . crude, that was it. The pottery itself seemed very crude. There was practically no decoration on the outer surface, and what little there was seemed no more than aimless daubs of ash or charcoal applied before firing.

Even the mix of the clay seemed crude to him. And Talks To Ghosts knew virtually nothing about the making of pots. That was a skill undertaken most often by people who lived dull, stationary lives, not the proud wanderers who were Talks To Ghosts' people.

Even so, Talks To Ghosts was familiar with pots and pottery. He had seen it, felt it, been exposed to it for virtually all his life.

Never had he seen anything remotely like this. It . . . felt wrong. The surface textures were gritty, and when he ran his thumb over one of the sharp, broken edges on this piece, the material was so brittle that it crunched and crumbled away from his touch. No wonder the pot was broken. It was poorly made to start with.

Talks To Ghosts tossed another handful of pine tips on the fire to revive the quickly failing light, then peered up at the black veneer that covered the stone ceiling that protected him from the elements beyond.

He could not help but wonder who the people were who came before him. And who would come to this place later when Talks To Ghosts and his people were passed from the world of air and water into whatever lay beyond. It was a daunting question, Talks To Ghosts found, and he completely forgot the discomfort that had wakened him.

What was? What would yet be?

The spirits were silent on both subjects he found as he turned the bit of broken pot over in his hands, over and over again, wishing vainly that the homely object would allow him access to the shades of whoever made it and whatever hand employed it . . . however long ago.

II

No matter how often he saw it, no matter how many times he did it, the fact was that the process was, remained, and probably always would be quite magical to him.

Talks To Ghosts' lips drew back into a smile as the bright yellow heat turned brown powdered bark into black curls. The curls twisted and writhed from the effects of the heat, and within moments the first tiny wisp of pale smoke rose from the spot.

Talks To Ghosts' smile turned into a grin as, lips pursed, he gently breathed on the wee, smoking coal.

A core of red appeared inside the focused yellow pin-point, and Talks To Ghosts blew again. Smoke swirled and was whisked away, and then in a sudden and dramatic transition there was a flare of newborn flame that appeared like a leaf bud, sprouted swiftly, and grew into a blossom of intense heat. Just that easily, just that quickly, Talks To Ghosts had the beginnings of a fire.

Pleased, he sat upright, rocking back on his heels and reaching for the shaved curls of dry wood he had prepared in readiness for this moment. He held one carefully over the newborn flame, keeping it there until it took fire. He dropped it and held another, then several, then a small handful of the easily fired kindling.

Moments. No more than that, and he had a brisk fire blazing. It was truly magic.

Talks To Ghosts chanted softly under his breath while he added wood to his fire and then began to heat the water that he would use to make a tea of herbs and to create a stew using the meat he himself dried from what Red Beard gave to him.

He still had meat and at this season there were berries to gather and wild onions to dig and cattail roots to roast and peel. He would not be hungry while he waited here for the people to pass by on their way off the grassy plains and back into the mountains that nurtured and protected them.

Better, he had decided, to wait for them to come to him rather than risk missing them on the huge, empty grasslands if he were to go in search of the band. Besides, Talks To Ghosts enjoyed this solitude, enjoyed being able to spend his waking time in thoughtful contemplation.

There was so much that he did not understand and that he wanted to think about. The experience of dying at the hands of the Kiowa. The coming of the brown-skinned white men. The strange behavior of Red Beard. And most of all the visions the spirits showed to him when he was dead. It was all very unsettling. There was much that he wanted still to know.

Chapter
Twenty-four

I

This was the day he'd been waiting for, the one in anticipation of which he'd worked so hard and carefully.

Aaron stood on the north bank of the Purgatory and watched the wagons rumble down the path from distant Raton Pass.

This was a mule-drawn train, not oxen, so he knew the wagons were not those of Mr. Matthewson. It was inevitable that Aaron would have to face up to Matthewson someday. But not today. Not now. And not, if Aaron had anything to say about it, until Aaron was in a position to negotiate reasonable terms for the, um, freedoms he'd taken with Matthewson's bale of trade goods.

After all, it never had been formally established—not exactly—that Aaron's pay owed was equal in value to the food and the goods that "left" the train at the same time Aaron did.

Still, this group of American traders now approaching was exactly what Aaron needed if his plan was to succeed. He stood with arms folded—and fingers crossed—waiting for the first of the wagons to splash through the rock-strewn ford and climb out onto dry ground again.

"Howdy."

"Howdy your own self." The driver of the freight rig squinted closely at the red-haired man confronting him, then turned his head and spat a thin stream of yellow tobacco juice. "Something I can do for you, neighbor?"

"Could be something you and me can do for each other."

"Izzat a fact?"

"If you're the wagon boss it could be," Aaron responded.

"Oh, I'm the boss, all right. Name's Sproule, Leon Sproule, but you can call me Mister." The wagon driver grinned.

"Aaron Jenks. But you can call me the fella who's gonna add to your profits."

"I dunno, Jenks. Keep this up an' I might could start liking you."

"Pull over in that grove there, Mr. Sproule, and give your teams a rest. I got buffalo ribs enough for you and all your crew laid out on the fires, and I've dug out a couple troughs where you can water your stock."

"Accommodating, ain't you. An' by the way, Aaron"— Sproule's grin got wider—"you can call me Leon."

"Obliged," Aaron said, turning to guide Sproule's lead wagon into the grove where everything—including all Aaron's hopes—lay in readiness.

II

"So you see, Leon, it's pretty simple. I sell my goods to you here in Mexico but you don't pay me for them until your next trip west. Then you pay me not in cash, see, but in other goods. Trade goods, gunpowder, lead, things like that. I'll use those goods to get more. Hides, dried meat, dried squash, and the like that I can get from dealing with the

Mexicans. Skins and more hides that I can trade for with
the Indians. Then on your way back east next summer we do
the deal again. You and me both make a profit, and everybody comes out ahead."

Sproule smiled and nodded and helped himself to
another succulent rib. His beard was already greasy from
the half dozen such he'd consumed to this point, but if it
bothered him he was able quite manfully to keep from
showing the discomfort. He buried his face cheek deep in
the dripping buffalo rib and chewed loudly for a moment
before he tossed the bone aside and, wiping his mouth on
the back of his wrist, belched loudly. "That was good, kid."

"So what do you think?"

"About you and me going partners?"

"I wouldn't call it partners, exactly," Aaron said. "I
wouldn't expect any such a thing as that."

Sproule grunted, gave a halfheartedly yearning look in
the direction of the remaining ribs, and reluctantly shook his
head. "Any more an' I'll bust clean open."

"You still haven't said—"

"Tell you what, kid," Sproule said as if he hadn't
heard.

"Yes?"

"I'm not interested in no partner sort of deal. But I tell
you what I would do."

"What's that?"

"I'd buy your hides and, say, four hundred pound o'
that jerked meat. Pay you cash right here on the spot.
Twenty-five cents for a buff'lo robe, ten cent for a deerskin.
And five dollars a hundredweight for the meat. How does
that sound to you?"

"That sounds like about twenty-five cents on the dollar
compared with what those items are worth."

"Worth to who? Not t' me. An' worth where, eh?
There's that t' consider. If they're worth more t' you then
keep 'em. I don't give a damn what you do."

"You're trying to take advantage."

Sproule shrugged, thought it over for a moment, and

reached for another rib. Aaron had the thought that it would not necessarily be a bad thing if Sproule did burst wide apart from eating this extra rib.

"I said—"

"I heard you," Sproule mumbled past a mouthful of fat meat. "You got somebody else t' sell to, do you?"

"That isn't the point," Aaron began, but Sproule cut him off with a grin.

"Course it's the point," the wagon boss said with obvious satisfaction. "You got no wagons t' carry your hides t' where there's a market an' you got no market for selling them out here. But if you wanta hang on to goods that you got no use for your own self and no way to sell, why, you do as you please. As for me, I made you the best offer I'm likely to. Now you decide what you wanta do, boy, because soon as my men and me finish eating we're pulling for Independence an' the Ewe Nited States. You understand me?"

Aaron understood. All too well. Sproule had him over the proverbial barrel, and both men knew it.

Aaron thought on it a moment and then, with a sigh, he smiled and looked Leon Sproule in the eye.

"Mr. Sproule, sir."

"Yeah, kid?"

"Go to hell." Aaron's smile got bigger. "*Mister* Sproule, sir."

III

"And that's my proposition, Mr. Donnels. It would be fair to both parties," Aaron said to the wagon boss who sat across the fire from him. Hugh Donnels was the third wagon master Aaron tried to trade with. Neither of the others had been the least bit interested in an honest deal. Although either would gladly have taken advantage of a one-sided agreement.

"Young fellow," Donnels said, leaning forward to ignite a sprig of straw in the fire and use it to light a clay pipe that long ago was stained dark brown by the combination of tobacco juices and sustained heat, "I'm going to be honest with you."

"Yes, sir?"

"You won't find a taker for your proposition."

Aaron tried to interject a comment, but Donnels stopped him with an upraised palm. "Wait a second now and listen to what I'm saying."

Aaron reluctantly clamped his mouth shut and waited for the lean Missourian to continue.

"The reason no one will take up your deal, reasonable though it would be, is that there's talk about you. I believe you know a man named Matthewson."

"Yes, I do," Aaron admitted.

"And he certainly knows you. He's told all the Americans in the Santa Fe trade that you're poison. Now maybe you are, maybe you aren't. I'm not gonna get myself involved in whatever lies between you and Matthewson, Jenks. I'll leave whatever is between the two of you to be worked out by the two of you. The thing is, I won't risk the goodwill of the others on this road by striking any bargains with you. That could come back on me at either or both ends of the road. There aren't so many of us involved in the trade, and we rely on each other's help. Get a bad reputation among the others, and it could go hard on one. A man could find his credit questioned in Saint Louis or his reliability in doubt in Santa Fe. You know what I mean?"

Aaron wasn't sure that he did, but he nodded anyway.

"Little enmities can grow into big problems. Especially when you're in a foreign country where the authorities aren't above playing favorites. All us Americans have to stand together in Santa Fe or none of us will succeed. So as much as I might like you personally, Jenks, and as much as I might think of your proposition, there's no way I'd risk making an agreement with you and alienating every other trader on the road. And the truth is that I think you'll find this true with anyone else you approach with your idea. It's a fine plan and it otherwise would have worked. But not for you. Not so long as Matthewson says you're a pariah."

"I thank you for telling me, Mr. Donnels. Have another rib?"

"You take disappointment well, Jenks."

"If I thought getting mad would make you change your mind, sir, I'd be hollering at you right this very minute."

"I wish you luck, Jenks. But I expect you'll have to look for some other business opportunity if you expect to cash in on that luck."

"Yes, sir. I understand."

The wagon master drew deep on his pipe.

Chapter
Twenty-five

I

Stupid bullheaded hard-nosed arrogant damned American, Emilio thought. Not for the first time. Aaron was a genuinely nice fellow. But he was dumb. Why could he not learn to speak a civilized language? Was his tongue so numbed from speaking the ugliness that was English that he could not see the beauty of Spanish?

The best part of an hour they had been talking—well, what passed for talk between them, which consisted as much of hand movements and broad arm gestures and contortions of the face as it did of spoken sounds—and still Emilio did not know what it was Aaron was trying to explain to him.

Something to do with the burros. That much he had figured out.

But what? Already he had agreed to loan Aaron the short-legged beasts. As he often did. Whenever Aaron wanted to go out in search of more meat to dry. So what was so very different about it this time? Emilio did not understand what it was Aaron was trying to convey with his mimed explanation. Something being chopped in half? A buffalo hide or pile of hides? Perhaps. Emilio was not sure. Over and over again Aaron made motions as if dividing something between himself and Emilio. Deer hides, Emilio thought, or buffalo robes. But why would he want to do that? It would serve small purpose to cut a buffalo robe in half.

Emilio shrugged. He gave up. He pointed to the gentle burros picking at grass contained in the hayrick in the corral. "Take them," Emilio said. "Go on. Do whatever you like. I don't care. Just stop trying to explain it all to me. You are making my head to hurt and it hurts enough already from the pulque. Go on. Take them. Do what you wish."

Aaron said something back to him—in incomprehensible English, of course—and Emilio shrugged and put his hands over his ears. "No more," he said. *"No mas."* He pointed at Aaron and made a shooing gesture, sending him off in the direction of the burros. "Go."

The American grinned and said something more, then reached down to grasp Emilio's right hand. He shook the hand with vigor, pumping it and grinning broadly. Then, with a final friendly slap on Emilio's shoulder, Aaron spun and hurried off away from the corral.

Emilio, only a little bemused, went about the business that brought him here, that being the task of seeing to his flock of fat, woolly sheep.

II

"Sometimes I think the others are right," Emilio said. "Sometimes I think our friend Aaron really is as crazy as they say. Do you know what he did today?"

Consuela stopped what she was doing and looked up at him. She was kneeling on the floor, busy washing their clothes and the coarse muslin sheets, the one from her bed and the one off Emilio's pallet. She paused in her work and looked up at him, and for the first time in a considerable while Emilio saw how difficult this new life was on her.

Consuela was still beautiful. Emilio doubted even time would conquer such a beauty as hers. But she was haggard now and thin in the face. Sweat beaded on her forehead and rolled down her neck so that it darkened the cloth of her shirt between her breasts and beneath her arms.

She looked . . . like a servant, Emilio realized with a jolt. Consuela, once so delicate, now looked and in large measure acted like a common serving girl.

That impression was only augmented by the fact that she waddled now whenever she walked. She was so large in the belly at this point that it was a wonder she could get around at all.

It had been difficult for her to get onto her knees to do the washing this evening, and he knew when it came time for her to rise either he would have to help her up or she would crawl to the table and use one of the chairs like a ladder to climb her way back onto her feet.

Consuela was no longer so fine to look upon, Emilio knew. It was impossible for him, once that thought formed in his mind, to avoid comparing her now with Serafina Martine.

Poor Consuela was huge in the belly, as if she carried a melon beneath her clothing. Serafina was slim. Consuela's breasts had become bulbous and doughy, soft and drooping as they filled with milk for the child. Serafina's were taut and firm and faintly salty of flavor.

Emilio looked almost accusingly at the so-called wife he would never touch and thought of the young woman whom every man was allowed to touch and fondle. The thought of Serafina, of her undoubted beauty—and of her equally undoubted availability—aroused him.

"Emilio." She had to repeat it several times before he blinked, returning from the journeys of imagination, and said, "Yes, what is it?"

"The American. Aaron."

"What about him?"

"You were saying he did some crazy thing today?"

"Oh, yes. That." Emilio shrugged. "He wanted the use of our burros again."

Consuela nodded. "Good. The meat he brings back with him is always welcome."

"No, you don't understand. This time I thought he would take the gun and go out as always to bring meat. But this time do you know what he did?"

Consuela dutifully shook her head, then ducked low to wipe her forehead and flushed cheeks with the hem of her apron.

"He led the burros to our old house where he had his hides and bundles of jerky piled. You know?"

Consuela nodded.

"He cleaned it out. All of it. Packed everything onto the burros and left."

"Do you think . . . surely he will not steal our burros, Emilio. Surely he will bring them back again."

"I did not think of that."

"Did he take everything with him?"

"The things from his own place, you mean?"

She nodded.

Emilio frowned in thought for a moment. Then shook his head. "No. He took only the things from the old jacal. I saw nothing of the things from his camp."

"That is all right then. He will come back for those and when he does he will bring the burros back."

"Yes. But why would he do such a thing as that?"

Consuela shrugged. "Who knows. It is said that all Americans are crazy anyhow, isn't it?"

"So they say." Emilio stood and reached for his sombrero.

"Emilio, please. You are not going out again tonight, are you?"

"What of it?" he snapped, his voice and his gaze both with a cold edge to them.

"I just thought . . . never mind." Consuela dropped her eyes and reached into the wooden bucket where a lump of wet cloth lay in water made milky with the sap of the ubiquitous soapweed that some called the yucca.

"Don't wait up for me. I might be late."

He turned quickly away, not wanting to see the look in her eyes.

But damn her. Didn't she know? Didn't she know how hard it is on a man when he must be without a woman—without a *real* one, that is—in his life? In his bed?

Emilio stormed out into the night and took the by now very familiar path to the Martine jacal. His pace increased as his sense of urgency grew and before he reached the grove of cottonwoods that lined the riverbank he had begun to sweat, although whether from exertion or from anticipation he was not sure.

III

They came for him at the worst possible time. Well, almost at the worst possible.

Emilio's head felt like it was stuffed with cotton wool from the effects of the pulque, and he was sure his tongue had fur on it. Still, he had been having a fine time. Serafina was beside him, her flesh hot and slick with sweat. He grabbed hold of her, turned his face to avoid belching beneath her nose, and squeezed, perhaps too hard, with his left hand.

"Emilio . . ."

"S-sorry." He let go briefly, then groped at her again.

Serafina pushed his hand away. "It isn't that, you idiot. Can't you hear?"

"Hear wha'?"

"Outside. Someone is calling for you."

Emilio giggled. "Tell them he is not here, this Señor Esca . . . Esca . . ."—he belched again—"Escavara." It had taken him a moment to remember.

"Emilio!" Serafina chided. "Answer them. Make them go away. Papa will be angry if he hears so much noise and commotion."

The threat was far from being enough to sober Emilio but it did serve to get his attention. He scowled and listened for a moment. Sure enough there were voices outside calling for him.

"You wait, eh? I won't be long."

He pushed the blanket back and stood, a trifle wobbly, while he pulled his clothes on and stepped into his sandals. This really was rude of whoever stood outside screaming for him. He should be angry. Indeed, he decided, he *was* angry. He would . . . he would . . . he did not know what he would do. Something. Of a certainty he would do something strong and decisive and . . .

"Emilio."

"Yes?"

"Go outside. Answer them. Make them go away. Please."

"Yes of course, my pretty one. I shall . . ." His voice trailed lamely away as he forgot the path his thoughts had been taking.

"Outside, Emilio. Please."

"Of course. Immediately." He left the tiny coop—it really was a coop, having originally been intended to house chickens; the chickens, however, had not lasted long here before succumbing to an assortment of owls, foxes, and perhaps other creatures as well—where the beauteous Serafina Martine spent most of her evenings of late.

Emilio stumbled outdoors and around the corner of the low roofed shed where he relieved himself with a sigh of considerable pleasure.

"Señor Escavara, is that you?"

"It is, child, what do you want?" There was enough light from the newly risen moon for Emilio to see that a pair of small boys was addressing him. Garcia's sons? Perhaps. He was not sure.

"My mama sent us for you, señor. Please come."

Emilio frowned. "Your mama? What would she want with me?"

"She doesn't want you, señor," the smaller of the boys said, which earned him a reproving look from his brother. "If it was up to her you should stay away." The larger boy poked the smaller in the ribs. "Ow! It's what she *said*!"

"You aren't supposed to tell that part."

"Why not? You heard her yourself. Mama said—"

"Boys," Emilio interrupted, leaning on the flimsy wall of Serafina's coop so he could maintain his balance. "What is it your mother wants me to do and why does she want this of me, hm?"

"It is your wife who wants you, Señor Escavara. It is her time, and some of the women are with her now. That's why Mama sent us to find you."

Emilio blinked.

"You know, señor. The baby."

"Is it . . . ?"

The larger boy shrugged. "You want to come now? You want us to help you?"

"Yes. Yes, I do."

Emilio's head cleared considerably with the news. It occurred to him that he should feel some degree of embarrassment to know that even the small children of the settlement knew where to look for him. But later. There would be time enough to stew about that later. For now he supposed he would have to do his duty and present himself outside the house where Consuela was in labor.

He hoped, though, that this did not take long.

He was not sure how much longer Serafina would wait for him before returning to her family for the remainder of the night.

IV

They led him inside, the foolish miserable old women. Like a gaggle of stupid geese, they were. They were all smiles and vacuous grins and dumb anticipation. They acted like they expected Emilio to be as pleased as they were.

Consuela lay on the small bed, a pile of bloody cloths

pushed partially but not quite completely out of sight beneath the bed. She was pale and seemed on the verge of an exhausted slumber.

Emilio was pleased to see that she was all right. He did, after all, love her deeply and truly and was sure he always would. Although not in anything like the way these miserable women thought he did.

As for the red and wrinkled thing bundled at her side, well, that was another thing entirely, was it not?

Emilio peered at it for a moment. Then it occurred to him to ask, "What is it?"

"Not an *it*, señor, *she* is a fine and healthy baby girl. A daughter for the firstborn to you and your wife, señor. A beautiful little girl."

At last Emilio permitted himself a smile. A genuine one.

The women, who all had been watching him with suspicion if not with outright disfavor, relaxed now and smiled with him.

Emilio supposed they thought he was smiling because mother and child both survived and were healthy and whole. In truth he smiled from sheer relief. It was not something he had ever been able to discuss with Consuela, nor with anyone, but he had been in fear that the baby, if it survived, might have been a boy.

And that would have presented an awkwardness, for surely everyone, including Consuela herself, would have expected the naming of a son to honor Emilio's father and other prominent persons in the family lineage as well. And who should have been so honored. Their true father who was no longer of their family despite the flow of the blood? Some imaginary link to the long-gone Escavara line? To whom? It would have been ... uncomfortable at best. Disastrous at worst.

Thank God the fat-cheeked brat was a girl-child and no one could possibly care how it was named.

"Go on," one of the busybody women insisted with a prod at Emilio's shoulder. "Kiss your wife and your daughter, then go find somewhere else to spend the rest of this night. They don't need you stumbling about. Go on now. Go."

Emilio allowed himself to be hurried out of his own house, glancing upward toward the moon as he returned to the crisp, cool air outdoors.

He wondered if Serafina was still awake and if so could he convince her to return to the coop with him.

Chapter
Twenty-six

I

They came. Up from the lowlands they came, the ponies heavy with the meat and the hides gathered through the summer months. The people moved slowly into the protection of the high country where soon the winter snows would close the passes and make them safe from all enemies.

They came. But there were not so many of them as there were in the spring when they moved down onto the broad, rolling grasslands.

Talks To Ghosts watched the dear, familiar shapes move closer and ever closer. He watched. And he mourned. For there were those who should have been with the people and were not and would not be ever again.

The Kiowa, of course. Talks To Ghosts felt a deep-seated heaviness in his chest because he had failed to warn the people. He should have known. He should have seen. Somewhere in the signs from the spirits he should have recognized what would come. The long-ago smoke where there was no fire. It was a sign. He should have read it correctly, but he had not. And it was the people and not he alone who suffered from his failure. The leaden tightness in his chest grew tighter still, and Talks To Ghosts intoned a silent chant of sorrow and apology.

And then, when the first ponies were near, he left his place of refuge and picked his way carefully down to the path where he had known the people must eventually pass.

He was, after so long alone, home again.

II

Friends, clansmen and even his sometimes foes crowded close around him. For they were all of the people and they were all brothers, and their rejoicing was loud and ringing amid the silence of the peaks and passes. Children shouted and women babbled and dogs barked, and the men circled close around him.

A fire was quickly built and a camp hastily made, and the elders demanded an accounting of all that Talks To Ghosts experienced since the day the Kiowa killed him.

And then, finally, his belly full and the day passed into night unnoticed outside the light of the great leaping fire, finally Talks To Ghosts was done with the telling of his story and was able to ask the questions that haunted him.

Yes, the dreams he dreamt were true ones.

Yes, he was not the only one of the people who died that day. The Kiowa slaughtered little Otter Tail and old Carries Water and they cut down Woman Who Waits. All that was true. Worse, the Kiowa carried away others of the people. They took Yellow Shells, who was Tall Man's woman, and the pretty child called Mouse and the boy-child Magpie and . . . oh, yes, so sorry, Talks To Ghosts . . . they took Sleeping Fawn.

None of the missing people had been seen or heard from since the Kiowa carried them off that far distant day. If any of them would have been able to escape . . . so sorry, Talks To Ghosts, so very sorry.

Black Otter, dear and faithful Black Otter, touched

Talks To Ghosts' elbow and led him away from the pitying eyes of the others and off into the darkness.

"Think of your woman as dead, Talks To Ghosts. It is the only way."

"But she is not dead, Black Otter."

"To you she is," his friend responded with a simple logic. "Mourn her if you wish but know that she is dead."

Talks To Ghosts looked at his friend and admitted the truth. "But you don't see? That is the saddest part of it. I cannot mourn the loss of a thing I never wished to have. Sleeping Fawn was my wife but she was never my woman. I should miss her, but I do not. And because I do not I dishonor her now and dishonor the brother who knew her before me."

"Then think of this as freedom, Talks To Ghosts. In the privacy of your heart, think of this loss as an opportunity to find happiness for yourself."

"That would be even worse, don't you think? That would be even more shameful."

Black Otter shrugged. "I have never known a man more honest than you, Talks To Ghosts. Accept what is and move on."

Talks To Ghosts nodded. "Perhaps. We shall see."

"In the meantime, old friend, you will come stay in my lodge. There is always meat in the pot for you to share and a place beside my fire. You know that."

"Ah, Black Otter. What would life be without friends, um?"

"That is something you will never know, Talks To Ghosts. Not as long as I live. Nor will I know it for so long as you live."

"True." They walked back toward the great fire and the gay, noisy celebration, and Talks To Ghosts tried to feel regret or sorrow or some sense of loss at the absence of Sleeping Fawn, but he could not, and that continued to trouble him.

III

"We must find another route to take each spring and each fall," old One Stone said after drawing deep on the pipe.

"Why would we change now? We have followed this same path since the time of our grandfathers' grandfathers. We know every step of these trails. We know every watering place and shelter. I do not think there is reason to change."

"Horse Camp is no more. It is lost to us. If we do not change our path, what are we to do about Horse Camp?"

"Just because the straw hats are there is no reason to change. The straw hats are afraid of us. You saw how they all hid when we passed by them. They have no guns. They are no danger to us."

"Besides, there is the pale-skinned man with the red hair who is there now."

Talks To Ghosts' interest quickened when he heard that comment. Surely they were speaking of Red Beard. Who else could it possibly be if not him.

"That one has many things of value to trade," someone else put in. "You heard him yourself. If we bring furs to him he will trade with us. Only with us, I think. The Arapaho will not come so far south just as we do not dare go into their country to trade with the white men on the stream they call Fountain. If we trade with Bent or St. Vrain the Arapaho will find us and there will be sadness in the lodges because surely they will kill us unless we kill them first. Just the same, if we go far to the east to trade with the voyageurs on the Arkansas we may be found out by the Kiowa or even worse by the Comanche. But if we bring furs to the American at Horse Camp we will have the things we need. We can buy guns to shoot the Kiowa and the Comanche and blankets to keep our small ones warm and pretty things to keep our women happy. The American will buy furs, he said, or meat if there is enough to spare. And he will pay in goods. Gunpowder and knives. Mirrors and burning glasses. Fine beads and powdered vermilion. Even guns, I think, if we have enough furs to please him."

"I saw no guns at the red one's store."

"But we did see blankets and knives and burning glasses. We all saw those things, did we not?"

"We did," the skeptic admitted.

Talks To Ghosts thought about the burning glass that lay within his own pouch. It came from Red Beard. And many, many times he had seen the fine goods in Red Beard's bale. They were as the council said.

But what was this about a place where the people could trade for the goods they needed? There had been nothing like that at Horse Camp when Talks To Ghosts left Red Beard to make his own way home. A store? Talks To Ghosts remembered nothing like that when he lived with Red Beard.

He leaned forward, reluctant to speak up after being away from the people for so long but eager to learn of all the things that took place while he was dead. Including the things that took place with Red Beard at Talks To Ghosts' beloved Horse Camp.

It would be good, he knew, if the people had a place where they could trade. Especially if they had a place that was safe—or as much so as was possible—from their enemies like the Kiowa and the Arapaho and the Comanche.

Perhaps this, then, and not the summer's dangers was the meaning of the smoke where there was not fire.

Talks To Ghosts pondered all this in silence. He would bide his time, and when he thought the moment was right he would add his reasoning, and that of the spirits who guided him, to the discussions of the council.

Chapter
Twenty-seven

I

Aaron used to think he knew what cold was. Huh! Back in Pennsylvania he hadn't come close to understanding it. Now this . . . this was cold.

He was wearing big, bulky, awkward mittens made of wool and lined with rabbit skin, the fur side in contact with his skin . . . and still his fingers were numb and so cold they stung and ached from it.

His head was swathed thick in wool blanketing that he'd cut into eight-inch-wide strips and wrapped around so that only his eyes and nose were exposed. Yet the hairs inside his nostrils were frozen and stiff and hurt with every tiny movement while his eyes burned and watered, and thin slivers of ice built on his cheeks and in the cloth from the tears.

He hadn't had any sensation in his feet for several hours in spite of the soft, loose booties that fit over his moccasins— a seemingly barbaric fashion but infinitely more comfortable, especially in winter, than hard boots—and came to his knees. The overshoes were sheepskin, sewed with the fleece side in. Even that was not enough to keep his feet warm. Not when he was riding. It would have been better if he'd been afoot. But then that would have meant staying out in the cold that much longer. The plain truth was that there was no genuinely good solution available to him. Except, perhaps, to remain indoors until next spring. That would have been just fine, Aaron thought, in fact it would have been ideal, if he'd had a woman to stay indoors with.

Particularly if that woman was Consuela.

Since the baby was born, Consuela had become even more beautiful. If that was possible. Aaron ached with love for her every time he thought about her. He couldn't help it. Never mind that she was his partner's wife. She was simply the one woman in the world who was meant for him. He believed that. Couldn't do a damn thing about it, of course. But he knew that it was true.

Now he rapped sharply on the door of the stone house that he and Emilio together had built . . . and that they twice enlarged in the several years since.

It had been . . . what? He had to count back . . . four years since Emilio and Aaron both found themselves in the settlement—more like a town these days—that was coming to be known as El Rio de Las Animas but that some people were calling El Trinidad in honor of the Holy Trinity. Four years and a bit over, he finally decided.

Four years. And damned good luck that the American teamsters hadn't been willing to haul Aaron's hides that first season.

The partnership that grew out of convenience was a good one.

To begin with Aaron supplied the goods while Emilio contributed the transportation in the form of his shaggy little burros.

The burros had since been replaced by bigger and much stronger mules. And nowadays Emilio acted as factor, staying in place at the stone store Aaron built beside the ford and wagon road, while Aaron made the necessary trips down to Santa Fe or, twice now, all the way back east to the States so they could sell their furs and hides for cash and in

turn buy trade goods they could use to obtain more furs and
hides.

It was not a bad business. The Indians each spring
brought in furs by the bale—beaver, otter, mink, and marten,
anything the mountains might provide—and in fall when they
came back off the plains those same Indians had hides to
trade—bison, antelope, deer, and coyote—for the cheap
goods that they so prized.

The profits were wonderful. Almost embarrassing,
Aaron sometimes thought. An elderly flint musket worth a
dollar fifty in St. Louis or perhaps two dollars in Santa Fe
would trade for furs or hides worth twenty-five or as much
as thirty dollars on the banks of the Purgatory. And oddly
enough, a fine percussion gun with a rifled barrel and
modern lock would sell for perhaps twelve dollars, even
eighteen if especially well made, back in the States but
would hardly win a glance from an Indian, largely because
the Indian could find and flake his own flints to fire the
musket but would have been reduced to purchasing supplies
of the delicate percussion caps for the more modern and
presumably better weapon. That was just one of the many
things Aaron and Emilio had been required to learn in the
pursuit of their trade. That and . . . come to think of it,
Aaron scowled, just where was Emilio this evening? It was
damned cold out here.

He knocked on the door again and stamped his feet, as
much from impatience as with any hope that he might raise
some feeling in them.

"Emilio? Dammit, Emilio, open up and let me in."

II

It was Elena who opened the door. Tiny, wide-eyed,
bubbling Elena, the darling of all El Rio de Las Animas. For
after all, who could fail to be captured by such a delightful
child as Elena Escavara. Certainly she held her tio Aaron
wrapped tight around the smallest of her wee fingers.

The little girl chortled and cackled when she saw who had come calling. She threw her arms into the air demanding to be picked up and cuddled, and what choice did Aaron have but to comply? Gladly. He grabbed her up and swung her high into the air.

The child shivered and giggled, not minding the snow that fell from his capote to dust her warm flesh with cold flakes, hugging him fiercely despite the deep chill that clung to him.

Aaron laughed with her. And wished he could as openly embrace the mother as he did the child.

Consuela, as quietly beautiful still as her small, ebullient daughter, sat smiling in a rocking chair Aaron had made for her two winters past. She had a garment, one of Emilio's shirts perhaps, open in her lap and a sewing basket on the floor at her side.

The house was warm and lightly scented with the delicious odor of burning pinyon.

"You are safely home from Saint Louis, I see," she told Aaron. "I'm glad." Only then did she add, "Did all go well?"

"Couldn't have been better," Aaron told her, refraining from adding "now that I see you" as he might have wished. "We got a good price for our fur, and I've brought back enough goods to buy every hide from here to the Northwest Company's posts." The language they spoke was an amalgam of English and Spanish with Spanish perhaps taking the upper hand, as practically no one else in the town had any reason to learn English.

That, the almost physical comfort of being able to speak his own language without forethought or worry about misunderstanding, was one of the things Aaron most enjoyed about his visits back to the States. And this, the beauty of Consuela and the sweet warmth of little Elena, this was what he missed the most.

He was glad to be . . . home? Yes, he supposed this was his home now. El Rio de Las Animas, that is. Not this house. Although if only . . .

"Where is Emilio?"

Something—pain? unhappiness?—flickered briefly behind Consuela's eyes. Then her smile returned ... it never truly left her face, but for a moment there the expression was but a mask ... and she said, "He is with the other men this evening. You know?"

Aaron nodded.

"You look frozen to the marrow. Would you like coffee and something to eat before you go out again?"

He would have stayed just for the pleasure of the company, never mind that he was famished. He nodded.

"Elena dear, jump down and go get a cup and plate for Tio Aaron."

Aaron gave the child a peck on the cheek and planted her onto her own feet again. "When you're done, Elena, you will see what I brought for you from the Estados Unidos."

"For me? A present?"

Aaron couldn't help but laugh. The tot almost made him believe she was as surprised as she pretended. But when had he ever gone anywhere that he failed to bring a treat back to this little one? He bent, gave her a tap on the bottom to send her on her way, and then began digging in his pockets for the package of sweets he'd bought in distant St. Louis and carried on his person ever since. One couldn't be too careful, after all. If he'd encountered hostiles on the trip west he might have had to abandon the mule train and all their goods. But he would not have wanted to relinquish Elena's treats.

III

Sated, the fire back in his belly again thanks to Consuela's cooking—and thanks perhaps even more to Consuela's presence in the same room while he ate—Aaron pulled on his capote and overshoes and thick mittens. He bent to ruffle little Elena's sleek hair—it was already so curly there was no worry that a little more tousling might be objectionable—and gave Consuela a look of naked longing that he remembered too late to cover.

"Thank you for . . . everything."

"It was our pleasure, Tio Aaron." Her use of the word "uncle" put him gently back into his place. He was Emilio's partner. He was a friend of the family. He was, in a way, almost as if family. But there were things that he most definitely was not. And those forbidden areas should not be forgotten.

"Yes, well . . . I'll see you again, uh, soon."

Consuela nodded serenely and dipped her gaze to her sewing.

God, she was beautiful, Aaron thought in silent, useless anguish. So beautiful.

He felt a tug at his knees. Elena was giving him a hug good-bye. He picked her up and in addition to the hug was the recipient of a kiss that was sticky with the residues of candy on soft, tiny lips.

God, how lucky Emilio was. The most fortunate of men. And the most unappreciative.

Aaron went out into the cold wind once more, hunched deep into the hood of the capote, and turned toward the *taverna* started two seasons ago by Porfirio Mendez.

Chapter
Twenty-eight

I

God, he felt lousy. Sick and miserable and just plain lousy. His head ached, his belly was sour, and his tongue tasted like every sheep he owned had just crapped on it.

Emilio felt well and truly sorry for himself.

The real problem, though, was not the liquor he'd been drinking nor even the problems he was having with Serafina—damned woman insisted on going with every stinking peon who had two pesos in his pocket . . . and was willing to part with one of them—but with that damned redheaded gringo son of a pig over there.

Emilio's knees sagged and he had to hold on to the bar to keep from melting onto the floor. He blinked, his eyes rheumy and moist, and sent a baleful glare in Aaron's direction.

God, he hated Aaron. No, it was not hatred that he felt. In truth it was not. It was . . . envy. That was the truth of the matter, was it not? Emilio asked himself. Aye, of course it was.

Aaron was so easy with the child. Always laughing. Always smiling. No matter what.

Why did he ever agree to name the child Elena? It had even been his own idea, had it not? A bad idea, a terrible one . . . all the memories, all the reminders of what once was but was no more . . . God! When the damnable abomination of a brat was tiny it was Aaron who rocked and held her and who never so much as frowned when it puked on him. Even when his shirt was clean and freshly washed he scarcely seemed to notice and certainly never objected when the loathsome little bitch threw up on him.

Puked up the milk from Consuela's breasts. That was it, wasn't it? That was why the gringo did not object. The man was in love with Consuela. In truth he was. Emilio could see. He was not blind.

And Emilio could feel.

All this time and Aaron was in love with Consuela and thought Emilio did not know. Ha! He knew. He knew and he resented and yet . . . and yet there was nothing to be done about it.

Because even if Aaron was taking Consuela to bed—was he? Emilio asked himself for the ten thousandth time, was he really?—even if the two of them made the beast with two backs twice each night and three times on Sundays, there was nothing Emilio could or should do about it. Because no matter what his "dear" Consuela did or did not do, Emilio was not and never could be the cuckold that people would believe.

Emilio resented—no, dammit, he did *not* resent; or did he—the brotherly impulse that made him run away with Consuela and ensure that her child would not be a bastard.

But . . . but what of Emilio? What of the brave "father" who was not and never would be a father. Not to this child and not to any other.

Consuela had her child. And she had—oh, she never admitted to it, never even hinted of it; but Emilio knew the truth nonetheless—she also had her own passions, did she not? Aye, she did.

In the depths of her heart Consuela felt toward the gringo exactly as the redhead felt toward her. Emilio knew this was so. It was not a thing they would discuss. Never. But he knew. He was her brother. And he was a man. He knew. Consuela, the whore, would have given herself to the gringo just as she opened herself to whatever stinking whoreson it was that fathered her bastard.

Damn her, did she never once think of Emilio and *his* needs?

She complained. God, she complained all the time. Every night, almost. She complained of his drinking. She complained about Serafina.

Did the woman not understand that a man has needs? And not merely for the physical releases. Serafina gave him that. But that much he could have gotten alone on his pallet in the long nights. What he wanted . . . what Emilio *needed* . . . was . . . closeness. Warmth. The touch of a woman who *cared*!

And this Emilio did not have. This Emilio could not get. Not from Serafina. Not from Consuela. Not from . . . anyone.

Emilio stared blankly across the small *taverna* toward his friend and partner Aaron, and, unnoticed by anyone including himself, fat and shiny tears began to flow slowly across his cheeks.

II

Emilio bent, paying a harsh price by way of the throbbing in his head, and filled his arms with split aspen. The wood was powdered with snow, but he did not try to knock the snow away. Any extraneous movement was sure to cause him more pain, and he had enough of that already without inviting any extra.

He had slept badly, what little sleep he got, curled on the hard pallet on the floor of the stone house. There were times when he thought Consuela most thoughtless and inconsiderate. She should have taken the pallet last night and given him the comfort of the bed.

His head pounded now and there was a greasy queasiness in his belly that kept him from wanting anything to eat just yet. Maybe later. Very much later.

Consuela had offered to cook for him before he left the house. Judging by the smirk on her flat face she knew how he felt and was only taunting him. She hadn't meant to be nice to him. There were times when Emilio despised his own sister. Wife, that is.

When he left she said something about him bringing in water and an armload of firewood, but Emilio pretended not to hear.

Here at the store, however, he wanted to make a proper impression. He hadn't liked the looks Aaron gave him last night.

Emilio did not want Aaron to think that Emilio was losing control. As of course he was not. But who knew what might be in the mind of a gringo? They could be so strange. And never easy to understand. Aaron was better than most. But a man never knew where he stood with the yanquis. Not really.

He gathered the armload of wood from the rick behind the store, then shuffled through a knee-deep drift to get around to the protected front of the place. Carefully balancing the wood in one arm so he would have a hand free, Emilio let himself into the store.

A collapsible sheet-iron stove—not so fine as a cast-iron stove but infinitely better than any mere fireplace—purred and crackled at the back wall. A counter was to the right of the stove, also tight against the wall so no one could get behind whoever was on duty as clerk. To the left hung a partition of trade blankets that shielded the cot where Aaron slept whenever he was in Trinidad. Which in truth was not so often lately.

Emilio made an effort to be quiet, but his balance was not what it might have been. He stumbled, coughed, dropped a firelength of the dry aspen onto the top of the stove with a resounding clang.

"I'm already awake," Aaron's voice came from the far side of the blankets.

"I was trying to be—"

"Yeah, sure you were."

"Truly," Emilio protested. But he knew Aaron did not believe him.

"Did you see to the mules?"

"Not yet. I will get to them."

Emilio heard a grunt and the scuffling of feet on the hardpan floor—mud from the river bottom mixed with cow manure and allowed to dry into a durable, plasterlike surface—and a moment later Aaron pushed the blankets aside and came blinking out into the store, where now their goods were piled and where soon there would be bale upon bale of fine furs. The rougher, coarser green hides would be stacked outdoors, but the valuable furs would be kept here, both to preserve their value and to forestall theft.

"You look like hell," Aaron offered.

Emilio grinned at him. "Which is twice as good as you appear this fine morning, amigo."

Aaron grinned back. He too had imbibed more than a little last night. "What time is it?"

Emilio shrugged. "Does it matter?"

"That late, huh?"

Emilio chuckled. He pulled the fire door open and stuffed the box full of wood, then slammed the door closed with the side of his foot and dropped the remainder of the wood into the box that sat on the floor nearby.

Aaron pulled on his overshoes and took his thick red capote down from its peg.

"Where are you going, eh?"

"To feed and water the mules. For damn sure you wouldn't get to them soon."

"Did I not say . . . ?"

"Never mind. I'll do it myself." He held a hand up, palm outward. "And no, I'm not mad. Just don't want them to wait any longer. I pushed 'em pretty hard getting here in this weather."

"As you wish."

"While I'm doing that, Emilio, whyn't you start unpacking this stuff and arranging it where all those noble savages can see, okay?"

Emilio nodded. There was no hurry with any of that. And it was surely better to be busy indoors next to the stove while Aaron labored in the cold of the mule shed.

"And put some coffee on too, willya? I'll be wanting something hot when I get back."

There was a sharp-edged surge of cold when Aaron opened the door to go out, then blessed warmth again as the stove hissed and spat the snow that had been clinging to the firewood. Emilio surveyed all that needed to be done. Then he pulled a stool close to the stove and settled comfortably onto it. There was, after all, no hurry.

III

Emilio was spitting mad. His fury was so great that he trembled from the effort of trying to hold it all in.

He stood ankle deep in a pool of trade goods. Scattered on the floor all about him were opened bales and broken bundles. A packet of glass beads had broken open, and they spilled across the floor in a glittering torrent of red and blue and green.

Magnifying glasses, carving knives, awls, brass tacks, tortoiseshell buttons, and bullet molds were tossed willy-nilly about the place. Four crates of flintlock muskets had each been opened, and the stubby, ugly, smoothbore arms dumped out like so many oversized pickup sticks. A dozen brass-barreled kaleidoscopes lay nested in a tangle of calico cloth. Blankets—red blankets, gray blankets, brown blankets, blue blankets, white blankets, and mustard-yellow blankets—spread from one end of the building to the other.

Coarse gunpowder from Ohio, sensibly packed in canisters of lead so the containers could be melted down for shot, was stacked in tidy pyramids among the disorganized clutter of all the other goods.

All the things the Indians loved to trade for littered the floor of the Escavara and Jenks store.

Emilio whirled at the sound of the front door opening.

He scowled when he saw his partner return.

"Damn you," he snarled.

"Something wrong, amigo?"

"You know there is."

Aaron crossed his arms and stood defiantly at the entry.

"This was deliberate. You mock and insult me, Aaron."

"I used my best judgment, that's all."

"I am an equal partner, no? Or is that it? I am not truly an equal in this partnership. Admit it."

"What I admit is that you're wrong. And that yes, I deliberately didn't buy any damn alcohol. Didn't this time and won't the next trip either. Or the one after that or the one after that or . . . dammit, Emilio, we been over this a hundred times. Point is, amigo, I won't trade liquor to those people. It's cruel to them and dangerous for everyone else."

"I demand—"

"You go ahead and demand all you damn want, Emilio. No matter how loud you yell, though, it won't change my mind. I'm not selling no damned liquor to Indians. It's wrong, it's dangerous, and it's just plain stupid. Now leave it be. You hungry, Emilio? Your wife came by and said your lunch is ready. Said I should come too. Or maybe you don't want me in your house right now. What's it gonna be, Emilio? You want to take a break from your, uh, *work* now and have something to eat? Or d'you want to sulk awhile first?"

"Go to hell," Emilio spat.

"Likely," Aaron said agreeably. "Likely I will. But not today." He turned and went outside again, leaving Emilio to fume and complain if he wished but leaving Emilio really with no choice in the matter. What was done was done and it was too late now to add anything to Aaron's shopping in distant St. Louis.

Probably, Emilio thought sullenly, the damned yanqui was on his way this very moment to Emilio's own home so he could take Consuela onto the bed and rut with his best and only friend's wife. That was the sort of ingrate the gringo was. The sort they all were, surely, one just as bad as another.

Emilio kicked at the object nearest him and a cylindrical kaleidoscope went flying end over end the length of the store to smash itself into a shower of crumpled brass and bits of colored glass that fell like confetti onto the floor.

Emilio grabbed his coat and muffler and hurried out into the bitter cold. He headed not toward home, where that damned Aaron was undoubtedly putting the horns on Emilio, but to the *taverna*.

A drink or two to settle his stomach. He needed that. And then, when he was feeling better, he would call upon Serafina. She would make him feel better.

And for a little while, for the time it took him to walk from the store beside the ford across the Purgatory to the tavern built on the east bank of Raton Creek, for at least that much time Emilio believed everything that he told himself.

Well, almost everything.

Chapter
Twenty-nine

I

His head was light but his thoughts clear on this third full day of fasting. Talks To Ghosts stood at the edge of the sacred grove. Beyond the grove lay the slopes of the Huajatollas, the great twin peaks, shaped as if woman's breasts to symbolize their power and their beauty, for it was from these same peaks that the rain-giving clouds were born, it was from these peaks that First Man and First Woman emerged, and it was upon these peaks that the greatest of all the spirits lived.

It was spring, the time of awakening, and there was no better time to speak with the spirits.

Talks To Ghosts had been pondering this trip for a long while, and although it was dangerous—for who knows how a spirit will react to being disturbed by mere man?—it was a thing he wanted badly to do.

And if he did not return, well, there were worse things that could happen. He had no children to leave behind as orphans, and his friends—in this he was blessed—his friends would know that he died with their best interests at heart. There were indeed worse ways in which a man could be remembered than that.

Black Otter, truest of true friends, stood in close attendance at Talks To Ghosts' side. Black Otter had been with him more than a week now as they hurried ahead of the people on the annual migration down to the grasslands.

It was Black Otter who hunted for them until such time as Talks To Ghosts began his fast, and it was Black Otter now who emptied the tepid water from the goatskin bag and bent to fill it with fresh, clean, cold water from the stream that came bounding and bouncing down from the mighty Huajatollas.

Black Otter handed the skin to Talks To Ghosts, who drank deep of the chill liquid. The coldness of the water made his belly churn sourly but he was glad for the strength it also brought. Strength he would need in abundance in the time to come.

"You are ready?"

"Yes, I think so."

"I can go no further with you."

"I understand."

Not having fasted, Black Otter could not enter the sacred grove with him. And the path to the peaks and thus to the spirits passed through the grove.

"Are you sure you won't . . . ?"

Talks To Ghosts smiled weakly. "I will not change my mind, old friend. I cannot."

"If you are not back in so many days"—Black Otter flashed all his fingers on both hands—"I will come find you."

"No. You mustn't. You haven't been fasting, and . . ."

"I have said I would come. If you do not return, Talks To Ghosts, I will come."

Talks To Ghosts nodded. He drank again from the goatskin and, while Black Otter filled it once more, Talks To Ghosts wiped his lips and then carefully scrubbed his hands upon his flesh as if wiping away some impurity or defilement. He did not know where the impulse came from, but it was irresistible.

"In so many days. No more," Black Otter reminded.

"You will be here still?" Talks To Ghosts asked.

Black Otter smiled. "Where else?"

Talks To Ghosts nodded and reached out to touch his friend lightly on the point of his shoulder.

Then, steeling himself for whatever ordeal lay ahead, he untied the thong that held his breechclout at his waist and kicked his moccasins from his feet. A supplicant to such spirits as these should approach without defense or artifice, as naked as in birth, as pure of heart as man is capable of making himself.

Without uttering any good-byes—none at least that were audible—Talks To Ghosts walked slowly forward and into the shadowy grove at the foot of the Huajatollas.

II

"I see the smoke, Talks To Ghosts. Do you see it? There. Look where I am pointing. You see it too, yes?"

Black Otter did not wait for an answer. But then by now he probably no longer expected one.

It had been—he had to think for a moment to work it out—five days since Talks To Ghosts came back from seeking his vision at the navel of the world. In that time he had yet to speak. But he had much to think upon.

He allowed Black Otter to guide his mortal sight, and Talks To Ghosts too saw the smoke.

Ah, but this smoke was ordinary smoke. It came from fires. Many fires. In the stoves and upon the hearths of the pale ones they called Americanos and the hearths and the ovens of the brown-skinned white men they called Mexican.

The smokes rose above what once was Horse Camp. But Talks To Ghosts knew now beyond question that this place would never again be the Horse Camp he remembered of old.

The world was forever changed now. He knew this. And he feared it.

"Do you see where the people are camped, Talks To Ghosts? Look. Follow my finger. Upstream along the Purgatory, above the store where your friend waits. Do you see now? Those smokes are from the lodges of our people. Tonight we will sleep beside our own fire, Talks To Ghosts. Tonight we will eat well of fat dog and cattail root." Black Otter grinned. "And sugar, Talks To Ghosts. Tonight there will surely be much sugar and coffee in our lodge and heat in our bellies. Tonight we will be home."

Except, Talks To Ghosts thought in silence, tonight we have no home.

III

Talks To Ghosts was able to lay the visions aside finally when he saw Red Beard. Or, more properly, He Runs.

Thin Weasel, who learned the white men's language one winter at the post of the Bents, was able to talk with the red-haired man who was so kind to Talks To Ghosts after the Kiowa killed him. Thin Weasel explained that the white man called himself I Run, and so the people obligingly named him He Runs in their own tongue. But the truth was that Talks To Ghosts continued to think of him as Red Beard and probably always would.

Talks To Ghosts was pleased to see Red Beard behind the counter at the trading house and could not help smiling at this tall man who was truly a friend.

"Talks To Ghosts! Welcome." Red Beard dropped the marten pelt he had been examining and hurried out to grasp Talks To Ghosts warmly by the elbows. Talks To Ghosts could not help but feel a sense of pleasure at the greeting. There was a twinge, the smallest only, of regret as memory of the visions intruded.

And then the two were able to talk again, to exchange news and visit memories. Talks To Ghosts had no English, of course, and Red Beard did not understand plain language. Even so, they shared some words of the brown-skinned white men who although they called themselves Mexican spoke a language they called Spanish. It was all very confusing to Talks To Ghosts, and he was not sure he always understood. But some common ground was better than none.

And Red Beard was not to blame for what Talks To Ghosts had seen in the visions. Talks To Ghosts reminded himself of that several times during the course of their visit.

Chapter Thirty

I

It never ceased to amaze Aaron. Damned if the pretty little grove of cottonwoods that he first saw hadn't become quite the little town.

There must have been a score or more of houses. And that was not even counting the commercial structures like his and Emilio's store or Mendez's tavern or Del Garza's budding mercantile or Jess Tomkins's smithy. Trinidad—no one called it El Rio de Las Animas anymore, hadn't in years—was growing into a regular city.

Aaron slowed his horse to a walk on the lumpy, winding road that dropped from the clouds at Raton Pass onto the soft and pretty land along the Purgatory. He slowed to allow the mules behind him plenty of time to pick their way along the path. But the truth was as much that he was enjoying the view before him as that the mules needed the time he gave them.

He was on his way back from Santa Fe where he had taken virtually all the wool crop from the spring shearing. The price at Santa Fe was good this year, and the firm of Escavara and Jenks had turned a decent profit.

For the return trip his packs were loaded with a few things for their own store but mostly carried freight for Mendez and Del Garza and the few other merchants in town. It was a service that benefited all in the community, and Aaron and Emilio had agreed long ago that they would not try to take much profit from the carrying of consignments for their neighbors.

Lord knew they made enough from their trade with the Indians as it was. There were times when Aaron felt about half ashamed at the amount of markup they took on their goods. Still, their prices were in line with—and often a little below—those charged by their competitors farther north on the Fountain or east on the Arkansas.

Aaron reached the flat and splashed his train noisily through little Raton Creek, then bumped the horse into a slow lope for the last short distance to Trinidad.

He turned the mules into the corral beside the old jacal storage building and called to young Joaquin Bonafacio to unload and water them. Aaron dismounted and tied his horse outside the corral, then unstrapped his saddlebags and carried them toward the house.

He had a present to deliver. And despite all his resolve to the contrary, his heart was racing faster and faster and his cheeks were beginning to burn. He simply couldn't help it.

II

"Tio Aaron!" The little girl came flying out to greet him, arms extended and skirt swirling madly around brown and dusty legs.

Aaron bent. Caught her up. Swept her high into the air. Well, as high as he could manage nowadays. Laughing, he put her down again.

"You're getting too big for me to do that much longer, *querida*."

Elena's response was to plant a kiss on her uncle Aaron's forehead, avoiding the red bristles of his beard.

"What did you bring me, Tio Aaron? Did you bring candy? A doll? A pretty necklace for me to wear?"

In the months since his last trip the child—she was eight now and possessed of a bright and delicate beauty—had managed to request each of those presents. Should he find it convenient, that is.

She knew, of course, that he would always find it perfectly convenient to grant her every whim and wish. And so he had again. He unbuckled one side of the saddlebags and reached inside. After a moment he frowned.

"What's wrong, Tio?"

"I can't find . . . no, wait a minute, wait. . . ." He pulled out a small paper bundle tied with string. "I'm not sure what this is. Why don't you open it and see."

Elena happily began the rituals of unveiling the many treasures that were hers.

And if there were other gifts Aaron would have liked to bring back with him in the hope of putting smiles onto another—but not altogether dissimilar—face, well, some things were permissible. Others were not.

Best to be content with what he had and dwell as little as possible on what he did not.

III

"I'll make you something to eat. You must be hungry."

"You don't have to do that."

"I don't mind."

Aaron gave Consuela a hopeless, helpless look of undisguised yearning. But not until she had turned her back to go to the stove and fix something for him.

At the other side of the small room Elena was admiring her new necklace and rings, using the hand mirror Tio Aaron brought her two trips back. The mirror was ornate and pretty and just right for a little girl.

He almost hated to ask, considering the many possible answers, but convention demanded it. "Where is Emilio?"

"At the store." Consuela hesitated, leaving her back to him so that he could not read her expression. "He hasn't had a drink since before you left, Aaron. Not one. I am sure of it."

Aaron nodded. He was pleased, of course. Small credit, though, to Emilio. Before he left for Santa Fe Aaron had a few choice words with Mendez at the tavern. There would be no credit extended to Emilio or there would be no more buying and hauling of alcohol for Mendez by Señor Jenks in the future. It was a simple enough arrangement. And neither Emilio nor Aaron ever saw much in the way of actual cash money.

Perhaps this was what Emilio needed, though. In Aaron's opinion Emilio swam entirely too deeply in the liquor keg. He needed to stop leaning on it to exorcise whatever demons haunted him.

Aaron sighed as his thoughts revolved around his partner and, yes, still his friend. Truly Aaron could not understand the man. He had the most beautiful wife in Christendom, bar none. And while no outsider could ever know what went on inside another's household, Aaron firmly believed that Emilio had the most gentle, kind, and completely good wife anywhere, not only the most beautiful.

He had Consuela for a wife and yet night after night drank himself sodden and then tumbled into Serafina Martine's sweat-soaked and much traveled bed.

Dammit, for that matter Emilio had the most loving and lovely daughter Aaron could ever imagine. And yet for the most part Emilio ignored the child. On those few occasions when he was not ignoring Elena he was yelling at her.

For years—up to and including this trip just concluded—Aaron brought presents to Elena that she asked for and a trinket or two from himself and always, always one more particularly nice gift that he told Elena her papa had requested that he buy especially for her.

The truth was that Emilio never once had asked Aaron to bring back a gift for the child. Nor, for that matter, had he ever asked Aaron to shop for Consuela. Emilio seemed to think very seldom about either of them. Aaron could and would do nothing about Emilio's indifference toward Consuela, but he could and did try to make up for the man's coldness to Elena. He wondered sometimes if Elena still believed his lies about how and why the gifts were chosen. But of course he could not ask.

He sat in comfortable silence for a while, enjoying the small exclamations of preening pleasure from Elena's side of the room and enjoying even more the small, domestic noises of a good woman tending to a man's needs in her kitchen that reached him from the stove.

He should, he supposed, go out and see to the unloading of the mules and the distribution of the goods he brought back to the townsmen and the merchants of Trinidad. Later. Joaquin would see to the comfort of the animals. Later Aaron could tell Mendez and the rest that their goods had arrived. For now there was an emptiness in him that Consuela would assuage with a supper prepared especially for him.

Chapter Thirty-one

I

At last. Aaron finally listened, at long last he'd paid attention to Emilio's pleas and explanations and outright demands. At last.

There were . . . how many? . . . eight, twelve, no sixteen kegs of alcohol here. Enough to make an incalculable amount of trade whiskey. Surely not all of this . . . no, of course not. Mendez must have ordered some. Of course. That would explain why there was so much. Sixteen casks. How much then . . . half? Probably. Half for Mendez and half for Escavara and Jenks. This was more like it. Oh, so much better.

Now they would truly prosper.

Everyone knew. Not everyone admitted it, but everyone knew. Indians love whiskey. Nearly all the filthy savages do. And not being accustomed to it, they are all quick to drink and even quicker to become drunk. Stupid to begin with, Indians lose all sense once they have a drink or two inside their heathen bellies.

Oh, yes. Emilio knew. Toll them in with promises of free drink. Two cups per man, no charge. Two cups per man and there would be no limit thereafter. Two cups of whiskey in an Indian and he will pay anything he owns, even his wives or daughters, for another cup and for one more after that.

Two bales of beaver for a musket worth two pesos? Bah. Two pesos' worth of thoroughly watered whiskey is enough to drown an Indian, much less intoxicate him. For that much liquor an Indian would hand over his entire year's catch and throw in the services of his youngest wife besides.

Oh, Emilio was happy now. Truly happy.

He slapped Joaquin Bonafacio on the back and told him to run fetch his brothers.

Eight casks of alcohol to Mendez at the *taverna, por favor,* and the other eight to the store.

Quick, though. Garcia's nephew stopped by a little while ago to report that the Indians were already coming down from the mountains. They were but half a day's ride away when Garcia spotted them, and if they came right on could be there to start the season's trading as early as this very evening. Emilio would have to hurry to get his whiskey ready for their arrival.

II

"Come in, come in, my friends. See what we have for you this season, eh. See what changes we have made. Whiskey, my friends. On the house. It is an expression, yes. It means for this there is no charge. You are such good customers we give to you this whiskey as a gift. Yes, truly, it is free to you. Two cups for each one of you. Yes, please, help yourself." Emilio smiled and pointed. Yes, by all means.

He was sure . . . fairly sure . . . that they understood. They had learned a little Spanish over the years, and he and Aaron had learned some of the sign language that all the tribes seemed to have in common whatever tongue they otherwise spoke.

"Help yourself. Don't be shy. Nothing wrong with

this whiskey, no indeed. You want me to show you, ha ha? Here, give me the dipper. I'll have a taste myself. See? Ah, now that's good. Puts a burn in your belly, I tell you. Good. See? Now you have some."

The dipper passed briskly to and fro.

And every so often Emilio would laugh and chuckle and grab hold of the ladle so as to help himself to a small portion of the fiery concoction.

He'd put in . . . he couldn't remember exactly. Alcohol from the casks Aaron brought from Santa Fe, of course. Water. But only good well water. No river dippings for this mixture, no indeed. Some gunpowder and quite a lot of tobacco. Everyone used those, of course. Chilies too. Hot chilies to give it authority and molasses to smooth off the flavor and, too, to add some color. If he did say so himself, Emilio did a first-class job, an absolutely magnificent job, of turning raw alcohol into most excellent whiskey.

"Here now, don't be so greedy with that, you stinking savage. Give here now. It's my turn. Damn you, Indian, don't you dare pull that away from me or I'll . . . I'll . . . you'll regret it, Indian, that you will."

Emilio snatched the dipper away from the ugly red man and plunged it into the keg. Helped himself to a drink and then had another. One of the Indians, perhaps already drunk or else anxious to become so, shoved Emilio roughly away from his position beside the keg. The Indian shouldered his way to the keg and drank. Dipped. Drank again.

"That's all for you, Injun. No more. Go on now. No more unless you pay. You savvy? Pay for more if you want to drink now. Pay all you own, damn you, you filthy get of a goat. Pay me everything you own, that's right. You got a woman? Probably not. Ugly bastard like you wouldn't have a woman. But you got furs, yes? What you got? Beaver? Buff'lo? Elk robes? Eh? You bring them to me. You bring all them to me if you . . . if you . . . if you want more, damn you."

Emilio tried to wrest the dipper from him. The Indian held up, pulling back and easily keeping his grip on the ladle.

There was a loud, incomprehensible babble from the Indians.

Too many of them had crowded into the store. Not so many. Not good to have so many inside at once. Everyone knew that. Only few at a . . . few at a time. That was it. Only few.

Emilio staggered, blinked, roared at the Indians. Cursed them and swore and told them all to leave. He would reopen for a few of them, but only a few, at a time. Damned Indians were paying no attention to him.

Emilio reached out, intending to take the liquor cask away until he could restore order. The cask wasn't there any longer. He had put it . . . there. Hadn't he? He was almost sure that he had. Yes, on the counter right there. So where had it gone? He shuffled closer to the counter, holding on to it to maintain his balance.

Must have fallen behind. Except wasn't there either. Wasn't . . . couldn't find it.

There. There it was. And over there too.

Emilio was confused. He was not, absolutely was not seeing double. Two casks. That Indian had one. So did that one there. And a bunch of them were squatting around another cask in the corner. Weren't they?

Crazy damn Indians were drinking out of the wrong kegs. Now wasn't that just the stupidest thing he'd ever seen or heard? Course it was. Ignorant damned savages. Broke open the wrong casks, that's what they did.

Those kegs weren't even whiskey. Plain alcohol. Huh! Joke was on the stupid Indians. No taste in straight grain alcohol. Lot of heat. But no damn taste.

Had to stop them. Just . . . get things back under control here. That's all he needed. Get things back the way they should . . . not so damn many inside all at once, no . . . get things back. Drink a little whiskey, not alcohol. Get things back. Everything will be just fine. Yes, of course.

Emilio picked up a trade musket. Back under control. Had to get things back in control. Yes, of course. He fumbled a load of powder into the barrel. Shot. Dropped some but

some went in. He saw it. Now the priming powder. Yes,
there. That was where it went. There.

Emilio's face felt hot and the tip of his nose was numb.
He had to concentrate to make his hands do the things his
mind wanted done. But he could do it.

Get things back under control. Then sell . . . then sell
whiskey. Take in every fur and robe every one of these bastards worked for the whole winter past. Take in all the stuff
and a nice-looking girl or two if he could find some that
weren't covered too thick in grease.

Emilio firmed his shoulders. Took a fresh grip on the
musket in his hands. He held the musket with the muzzle
wandering aimlessly back and forth toward the mass of
Indians packed inside the store.

He tipped his head back, almost losing his balance again
as he did so, and roared as loud as he could. Didn't work.
They didn't pay attention to him, damn them. Hunched over
the casks of alcohol. Drunken bastards. Nothing worse than a
drunk Indian.

There was a sour taste in Emilio's mouth and a roiling
queasiness in his stomach and a ringing in his ears. His
vision seemed clouded and his equilibrium gelatinous.

Indians. Damn Indians. Their fault.

Emilio leaned hard against the counter, bracing himself
there so he would not slip down to the floor. Couldn't do
that. Not now. Had to take charge. Drunken damn Indians.
Their fault. He closed his eyes. And dragged the cockpiece
of the musket back with a thumb that felt like it surely must
have belonged to someone else for all the sense of feeling
left in it.

Chapter
Thirty-two

I

Talks To Ghosts did not like this. The thin brown-skinned man was drunk and so were all the men who crowded into the store. Red Beard never permitted this sort of thing. But Red Beard was not here. There was no sign of him, and Talks To Ghosts was worried.

The men were drinking. Taking things. Talking rudely.

Not that Red Beard's partner could understand. The men were not so drunk that they would say the rude things in Spanish so the Mexican could understand. They might be drunk but they were not stupid.

The Mexican took up a gun and loaded it, but no one paid any attention. He shouted and swore and no one paid attention to that either.

Talks To Ghosts helped himself to a bag of sugar, dark and moist and delightfully sticky. He dipped two fingers into it and licked them clean and then helped himself to some more.

The others in the room were taking more than just sugar, of course. All manner of goods were quickly disappearing, men with their arms full darting outside only to give the articles to their women so they could return for more. And most of all, of course most of all, they took the whiskey.

There were—Talks To Ghosts could not tell exactly how many; too many—there were many, many casks of whiskey in the place and the men found and breached all of them. Already Black Otter and Two Tails lay in a stupor atop a pile of blankets, and Dog Tooth was engaged in throwing up into a box of cured tobacco twists.

Poor Emlion—or something like that; Talks To Ghosts never could remember how his Spanish name went, but the people sometimes called him Sad Man—the poor man was practically berserk now at the sight of so much profit being lost to his own foolishness.

He shouted and swore and waved the gun in the air. No one paid any attention to him, of course. He was not the sort of man to lead other men anyway, and now all the people were interested in the liquor and in all the wonderful things that were there to be taken.

Everyone was having quite a nice time, actually.

Everyone except Sad Man.

Everyone was having a wonderful time. Until poor Emlion ruined the fun.

There was an explosion. And smoke. Oh, so very much smoke that it was difficult to see and the air was stinking and hard to breathe. And there was silence.

And on the floor. There not three paces distant from where Talks To Ghosts stood with his bag of sugar and his two fingers sticky and coated with the sweet, there on the floor lay Big Stones. So wise and forceful. So much the leader. So brave and cunning. Except now all Big Stones' wisdom and cunning and bravery spilled forth in ropy clots of red and gray brain matter that flowed onto the floor beside him and speckled those that had been standing near.

Balls from weak and ineffectual little Emlion's gun had struck Big Stones flush on the temple and opened up the other side of his head like an overripe melon dropped onto hard ground.

There was a period of shocked silence when even the

most drunk and unaware of the people stood rooted and immobile. And then—it was a thing Talks To Ghosts had heard before in the past but seldom, seldom—then there was a deep, collective roar from the men of the people.

And stupid, drunken, so very foolish Emlion who was Red Beard's partner disappeared beneath a wave of enraged warriors. Knives jabbed and clubs rose and fell and newly grabbed axes and mauls pummeled and pounded.

In minutes, no more, it would have been difficult for someone newly arriving to decide what sort of animal it was that was butchered on the floor of the trading house. All that remained once the fury was spent were red, tattered scraps of meat and cloth and bone.

II

There was another silence, this one deeper and more awful somehow, as the men stood in contemplation of what they had just done.

Not that anyone regretted it. Oh no, not at all. The feeling was more that of a great and wondrous accomplishment. They had overcome. And they had taken much booty as their reward. Their enemy, the man who attacked them when they were merely being playful and innocently enjoying themselves, this man lay dead now as an enemy of the people rightly should be dead.

A few, particularly among the younger men, came forward to flash their buttocks toward the corpse of dead Emlion, and others spat on the gore that remained of him, and even outside where the women waited for the riches to be carried out to them there arose taunting chants to proclaim the victory.

And it would have been all right, Talks To Ghosts thought, if only it stopped there, but it did not stop. Too much liquor had flowed and more remained in the kegs and the blood of the men was fiery in the strength of victory.

Someone shouted a high-pitched ululating cry and

someone else took it up, and within seconds the silence of
the place had become a yelling, yammering chorus of undirected rage.

The cries became louder and louder and Talks To
Ghosts knew what soon would come, what soon must come.

He dropped his bag of sugar unheeded to the floor and
slipped quietly outside, while indoors the men shouted and
stamped their feet and began to boast and brandish clubs
and scythes and whatever came to hand.

Talks To Ghosts pushed rudely through the women
and small ones who crowded close around the door trying to
see what went on within. He did not even take time to apologize for his rudeness.

Because he knew.

His heart was cracking apart within his chest, and hot
tears gathered behind his eyes. Because he knew. The
visions, the spirits, told him, and every season since he
waited and was most pleasantly disappointed until he began
to think the flow of the circle was altered somehow and this
time the vision would prove untrue.

But that was false. It was coming now. Just as he
feared. Just as he once saw. And now there was nothing he
could do but to repay his debts and accept fate. His own
fate. And that of his people.

With an aching heart he pushed free of the crowd of
women and immediately broke into a run. He ran fast, feet
barely skimming the broken ground, lungs burning, shattered heart pounding.

He ran and ran, and before he reached the cottonwoods
of his beloved Horse Camp beyond the wagon trail he could
hear the roar of fury as the war cries of his people sounded
behind him inside the stone walls of the trading place.

Before him lay windows and lights and people taking
their ease in the early evening.

Behind him the men had blood on their hands and
blood in their hearts and a raging appetite for more blood in
their voices.

Chapter
Thirty-three

I

Consuela screamed when the Indian with half his face a mask of scars came crashing into the house without warning.

She grabbed up a pot of boiling water from the stove and threw it at him, following behind it to snatch Elena by the arm and pull her back to safety.

"Hey. Whoa! It's all right." Aaron took a moment to try and reassure Consuela and the suddenly frightened Elena, then turned to his old friend who was gritting his teeth against the pain of the water that burned his arm and shoulder.

"What's wrong, Talks To Ghosts?"

"Come, Red Beard. Hide."

"Why?"

"Fight. Big fight. My people kill you people. All fight. All kill. Come now. Hide."

Aaron frowned. He couldn't ... surely Talks To Ghosts couldn't be right about that.

Aaron stepped to the door, standing open to the newly fallen night after Talks To Ghosts crashed through it. To the

west, over toward the store, he could see a bright glow
beyond the trees. Yellow light shimmered and became
stronger.

Something had been fired there. And there a bit to the
right. And there, closer. Many fires. And shouts. Screams.
Shouts of war and screams of terror. And of pain.

He heard a gunshot and another. But mostly he heard
screams. They ripped and tore at the fabric of the night and
they chilled Aaron as he thought about Consuela and Elena
in such agony as would cause screams like those he heard
now. The Indians were out of control for some reason.
Marauding as he'd been told wild savages could do.

Except . . . it was strange, painted hostiles who were
supposed to do that. Not people with whom he had traded
and laughed and shared meat for nearly a decade past. These
people were if not friends then certainly not enemies. And
Talks To Ghosts. He was a friend. As he was proving this
night, Aaron conceded.

Quickly, his mind awhirl, he stepped back inside the
house and slammed the door closed, bolting it securely shut.

A musket. That was what he needed. Surely Emilio
kept a musket somewhere in the house. Emilio. Where the
hell was Emilio? At the store? The tavern, more likely.

Safe, Aaron hoped. For the first time ever Aaron found
himself hoping that Emilio was safe in Serafina Martine's
bed. And that he would have sense enough to hide there
until this awful thing blew itself out like some furious but
brief prairie storm.

Aaron dashed about the stone house he had built for
Emilio—and for Consuela—closing and bolting the shutters.

He felt a tug at his elbow and pulled away and felt it
repeated again.

"What is it?"

Talks To Ghosts pointed to the shutters and the barred
door. "No good. Break . . ." He paused, searching for the
few Spanish words he possessed. In his frustration he
spewed a rapid string of his own words, then stopped and
more calmly tried again. "Door break. Wood things," he

pointed to the shutters, "break. Fire." He pointed to the ceiling.

Aaron looked up and realized what Talks To Ghosts was trying to tell him. Yes, the walls of the house were of stone. No, those walls would not burn. But the roof would. The door would. The shutters were dry and would soon burn away if fire were introduced to them.

The safety of a bolted door was a false safety, and if someone seriously wanted in then they would come in. And one man, with or without a gun, would not be able to stand against them.

"Come," Talks To Ghosts said. "I give you back the life you gave to me."

Aaron swallowed. Hesitated only a moment longer. Somewhere not far away . . . not nearly far enough away . . . he could hear shouts of triumph, shouts of rage, screams of unimaginable horror and pain.

"Quick," Talks To Ghosts said.

Aaron put an arm around Consuela's shoulder and pulled her and the child to him. "We have to go now."

"With that Indian?"

"Exactly," Aaron affirmed. "We will go with Talks To Ghosts."

II

Talks To Ghosts led them past the corral where the mules picked desultorily at their hay and beyond the sheep pens where the naked, newly shorn ewes stood spraddle-legged over their lambs and up onto the hillside to the south.

Behind and below them now there were a dozen fires or more, and the screaming continued. Aaron heard a woman's voice, tremulous and quavering. Her agony rose and rose and chopped abruptly short. The sudden silence seemed even more terrifying than her pain had been.

He looked at Consuela, pale and trembling with Elena wrapped tight in her arms. Aaron pulled both of them into his embrace—scant comfort there, he thought, and no protection whatsoever—and held them as much with his heart as with his flesh.

Talks To Ghosts motioned them to the ground, then lay down beside them, all of them out of sight behind a pair of small boulders and some clumps of wild grasses that sprouted between the stones. From below they could not be seen even had it been daylight, and that was likely the best protection they might hope for.

"What happened?" Aaron asked softly once he was certain they were far enough away from any marauding force so they could not be overheard.

Haltingly, choosing his words with great care, Talks To Ghosts attempted to explain.

And below, along the banks of the Purgatory, the homes of Trinidad burned and the people of Trinidad died under the knives and the clubs and the swinging axes of men who they once thought of as friendly.

III

Dawn came like blood creeping over the horizon. But far less blood than lay on the earth below.

Aaron and Talks To Ghosts were awake to see it. The two men had talked quietly through the night, but hours earlier both Consuela and Elena let exhaustion overcome their fear and dropped into fitful, nervous sleep.

Aaron hated to wake them now, but he supposed he really should. There was much they needed to do. Burials first of all.

Surely there would be others who escaped the fury of the Indians. But there would be many who had not, and those would have to be found and tended to.

There were houses to rebuild and inventories—of both the living and their looted possessions—to be taken.

Already Aaron was sure he was ruined. Emilio was dead. Talks To Ghosts told him that. There was no possibility that poor Emilio could have survived. The store was surely gone and all the things that had been in it. Emilio's house—Consuela's house—still stood. During the night Aaron watched the roof burn and collapse, but at least some of the things inside might yet remain.

He would rebuild the house for her and for Elena. And, if she would have him, for himself as well.

With Emilio gone . . . he shook his head angrily. It was too soon to talk with Consuela about that even though he had loved her from the first moment he saw her. Too soon to talk about it. But not too soon to think it within the privacy of his own silent heart.

For now, there was a town to rebuild.

And revenge . . . he didn't know. They could ask for soldiers to pursue and punish the savages. Not that it would do any good.

From the Indian point of view, as Talks To Ghosts tried to explain during the long night just past, the events of last night were momentary and, in a manner of speaking, hardly of importance. Talks To Ghosts' people would go away, and in the fall they would return and expect to be greeted as ordinary visitors and be dealt with the same as any others who had robes to trade and goods to buy. Aaron did not know how he and the people of Trinidad would handle that when the time came.

When the time came, he repeated to himself. That, he suspected, was how to handle it. When the time came. Not before. Not in heat at this moment but dispassionately and when the time came.

For now . . . he turned his head to peer with loving wonder at the incredible beauty of the woman who slept at his side and at the round, cherubic face of the child who was hers. So beautiful and so innocent, the both of them.

Aaron hoped . . . no, he prayed, he really did, he prayed that when this pain was ended Consuela . . . and Elena too, for he loved the child almost as completely as he loved the mother . . . would accept him into their lives. If that were to happen he would consider himself the most fortunate of men.

On an impulse he bent his head to lightly kiss the softness of Consuela's temple.

He turned with a smile and to Talks To Ghosts said, "Let's go down now and see what's left, eh?"

The Indian clasped his friend's shoulder and, groaning from the pain of stiffened joints, stood upright to stretch.

Far below, somewhere in the vicinity of Emilio's sheep pen, there was a shout and a voice floated up the slope, "There's one!" and a gunshot loud in the morning calm.

Oddly, Aaron heard the strike of the ball before he heard the report of the shot.

There was a sound like raw meat being pounded with a tenderizer and a grunt followed closely by the sound of the gunshot.

Aaron jumped to his feet. But too late.

Talks To Ghosts stood swaying slightly, a reddish purple depression the size of a fired clay marble pulsing wetly on his stomach just beneath his scrawny breastbone.

Talks To Ghosts looked at Aaron and, oddly, smiled.

"You knew? You . . . expected . . . ?"

Talks To Ghosts nodded. Aaron reached for him, but too late. Talks To Ghosts slumped to his knees, looked out across the plains where the buffalo grazed . . . a film clouded his eyes and Talks To Ghosts fell to the ground dead.

IV

They stood on the hillside where months earlier they had lain in fretful hiding, a tall red-haired man and a slender woman with hair like a raven's sleek wing.

Aaron laid a bundle of sage and tobacco beside the small cairn that marked the grave of Talks To Ghosts.

Consuela hooked her arm into the crook of Aaron's and pressed her cheek warm against his shoulder. "Tell me again," she asked.

"Cattle," he said. "White men's cattle spreading across all the miles of grass. More cattle than there are buffalo now. And the smoke from many chimneys. Stone houses beyond number. But no Indians. No more will his people come here to hunt and no more will there be Indians at the place he called Horse Camp. Wherever that is."

Consuela shivered and hugged his arm all the tighter. "You don't think he really saw . . . ?"

Aaron shrugged and shook his head. "I can't tell you what he saw. But I believe that *he* believed whatever it was he *thought* he saw." He smiled. "If that makes any sense to you."

Consuela nodded.

"Smoke where there was no fire . . . ," he started.

But he saw that Consuela's attention was not on some dead Indian's dreams but on something much closer. She was looking down toward the sheep pens where Elena was playing dangerously close to a foul-tempered ram. Down where there were sheep that would soon need shearing again and a train of pack mules that needed to be fed and where, as ever, there was much work to be done.

"Let's go home now," Aaron said and led his wife down the slope.

ABOUT THE AUTHOR

FRANK RODERUS wrote his first story, a western, at age five, and says he quite literally has never wanted to do anything else. He has been writing fiction full-time since 1980, and was a newspaper reporter before that. As a journalist, he won the Colorado Press Association's highest honor, the Sweepstakes Award, for the Best News Story of 1980. His novel *Leaving Kansas* (Doubleday, 1983) won the Western Writers of America's Spur Award for Best Western Novel. A life member of the American Quarter Horse Association, he is married and currently resides in Florida. Roderus and his wife, Magdalena, expect to divide their time between Florida and Palawan Island in the Sulu Sea.

CAMERON JUDD

Writing with power, authority, and respect
for America's frontier traditions, Cameron Judd
captures the spirit of adventure and promise of the
wild frontier in his fast-paced, exciting novels. In
the tradition of Max Brand and Luke Short,
Cameron Judd is a new voice of the Old West.

THE SHADOW WARRIORS

____57698-4 $5.99/$7.99 in Canada

BOONE

____57383-7 $5.99/$7.50 in Canada

CROCKETT OF TENNESSEE

____56856-6 $5.99/$7.50 in Canada

PASSAGE TO NATCHEZ

____57560-0 $5.99/$7.99 in Canada

The exciting frontier series continues!

～～～～ RIVERS WEST

Native Americans, hunters and trappers, pioneer families—
all who braved the emerging American frontier drew their very
lives and fortunes from the great rivers. From the earliest days
of the settlement movement to the dawn of the twentieth cen-
tury, here in all their awesome splendor are the RIVERS WEST.

____56511-7	THE HIGH MISSOURI	WIN BLEVINS
____29925-5	THE RIO GRANDE	JORY SHERMAN
____56794-2	THE PECOS RIVER	FREDERIC BEAN
____29772-4	THE COLUMBIA RIVER ($4.99/$6.99 Can.)	JORY SHERMAN
____56796-9	THE HUMBOLDT RIVER ($4.99/$6.99 Can.)	GARY MCCARTHY
____56795-0	THE PURGATORY RIVER ($5.50/$7.50 Can.)	FRANK RODERUS

each available for $4.99/$5.99 Can., except where noted

- -

Ask for these books at your local bookstore or use this page to order.

Please send me the books I have checked above. I am enclosing $____(add $2.50 to
cover postage and handling). Send check or money order, no cash or C.O.D.'s, please.

Name _____

Address _____

City/State/Zip _____

Send order to: Bantam Books, Dept. RW, 2451 S. Wolf Rd., Des Plaines, IL 60018
Allow four to six weeks for delivery.
Prices and availability subject to change without notice.   RW 7/97

The Spur Award—winning author of NICKAJACK

ROBERT J. CONLEY

Drawn from Cherokee legend and lore, faithful to his own Cherokee heritage, award-winning author Robert J. Conley brings to spellbinding life the tumultuous events that changed a proud nation forever. He tells of a people struggling to survive amid the wonders and terrors of an untamed land.

THE DARK WAY

___56035-2 $4.99/$5.99 Canada

THE WAY SOUTH

___56031-X $4.99/$6.50 Canada

Ask for these books at your local bookstore or use this page to order.

Please send me the books I have checked above. I am enclosing $____(add $2.50 to cover postage and handling). Send check or money order, no cash or C.O.D.'s, please.

Name _____

Address _____

City/State/Zip _____

Send order to: Bantam Books, Dept. DO51, 2451 S. Wolf Rd., Des Plaines, IL 60018
Allow four to six weeks for delivery.
Prices and availability subject to change without notice.   DO 51 7/97

From Dana Fuller Ross, the creator of WAGONS WEST

THE HOLTS
An American Dynasty

YUKON JUSTICE
_____ 29763-5 $5.99/$6.99 in Canada
As gold fever sweeps across the nation, a great migration
north begins to the Yukon Territory of Canada.

PACIFIC DESTINY
_____ 56149-9 $5.99/$6.99 in Canada
Henry Blake—a U.S. Government spy—undertakes
a dangerous secret mission.

HOMECOMING
_____ 56150-2 $5.99/$6.99 in Canada
The promise of a new adventure draws
Frank Blake toward New Mexico.

AWAKENING
_____ 56904-X $5.99/$7.99 in Canada
The dawn of an age of discovery and danger.